SIXTEEN STEPS

TO HEAVEN

By

Robert Slakki

Thank you to my family and friends for the support and encouragement to write my second novel. Especially the wife who is still waiting for jobs around the house to be completed.

CONTENTS

Death manifests itself indiscriminately upon humanity, slowly creeping and crawling towards darkness like a storm cloud on a bright summer's day. Lurking as a constant presence in the recesses of our subconscious mind, taking refuge in those sombre, unassuming places society neglects to discuss, a mere consequence of life. Death imparts no favours, no loyalty to the wealthy, sympathy for the poor, or blind eye turned for the young, the fit, the healthy. No pity is shown for the weakness of the elderly, the unpredictable fragility of the sick, or the innocence of the naïve. Mother nature establishes her undeniable authority upon mankind with a hand of uncompromising brutality. Then of course, the unnatural sinister aspect of death prevails, the violent, depraved, grotesque side with a disrespect for life, for emotion, devoid of empathy, then there is Murder.

CHAPTER 1

A midnight black M3 saloon BMW sat on the far side of the old cobbled market square carpark, away from any prying electronic eyes and under the vast shadow of an ancient bowing willow tree. A rusty amber glow from a nearby streetlight performed a flickering stage show with excited branches dancing in the gusting wind. Golden autumnal leaves swirled high towards the rolling shroud of darkness, descending to earth with a fluttering elegance, before scurrying in all directions like a hundred and one mice fleeing for their lives across the rain-drenched York cobblestones. The constant drumming of the late October rain beat rhythmically on the roof of the car, possessing an almost therapeutic quality. A new angel slept soundly in the passenger seat beside me, sun-kissed golden hair tumbling naturally around a bronzed face, before cascading in waves over her slender shoulders to a point in the middle of her back. High cheekbones, a button nose, plump lips and piercing electric blue eyes accentuated her model-like beauty. I had excelled myself again with the choice of young lady to fulfil my yearnings. She is a glorious picture of beauty, one I will never forget, an image to be treasured for all eternity in the memory banks of my mind. Her peaceful, angelic appearance raised a glowing smile within me. It seemed a shame to wake her.

"Come along my angel, the time has come for you to fly." She stirred from a brief slumber, her stunning sapphire animated doe-like eyes battling against a wave of drug-fuelled fatigue.

"I don't feel well, my head is spinning." The woman paused for a moment, swallowing back the contents of her stomach through an arid throat. "I think I'm going to be sick," the young bombshell slurred. "Why is my back so sore?"

"I have done what was required in preparation for your salvation."

"What was required? Slashing me to pieces, you fucking freak. Wow! Just Fucking Wow!"

"Now, now, stop please, enough of the profanities Hannah my love. I will not be subjected to such foul language. Why don't we partake in a walk through the park? I'm sure you will appreciate the fresh air."

"Why on earth would I want to go anywhere? It's pissing down outside, freezing and I feel like shit."

"We'll take a little stroll, it may clear your head. Let's get you out of the car."

"Are you gonna let me go? You promised you would let me go, remember? Earlier tonight you said I could go home."

"Young lady, we shall see. I want to make sure the night is safe for you first. The hour is extremely late you know. There could be numerous unsavoury characters on the city streets, and we don't want you coming into harm's way now do we?"

"What, more unsavoury than you? Please, I don't think so."

"Come on my darling, don't be like that, only the necessary preparation required for your salvation was employed."

"Seriously dude, you need fucking help, you're not right in the head."

"ENOUGH! I will not listen to your gutter talk any longer. Come, let us stroll, then you can wander off into the night to those trendy, affluent friends whose tedious details you insisted on boring me with."

"Really? Thank you," she said as a smile of false hope beamed across her face.

"Wait there my angel, I'll give you a hand."

The carpark was almost deserted, only three spaces were occupied by the vehicles of late-night drinkers who had consumed one too many of the favoured tipple and decided on the responsible option of a brisk walk or public transport rather than risk blowing down a tube for traffic cops. Torrential rain crashed heavily onto my parka jacket and splashed into ever-increasing puddles surrounding the vehicle.

I pulled a new pair of black leather gloves from the car door side pocket, purchased prior to the event, and placed them on my hands; their thermal qualities provided instant relief from the bitter driving wind. With my left arm I reached into the back seat for my large black golf umbrella, only ever used once before for a friend's funeral several years ago, placing it under my right arm for convenience. Next, the gift meticulously prepared for her which I inspected briefly before placing it under my arm along with the umbrella; the one remaining item slid into my inside jacket pocket out of sight.

The cocktail of drugs and alcohol had produced the desired effect of subduing the woman enough to be quiet but still rendered her mobile, preventing any unnecessary commotion. Although thanks to the bloody awful weather and the ungodly hour, the streets were almost abandoned even within London, a city which claims insomnia. In any case, from my experience, folk rarely concern themselves with the activities of strangers under the amber glow of the city night. In fact, they seldom take note of much at all, consumed within their own miniscule bubble of self-importance or a handful of modern technology.

"Come my angel." I opened the passenger side door to the elements of the night.

"My legs are funny – they're tingling, and my face is burning."

"I'll help, maybe it was something you drank," I replied, an attempt at humour that fell on deaf ears.

"Please, I don't like this, I'm gonna be sick, help me." She gagged a small splash of bile onto the cobblestones, legs jiggling with each wretch whilst holding her hair away from her face.

"Take some deep breaths my angel, the fresh air will ease the feeling of nausea," I suggested, taking her by the arm to steady her stagger, before steering her along the winding path from the car to the garden of angels under the canopy of my huge black umbrella which, in fairness, provided little in the way of shelter from the gusting rain.

"A jacket might be an idea; it's freezing out here." She shivered, folding her arms across her chest to maintain warm.

"Unfortunately, we left it at home my dear."

"That wasn't my fucking home was it? You took me from my home, remember?"

"Why the animosity? Please keep walking Hannah darling, we're almost there."

"Where?"

"Here, an oasis of natural beauty exploding from the throngs of the concrete jungle," I said, parading the snip of urban greenery swaying in the wind.

"What the fuck are we doing here?"

"Never mind my dear. Here, I have a gift for you, I hope you like it, you understand this took an eternity to make. Look at it then." She rolled the ornate silver band around in her shivering hands, examining all the intricate decoration painstakingly engraved before placing it at a jaunty angle upon her head.

"Wow it's beautiful, I love the design, is it a crown? Am I your princess?"

"No, my darling, it's your halo, you're going to be an angel," I answered, removing item number three from my jacket pocket with care, sliding the shaft through my hand until it reached its full length. A look of confusion passed across her stunning features. I composed myself with a long deep breath of the cool night air; the autumn rain continued to batter my face, driven by the icy northeast wind, cutting at my cheeks and keeping my senses alert.

The other person inside stirred into life, crawling from his dingey hole to invade my being, like a virus consuming my body, my mind, my movements and actions, trying to control everything I do. I'm forced to beat him back, this process requires precision – perfection must be achieved. Another pulse of pure rage surged through my veins for an instant; again, I resisted the impulsive reaction to cause harm until the target revealed itself. My eyes narrowed, focused on the area in question, as she turned away, admiring the utopic St Mary's Park.

And then the inner me erupted, plunging the hammer head deep into the back of her skull, breaking through the bone with a gut-churning crunch – once, twice, three times, four. A spray of crimson mist spattered across my face, warm with the usual metallic stench. The angel's body became limp and silent as she slumped to her muddy grave under the watchful eye of St Mary herself.

The clouds continued to lash their contents to the earth. I gazed upon her body with a contented smile as the life twitched and flitted from her soul; the inflicted injuries haemorrhaged blood into her brain, shutting down her basic bodily functions bit by bit, like lights being switched off in an office block before darkness descended. This woman's days had ended on a chilly wet October evening in a pile of muddled leaves and twigs, her short pencil skirt riding up high around her slim, silky thighs to reveal the pert cheeks of her arse, but dignity was no longer a concern. Freckles of Hannah's blood began to dry tacky on my cheek; a sterile wipe from my pocket removed them in a moment before I carefully placed the soiled item into a small plastic sandwich bag which I sealed, to be disposed of at a later date.

I inspected my work – the aim was precise, the hammer head had certainly completed the task with the first blow; the second, third and fourth blows were a consequence of the one inside and his lust for gratuitous violence. A desire for more aggression was stamped out before the increase in violence enhanced the chances of leaving a calling card for the police forensics. My mission for this lady was complete – she flies towards the heavens to meet her maker and line the passage with the others.

"Now you are free my angel, fly high."

CHAPTER 2

A telephone rang out breaking the relative silence across the small open plan office containing four workstations separated by royal blue acoustic dividers each customised by their usual occupant with various photos of loved ones, pets or their favourite scantily clad celebrity. Obscuring the only window space allowing natural light into the dim office sat a monster Hp photocopier/printer which sounded like a train leaving a station when set in motion. Situated furthest away from the exit was a one-person office that I used for those moments of required solitude. A cosy but effective space it was full to the rafters with box files of various cases, a couple of grey filing cabinets and the obligatory half-dead cactus, one of those good idea at the time purchases. On the well-worn desk were a number of family photographs – Mum and Dad, son Jacob as a baby, my aunties and finally my Uncle Ged. He had been the inspiration for the career I had chosen – a man who became a black detective constable, the only one in his station at the time, before his untimely cruel death from cancer.

"Dog and bone for you boss," DS Gary Turner shouted from his workspace, an area covered in an ocean of paperwork, biscuit wrappers, McDonald's packaging, scrunched-up A4 notes and used Costa coffee cups which resembled the contents of a skip rather than the professional workstation I would much prefer. Gary is a six-foot-eight gentle giant with a thick-set frame, size fifteen shoes and hands like shovels; he sports an impressive dense fawn beard with evidence of ginger and a drizzle of grey straggled throughout. A cherished whisp of cropped hair receded towards the rear of his scalp which he was desperately clinging on to before it disappeared forever.

"Bloody hell, I can't even make a brew in peace. Any ideas who?" I asked from the designated mess area, a box room next to my office containing all the amenities necessary to make hot beverages, a small chrome sink and not much else.

"God knows. Says he'll only talk to you, boss."

"Fantastic, as if I haven't got enough on my plate." I strutted across the office towards my desk, slopping tea onto the well-worn carpet before seating myself in the battered red leather chair which has been my sanctuary for years.

"Hello, DCI Lynch, London Serious Crime Investigation Unit, how can I help?"

"DCI Lynch, are you the coloured lass?"

"Yes sir, you could say I do have an Afro-Caribbean tinge. Now who's speaking please?"

"It's me, Mrs Lynch."

"Really! Come on, is that all you can muster? My capabilities as a detective exceed that of many others, I grant you that, but I will need a little bit more information than 'it's me'. The population of the UK is over sixty million people, so how about you elaborate and at least give me a fighting chase."

"Danny, Danny Walker."

"Better, that wasn't difficult was it? What can I do for you Mr Walker? Hold on, let me take an educated stab in the dark, shall I? Yesterday you were released from prison, again! And you need me to perform some sort of miraculous string-pulling to obtain a wedge of monetary funding or extra methadone in return for, at best, an unreliable snippet of information which might lead us to gang murders committed by the latest drug dealer who's pissed you off. Am I close?"

"Nah, nah, nuffink like that man, I've turned over a new leaf 'onest dude. No more drugs for this kid, I don't want t' go back t' prison, I 'ad a fuckin' shit time this stretch."

"Oh, joy of joys, has the penny finally dropped? So what are you telling me Danny boy? You're not robbing old ladies or shoplifting to order anymore to supplement your extortionate smack habit?"

"Yeah, that's exactly wot I'm saying, I'm clean man, 'ave been for months now."

"Let's not beat about the bush here. I wish I had a pound for every time those words have been uttered to me young Mr Walker. Let me assure you, I wouldn't be working for a living, I'd be on a beach somewhere blissfully warm, sunning myself with an ice-cold gin and tonic at my side, but hey ho, a girl can dream a little. So, 'new Danny', what can we do for you this time?"

"Well it might be wot I can do for you."

"Continue, I'm intrigued – please enlighten me as to what you think is so important I may be the slightest bit interested," I said with a subtle hint of sarcasm whilst taking a sip of my fresh strong tea.

"Well one o' me mate's man, he's on the streets."

"A bag head I'm guessing?"

"Yeah man, but he's tight, he's sound. Well he were, ya 'earing me?"

"Not really Danny, but carry on anyway."

"I found 'im this mornin', me mate Dec, in a right state, he's babblin' some real shit about a girl he's fucking seen man, he's frightenin me Mrs Lynch."

"It's DCI, and listen, he's aware I can't lay my hands on any drugs for him isn't he? You know, score here so to speak. Tell him, methadone is readily available from the clinic on prescription, he can acquire a fix with all the other drug-fuelled idiots."

"No, he's fine, he's not rattlin' or owt man, this is sommat he's seen wich has fucked with 'is head, do yer get me?"

"Stop playing games with me please, what does your mate think he might have seen?"

"Wer gonna need to set things straight first man, right? He don't want pickin' up by the coppers, I need yer word."

"Both of us know I can't guarantee anything. If he is reporting what he thinks is a serious crime, as per your somewhat vague allegation, someone will need to talk to him Danny. What I can promise is I will not nick him if he hasn't committed any offence, that's how the law works."

"But, but…"

"But what? Bloody tell me or I'll have you arrested for wasting police time. I'm an extremely busy copper at the minute and I don't have time for your shit right now."

"A body, a woman's body."

"Now I'm listening, tell me what, when and where?" I signalled Gaz for some paper and a pen; he rushed to my office door and threw them with an element of expertise ensuring they landed directly under my nose before returning to the seat at his desk, forcing a chocolate biscuit into his mush and taking a large gulp of tea with three sugars out of an oversized mug emblazoned with 'Top Dad' in bright green lettering.

"Me mate don't know wot's 'appened, straight up Mrs Lynch. All I know is he wer in St Mary's gardens lookin' for somewhere to get away from the pissin' dahn rain, he needed a rest from the chuffin' rain and a place to get warm. They do a soup kitchen three days a week."

"To shelter or shoot up?"

"Shelter right, he'd scored earlier in the day, wich is by the by. Listen, do yer lot wanna ear this shit or not?"

"Yes of course we do, carry on please."

"Thanks Mrs Lynch, this is 'ard for us, goin' on t' coppers."

"Again, I apologise, but look at this from our point of view – how many times have you concocted some elaborate plot for personal gain?"

"Yeah, but 'onest, this is the truth," he assured me with a wobble of emotion in his voice.

"Right Danny, calm down and continue. You need to provide us with as much detail as possible."

"He's seen 'er, the blondie, under those giant bushes, the ones wich 'ave purple flowers in summer."

"The rhododendrons."

"Yeah them fings, the woman is under one o' them big bushes. She scared the fackin' life out of 'im man, 'is 'ead's facked up, he says she were laid like a ghost, all covered in mud, and leaves, and shit."

"Danny, take a breath and calm down. He is positive of this is he? Your so-called friend wasn't on planet smack at the time, was he?"

"No, he wern't high and yeah he's sure awright. The lad plucked up the courage to go back and see if she were right, but she aint Mrs Lynch, she facking aint, he thinks 'er fackin' 'ead's smashed in."

"Right, relax and breathe again. Can you confirm he did not return to this woman to check her handbag for cash? Believe me, if this is a murder case and we discover any of his DNA at the scene, hair samples, prints, it will not be good, do you understand what I'm saying?"

"'onest Mrs Lynch 'e didn't touch owt. He's in a right mess. He ran out onto the street and puked up all over the friggin' pavement, I found 'im. So, I called yer because I didn't know wot else to do, yor about the only pig I trust man."

"Thanks for the twisted compliment, and I appreciate how difficult this must be. I'll have someone check out your story right away, I promise. Now, as I've said, calm down and give me your location – a squad car will pick you both up because we will require further discussion with your friend. We will need details for his witness testimony."

"I've told ya, he won't talk to the coppers Mrs Lynch, he's 'ad a bad experience wiv you lot, he gotta good 'idin' in the cells one night."

"DCI Lynch, not Mrs, I'm not married and don't intend to be any time soon Danny. It is important we speak to your mate ASAP, and I assure you he won't be getting a beating in my nick, Danny? Danny? The prick," I said, slamming the phone down in disgust at the silence on the other end.

"What's up Kell? Your boy hung up on yer?" asked DS Turner, grinning and leaning back into his office chair whilst adjusting the lumbar support with a couple squeezes of the hand pump for extra comfort.

"How did you guess? Listen can we send some uniform down to St Mary's gardens, Islington. Our mate Danny Walker is alleging a friend of his might have found a woman's body," I replied with a hint of sarcasm, holding my hands aloft and executing quotation marks, before realising I was performing the one thing which boils my piss at the best of times.

"What, you mean smackhead, scumbag, rob his own fucking granny for a score Danny Walker?"

"I think that is the general description, although he's now a self-proclaimed good boy."

"Yeah right, so we're taking the word of that twat after all the shit he's put us through in the past?"

"True Gaz, but still, let's have uniform check this out in passing. I don't know why, but he appeared genuine today, and alert the team we may need to move on this quickly."

"No probs boss, I'll do it ASAP – well, right after my chocolate hobnobs," Gary smiled, having already demolished half a packet before taking another slurp of tea.

For the next half hour, I added the final touches to the paperwork for a pending court case, a brutal premeditated attack on a senior solicitor. The suspect and his family were well known within the courts of London. Our victim had previously discovered his business partner had not only been skimming a considerable amount of cash from the company but laundering money through the books for a well-known drug dealer to whom he had become overwhelmingly in debt. Weeks later, the solicitor and his family were discovered in their home – they had been beaten to a pulp and an attempt at arson had been made to destroy incriminating evidence. Considering solicitors are deemed to be above average intelligence in society, this man was an exception to the rule, overlooking the most blatant evidence available during the incident – CCTV.

"Ma'am, confirmation from the scene. Danny was right, we've got a dead one," the DS informed me within thirty minutes of the initial call.

"Shit, cheers Gaz. Right, you know the score, instruct uniform to cordon the area off, no one in or out. Give Jenny McCabe a call, they'll need to start ASAP before any DNA evidence starts to deteriorate considering the shit weather and we'll establish the incident room here. DCI Evans at MIT will need to be informed but we will be taking this one no doubt. I'm sure that will please him and his enormous ego. I'll take my car down to the scene and attempt to establish an ID of the victim and meet you there later."

"Just got hold of Jenny, they are on route. Don't you want details of what we're dealing with before you go Kell?"

"Yeah go on, it would be an idea."

"The uniform report says we have a white female believed to be mid- to late-twenties, possibly early thirties, approximately five-foot-five, blonde hair, with possible head injuries. It appears she may have been under the bushes for a couple of days looking at the state of her."

"Cheers Gaz."

Before I had chance to leave, I saw DC Sally Glover stroll through the office door, hanging her dripping jacket on the coat hooks above a small but effective heater. Sally is an annoyingly fit young woman, in fact devastatingly so; it was bloody sickening. When she walked into a room, heads turned – and not only the men's – thanks to a combination of long flowing brunette hair, hypnotic green eyes, and a stunning figure she surprisingly managed to maintain despite her lack of exercise and the vast amounts of crap and alcohol she consumes.

Early in her career she acquired a bit of a wild child party animal reputation before joining our team, but I took a risk on her, and it paid off. I regarded the whole bad girl persona as a cry for help, like a bored puppy misbehaving and chewing your best shoes, destroying the couch, antique dining room chair, or pissing throughout the house. You can shout, bawl, stamp your feet and scream obscenities until you're blue in the face but the result is still the same – a chewed chair or a pool of piss on the kitchen floor. But if you walk them, play with them, give them something to do, train and nurture them, they don't destroy your designer shoes, they learn – and fast. Sally was the misbehaving puppy. I took a punt on her and gave her the chance to shine, and she grasped it with both hands. Now she doesn't chew shoes anymore – she has become a brilliant, instinctive detective and a committed wife (although how committed, I'm not sure but that's a different story).

"Sally, sorry to hit you with work before you've made a brew love, but we've got a body."

"No problem boss, someone will be having a shit day today without knowing. What do you want me to do?"

"Can you start with missing persons for the last few weeks? We're looking for blonde females twenty to thirty years of age. Start locally and if that doesn't bring up anything obvious, you and Jordan can look further afield when he arrives from dropping his kids off at school. And cheers in advance, team, there will be some late nights coming up."

"I'll warn the husband – mind you, he might be glad of the break," Sally said in her usual jovial manner.

"Obviously we have nothing to go on yet, but let's clear the evidence board and begin to build a profile of the potential killer from scratch. Jot down anything we come across – even if we believe it to be insignificant ATM, note it down on the board, anything at all; even if it appears negligible at the time it might link to something later. And rid your heads of preconceived thoughts and previous killers we've dealt with, they all present differently with diverse motives, so keep an open mind. The gaffer should be here by now, I'm sure he'll appreciate, 'Hi governor we've got a body and I'll need thirty of your finest officers, and some specialist investigators on top' first thing in the morning. Gaz, see if we can pick up Danny Walker and his mate – whether they like it or not we will need to talk to them."

"My pleasure boss."

"Finally, get hold of any CCTV coverage of the area in and around St Mary's for at least the last 72 hours. Any suspicious characters, run them through the facial recognition software. I'll get uniform to start a door to door, residential, bars, shops, etc, hit memories whilst they're still clear."

"On it Kell," Gaz said whilst Sally booted her computer into life to begin the endless trawl of mispers.

"Remember guys, the first thirty-six hours of any investigation are the most critical, DNA starts to deteriorate, and memories begin to fade. Work quickly, efficiently and it'll make the boss man happy."

"Yes ma'am," both Gaz and Sally mocked as I grabbed my jacket and scarf in anticipation of heading out to the scene.

"Kell, car keys," Sally shouted, throwing them across the small cosy office.

CHAPTER 3

The St Mary's crime scene was approximately a twenty-minute journey from the office across the busy city streets but that day there was a bizarre procession of slow-moving traffic, an endless stream of billowing buses, black cabs darting here and there, and delivery vans parked in obscure places, all damming the flow of vehicles, not to mention the endless sets of fucking traffic lights doubling the ETA.

All of which gave an abundance of time for my mind to contemplate the next few hours of grisly reality. A million and one questions regarding the victim manifested themselves in my brain. Who is she? Where is she from? What sort of life does she live? Is she an addict, alcoholic? Does she have dependents, family, etc? And finally, the big one – why her? I began to construct these thoughts into a question profile to store in a safe place deep within the grey matter for future reference.

From these lines of inquiry, we gradually build an image of a victim's life bit by bit and, before long, the whole picture reveals itself in full stunning glory. It's necessary to become intimate with the life of a stranger – their hidden secrets, addictions, debts, sexuality, lifestyle – discoveries which even close friends and family can be shocked to hear.

More thoughts come to mind concerning the victim's family, friends or lovers – some sit at home worried sick about their loved one, not sleeping or eating, resorting to alcohol and/or drugs to ease their way through the abnormality of their situation, whilst others momentarily find religion, praying to a superior being, whoever that might be, for the happy fairy tale ending we all realistically know rarely occurs in situations like these.

On the other side of the family and friends coin, there will be the awkward questions we will have to ask of sensitive loved ones or emotional friends from her vast social circle to help discover who has provided us with this horrifying and needless loss of life. A bitter ex-boyfriend? A current lover sick of their other half's flirtatious behaviour? A family member? The sickness of greed often makes people behave in peculiar ways they would never normally contemplate. A jealous besotted work colleague tired of their advances being ignored whilst she disappears off into the night with Casanova strangers, blasé to the angst she is causing them. And of course, the scenario we dread, the worst possible outcome for us – those who have no rhyme or reason for their acts and omissions. Members of society who show no remorse for the hurt and pain they cause. The beings who have a passion for the devastation they impose upon the world. Psychotic killers, animals manifesting their anger in the only way they consider reflective.

The built-in sat nav indicated that the crime scene was finally approaching; preparation for what I was about to witness in the next few agonising minutes was key. Images, smells and acts of violence no person should ever undergo. The brutality one human being can inflict upon another never ceases to amaze me. Seeing these horrifying scenes is a mandatory requirement of the job, and despite the nauseating jangling nerves, you do become hardened to the fact but never blasé; the sensation never leaves you but you do learn to cope in most situations. When a child is involved, then the anxiety increases tenfold – these are the cases all coppers dread, they are atrocious to deal with, especially for me, having a young teenager of my own. All deaths as a result of unnatural causes are devastating but a child's death is on another level for all involved, providing pictures which haunt the mind and never seem to fade with time, waking you from a deep slumber with a pounding heartbeat, all a-quiver in a cold sweat for no apparent reason. The workings of the human brain are not only peculiar, but sadistic – a horrific crime scene remains imprinted in my memory for years but recollecting the kind, loving face of my nan is an impossible task.

St Mary's gardens surround the twelfth-century church of the same name in the borough of Islington. Nowadays, as well as a sanctuary of prayer, St Mary's provides a place of solace and shelter in the form of a social centre and a soup kitchen for the homeless waifs and strays, smack rats and anybody else requiring a warm refuge. The gardens themselves cover approximately four acres of decommissioned cemetery, mainly consisting of open expanses of pristine lawn which becomes speckled with snowdrops and daffodils in spring. These areas of green are dissected by various meandering gravel and tarmac pathways dotted with reflective benches leading to colourful herbaceous borders all under a canopy of lime and ash trees.

A string of blue and white police tape fluttered in the breeze across the entrance to the gardens. Directly in front was a police support vehicle, plus two squad cars and the forensics van, side door open exhibiting its entire contents. To gain access to the gardens I flashed my warrant card to the young uniformed officer securing the scene, who in turn logged my credentials and the time of entry with a respectful nod before lifting the tape for me to pass under and pointing me in the direction of the body. In the distance I observed a scurry of activity in and around the Gala tent erected to help preserve any evidence. Officers dressed in paper overalls, surgical masks and boot covers milled in and out, going about their business.

A friendly hand shot up amongst the swathe of activity, ushering me in the correct direction. The forensic pathologist Dr Jenny McCabe and I have worked together on more cases than I care to remember over the past three years, our specialist subject being murders.

"What we got Jenny?" I asked whilst donning the usual plastic blue covers over my sensible flat work shoes, paper overalls with the hood pulled tight over my hair, and a face mask and surgical gloves. Once suitably clad to reduce any possible contamination from my person, I followed Jenny into the tented crime scene, taking care to walk the route highlighted with tread plates in the footsteps of my colleague to avoid the contamination or disturbance of any evidence.

The woman's body lay slumped on her left-hand side at the far end of the white tarpaulin, wedged against the base of a huge, cavernous rhododendron bush. Her right leg was raised to her chest, itching up the short figure-hugging skirt and showcasing the cheeks of her backside and her black lacey thong knickers. Long, sleek golden hair tumbled around a ghostly white cyanotic face; sky-blue, doll-like eyes staring unnervingly into the distance were the only part of her which still identified a life. The flash of a SOCO camera illuminated the tent for a millisecond leaving bright dots floating aimlessly within my vision as one of the team photographed blood spatter patterns and points of interest on the body, horrors to be preserved and studied.

"Good morning DCI Lynch. We have a Caucasian female approximately five-foot-five and thirty years of age. As I'm sure you've already guessed, we've got ourselves a murder. I've not had time to work out all the fine details, but I can confirm death by suspicious circumstances, with a twist as you can appreciate," Jenny exclaimed, pointing to the head of the young woman.

"She's not been here long judging by the smell, it's still bearable."

"No, a day and a half, two maybe, for a guesstimate, but look at this."

"Is that a crown?"

"That's one option at the moment. From a distance there appears to be an engraved pattern which looks to be surprisingly intricate, perhaps handcrafted I'm guessing. More examination will be required."

"Yeah, a bit weird! She's very pretty too, or was. You got ID or anything else yet?"

"On the table, in evidence bag SM3 to the right. All her belongings were left next to the body in her handbag including mobile phone. My brother not with you today?"

"He'll be here soon, don't worry. Right, who we got? A Miss Hannah Craven, bless her – a name always brings everything into perspective, doesn't it? She becomes a person rather than a crime scene."

"Correct, she's not a body now, but someone's child, sibling or friend. Someone will care, they always do, even with the down-and-out drug addicts or kiddie fiddlers, there is always someone who cares."

An aluminium fold-up table with a powder-coated steel worktop was situated in the corner of the tent furthest away from the body. Unmistakable evidence bags sat in an orderly fashion, like soldiers on parade, all tagged with their unique crime scene ID. I examined them one by one, reading the description, acutely aware of the limited helpful evidence left at the scene by whoever committed the crime, whereas there was an abundance of evidence to identify the victim.

"A travel agent with Norris brothers, not much else though, poor woman. A bank card, driving licence and several twenty notes, what are we looking at, sixty quid?" I said, scanning the individual articles through the translucent plastic.

"We estimated similar."

"So, we can omit a failed mugging from the investigation, judging by the cash?"

"Most definitely. This is much more than a foiled robbery. As well as the money, all her jewellery – expensive-looking rings, gold necklace with diamond pendant and matching earrings – is still present on the body, as well as what I've already mentioned."

"Interesting. What about a sexual motive?"

"From the preliminary findings, I'm disregarding that concept for the moment, only because her underwear remains intact, and her blouse and skirt are undamaged, although strangely her bra appears to be missing. In general, from experience, rapists are bred from desperation, they don't consider the inconvenience of clothing. Their only focus is the deed, satisfying their needs regardless of the consequence, often discarding clothes by any means in their frantic need to perform the desired act. They become blinkered by their hormonal demands, their own sexual gratification, the one thing at the forefront of their minds, with no regard for the dignity of their prey. Also, recent bedtime reading on research conducted into the workings of the rapist mind reveals that part of the thrill is the fear they induce in their victims – tearing the clothes and violence enforces a show dominance, they tend not to waste valuable time replacing clothing and often the indignity of their victim aids their escape. Additionally, from a forensics point of view, at first glance under the ultraviolet light we have no evidence of bodily fluids. But again, we will find out upon a full and thorough examination of the victim."

"And cause of death Jenny?"

"To be clear, without a coroner's report this is pure speculation, but initial impressions would indicate the cause of death to be our old favourite – the blunt trauma injury to the base of the skull. A hammer or something similar – see the bruising and matted blood in her hair here near the nape of the neck." Jenny's ballpoint pen emphasised the areas of interest. "In addition, we have evidence of spatter on the surrounding bushes, and a small amount in the mud here; we can bring the dogs in later to help identify further patterns. If I was a betting woman I would have a tenner on that being what killed her."

"Shit, nasty bastard."

"You need to comprehend the entire story. Walk this way. As we want to avoid moving the body until the examination of the scene is complete, we took these photos from the far side of the body where she's leaning up against the roots of the shrub." Again Jenny removed her ballpoint pen from her mouth to indicate the area of interest on the photographs. "The young lady appears to have been subjected to a degree of mutilation across her shoulder blades and down to the pelvic area. Again, I'm speculating at the minute, but I suspect a scalpel or Stanley knife – something extremely sharp has been used, see the narrow lines of blood patterning on her blouse? Had it been serrated or something like a kitchen knife I would expect to see broader injuries."

"Yeah, I see it."

"Problem is, as you can clearly see, her blouse is fully intact and distinctly lacking the profuse amount of blood staining I would expect to witness with lacerations to the soft skin tissue of the back. So, taking this into consideration, whatever injury was inflicted upon this woman, it was clearly done absent of her clothing and away from the vicinity of the fatal act. But we can clarify that when we return to the lab."

"Jesus, the poor woman was tortured."

"Yes, I would suspect so."

"Any DNA or owt else?"

"No unfortunately not, samples have been collected for analysis, but there's nothing glaringly obvious. The scene seems spotless, although it is early days. On first impressions it would appear whoever created this scene took care to plan with meticulous scrutiny, leaving no scraps to work with – no footprints or signs of a struggle, no defence injuries on the arms or hands of the victim, nothing. I don't regard this an opportunistic murder, had it been so, we would be presented with an abundance of evidence, because no thought has gone into the attack, no planning, it merely happens. This is different, I believe this was a victim of choice not chance."

"Shit, so we might have a proper lunatic on our hands?"

"Yep sorry, my opinion." Jenny held her hands aloft as if apologising for her words.

"Thanks, keep me informed of any developments."

"No probs and good luck catching this twat DCI Lynch."

"Alright Sis, how are you?" Big Gaz asked from the entrance of the tent.

"Tip top Gary, I love spending my day in the freezing cold up to my eyeballs in mud and dead bodies."

"You wouldn't have a job if we didn't have dead bodies, think yourself lucky."

"You really are a knob sometimes. How's Mum and Dad by the way?"

"Usual, still moaning about everyone and everything, so they must be fine."

"Your sibling love is so cute," I teased.

"I'm not sure about sibling love, more like a mutual tolerance ay Gary?" Jenny continued as she went about her business professionally.

"You love me really Sis," he replied with a beaming smile across his huge, grizzled face.

"I don't have a lot of choice do I? You can choose your friends but not your family. Anyway, haven't you two got a murderer to catch? Off you go, so I can concentrate on my job."

"Yeah, we have Jen, come on Gaz, I'll take your unloved arse away. While we're in the area we may as well have a snoop around, check for CCTV, ask some questions at the local shops and bars, jog some memories. But first, let's give Jordan or Sally a ring at the office and give them Hannah's identity info, so the police liaison officer can break the news."

"We should go out soon Kell, what do you think?" asked Jenny.

"Sod it, why not? Jacob is with his dad sometime soon, when he can be bothered to make the effort. I'll text you."

"Aren't I invited girls?" Gary quizzed.

"No, you're not," his sister replied with a comprehensive intent, whilst placing potential evidence into a clear plastic bag with a pair of tweezers and sealing and documenting it.

It may be a difficult concept for the everyday person to comprehend – that only minutes prior to arranging a night out on the lash we were in discussions concerning the vicious and brutal murder of a beautiful young woman on the streets of London. But you have to become hardened, because if you aren't, you'd end up in a mad house yourself. You train yourself to become immune to the violence, to the grotesque images you witness, the ones which haunt your mind, and never fade with time. You learn to turn it on and off like a light switch, one minute dealing with work and the horrors the job can deliver, and the next with home life, family, friends and normality. But life is never completely normal because you never entirely switch off – you do your upmost, but you can never forget the cruel violence of life that is impregnated within your mind. You're always awaiting a phone call because some psycho has manifested their brutality upon the regular people of society.

CHAPTER 4

The evening was starting to draw in; the daylight began to fade and streetlights flickered into action, spraying squat shadows in multiple directions. In all honesty any suggestion of sunlight had been at a minimum throughout the entire day. Wind-swept gun metal clouds continued to unload their contents with relentless enthusiasm. A northerly gust whipped them along at frenetic speed tumbling high above the city's concrete peaks as an inbound Jumbo with a cargo of bronzed holidaymakers broke clear of their grasp. In fact, the heavy rain had been present for days with little respite; the gloom was becoming depressing.

Diamond droplets exploded before me with a notable thud, colliding with the near freezing earth, decaying vegetation and graffitied park benches proclaiming that 'Jess Loves Arron IDST' and other indecipherable marker pen scribbled messages. Streams of rainwater meandered their way across the glistening damp paths and merged to form miniature rivulets which cascaded in the direction of the overworked gutters, gaining momentum en-route and sweeping the swirling twigs, leaves and discarded fag butts into the bubbling drains and then beyond into the abyss of the London sewers.

A male blackbird with sleek charcoal feathers and a bright sunset beak hopped across pristinely cut lawns and tended shrub gardens in the rapidly fading daylight, its head cocked to one side listening with intent for the slightest trace of its unsuspecting earthworm supper climbing to the surface through the rain drenched soil for a breath of vital oxygen.

A thicket of glossy evergreen flora provided the perfect camouflage to secure me from the manic bustling city life I so despise. Deep reassuring gulps of polluted air calmed my pulse, eighty-two beats per minute steadying to normality. The rat race simply passed me by, unaware of the interest being shown from the dreary hideaway. Double decker buses pounded the tarmac metres in front of my eyes, bellowing a haze of stinking dark diesel fumes high into the chilled evening sky on their perpetual quest for punctuality, transporting folk to destinations across London and the warmth and security of their humble abode. A constant stream of scarlet paintwork and advertising slogans promoting Chanel No 5 or the latest album to hit the streets by some talentless over-produced boy band. A shiver rippled its way slowly down my spine as the cool moist air bit at my motionless body. I pulled my collar against the icy draft.

It often amuses me to observe the behaviour of human beings in their natural state, at a point when they presume total solitude – singing to themselves, discussing silent thoughts aloud, picking their noses, scratching their private parts. On one occasion I witnessed an attractive young lady deep in conversation on her phone at an isolated bus stop, to a boyfriend, or possibly a girlfriend in the modern era, masturbating herself to climax, totally engrossed in the importance of her situation, ignorant to the chaos surrounding her until the point of satisfaction was achieved. Only then did it cross her distracted mind to check the world outside her ecstatic orgasmic bubble. Oral sex is a common occurrence, notably later in the evening when alcohol has quashed any of the usual inhibitions. The icing on the cake – full-blown penetration on a deserted railway platform bench: a young beauty I followed from her place of work, coils of golden hair cascading down an impressive slim figure, lifting her long floral summer dress around her lily-white thighs, straddling her man friend,

28

lowering herself onto him and riding him rampant to ejaculation in a few short minutes of unbridled passion. A couple on a late-night rendezvous weakened by the desires of the flesh and at the mercy of their hormonal demands, unable to bridle their sexual urges until they were within the privacy and sanctity of their own four walls.

It's a bizarre notion to comprehend that society makes the presumption their privacy is secure – they are not invisible for Christ's sake, far from it. Of course, I am not alone in observing mind-blowing antics from my hiding places. Oh no, we are on view constantly, there are limited chances of avoiding a camera – CCTV is everywhere in towns and cities these days; shop fronts, traffic lights, street surveillance, ANPR and house doorbells as advertised on TV are watching us 24/7, every single footstep we take, each lungful of air we breathe. Hence, why I am meticulous with my adopted life, why I plan beforehand to the last miniscule detail, choosing my places strategically away from the prying eyes of the cameras to limit any danger of appearing somewhere on a fucking screen. Risk taking is not an option, neither are mistakes. There are plans to manifest themselves, important objectives to complete, a program to execute before my demise. The Old Bill will no doubt attempt to hinder my agenda, trying their upmost to ensure I do not finish my mission, but they will only close in when I allow them to. I am far too intelligent for them, fact. Each step is planned to keep ahead of them, a sly fox on the prowl waiting patiently, and planning.

A tip tap of high heels on the pavement broke my moment of reflection. A new angel was on the way. The one I had been expecting for an hour in the cold wet mirk. Through the dripping leaves dancing with the wind in front of my eyes, I admired her catwalk figure striding with an elegance towards the bus stop. An instant surge of adrenalin filled my veins, elevating my pulse, eighty,

eighty-five bpm to a crescendo, banging out in my chest. Today's attire, a figure-hugging platinum pinstriped suit thoughtfully hand-plucked from a vast wardrobe, flowed stylishly around the contours of her body. If I'm going to be honest, the skirt is provocatively short, almost slutty, providing every man and his dog with a more than generous view of tanned thigh. The jacket opened with a sudden gust, revealing pert, symmetrical, globe-like breasts alongside a hint of nipple glimpsed through the silky white blouse. Unusually her golden honey hair was sleeked back away from her face and tied high in a neat bun, enhancing her beautiful features along with a liberal smattering of copper eyeshadow, rose lippy and deep berry bronzer. A pair of Gucci cat eye spectacles perched studiously on her small button nose finished the chic fashion parade. The woman dressed to impress, to thrill and tease society with forbidden treasures, to bowl over her potential clientele, tempting them into parting with their hard-earned cash for bricks and mortar. One must admire the fact she's not coy about showing a flash of flesh to achieve her goals, and the confidence she exudes.

A Prada handbag hanging over her slender shoulder dropped to the pavement with a thud, scattering half its contents across the path as she tried desperately to shelter herself from the torrential rain under a red and black polka dot umbrella. A mischievous wind ripped it from her grasp whilst she tried to recover the designer bag plus its contents and continue on her quest for home.

I thought back for a minute to our time together, our one night of passion, recollecting her gorgeous, curvaceous body adorned with a cherry blossom back tattoo which meandered to a point between her shoulder blades. An intricate red rose blossomed on one of those fantastic plump breasts, also expertly applied in ink. Her hips had weaved back and forth, her fingernails digging into my back as she enjoyed my manhood inside her. Testosterone rapidly replaced adrenalin and my penis sprang to life as I continued to ogle her impressive figure, appreciating the glimpses of thigh that were strutting purposely towards me in my leafy hideout. Becky Holt, you are about to become special, incredibly special.

CHAPTER 5

As my fabulous work colleague commented, "Becky Holt, you are such a fucking idiot." And she's right. I must have "Gullible cow" written across my forehead, or "Come and talk to me, buy me a vodka or two and I'll sit on your dick." But I guess I only have myself to blame – it's not like I was egged on by friends or colleagues. I was drawn in completely by a handsome face, a fit body, charming conversation and a wad of crisp notes. One can only wonder if the bastard knows what he's done to me or if he cares about the way he's made me feel. Was I playing my part in an elaborate bet with his mates or something similar? Blokes do that sort of thing for amusement or to promote themselves to the dizzy heights of the alpha male.

Well, whatever his agenda on the evening in question, I'm guessing he's satisfied and laughing all the way down the walk of shame with a sense of achievement and empty balls. One pro from all the cons emerging from our night of unbridled passion was that he was insistent on wearing a condom. If I'm honest the topic of safe sex had never crossed my mind, I was so caught up in a hormonal induced haze. All the girls at work guessed something was amiss, and after hours of prodding and probing me into submission, I confessed the weekend's antics with the handsome stranger. Both Sarah and Jenny were of course supportive and understanding, lacking the judgmental attitude I had not only anticipated but also dreaded, whereas others sneered or found amusement as they targeted my prudish attitude. I'm relatively sure all their true feelings regarding my weekend exploits have already bubbled to the surface of the company gossip column.

Friendly support aside, it doesn't numb the feeling of exploitation, stupidity or the extremely foreign concept to me of being a slag, having never done the one-night stand thing before. In fact, I usually take pride in myself for not indulging and bowing to the peer pressure of friends who participate on a regular basis in such practices. The thought of a consensual, unsatisfying thirty-second sticky fumble with a total stranger not only fills me with dread, but goes against all my moral principles. "Respect yourself, respect your body or no one else will," my nan always told me, and I had managed to reach the ripe old age of thirty-two with this attitude. Now I may as well be one of those two-a-penny ladies of the night you spot on the street corners who will dish out a blow job for a bag of spice or the odd tenner. I mean, think about it, what is the difference? He put his hand in his pocket for everything on the night – bar snacks, bottles of prosecco, gin and tonics, shots, all paid for with a wedge of cash, no plastic with this guy. Jesus, I also succumbed to a line of coke with him and it's years since any illegal substance has entered my bloodstream. If I must find a positive concerning the whole situation, he was fucking fantastic in bed.

Right Becks, pull yourself together girl, stop moping over spilt milk, shit happens, you will know better next time. I'll go home, take a long hot bath with bubbles, the type which makes my skin turn to shades of scarlet, climb into my baggies under a quilt, order a huge meat feast pizza from the shop down the road, find a crappy romcom on the box and drink wine until I can't stand up. Oh, and I might indulge in some chocolate as well to cheer myself up. I hope my bus is here soon for god's sake, this weather is rubbish again.

CHAPTER 6

This woman is incredible and unaware of how important she is. The next angel, one to satisfy my addiction, to ease my craving. Becky is going to be a pawn in my game, a cog in the process, she will play the part selected for her like an Oscar winning actor in a hit movie.

Social media platforms provide me with the required criteria, while dating sites lend a plethora of ladies from all social classes, ages, colours, sizes and societal statuses. This young woman I plucked from the depths of the internet; she shared far too many details about herself, making it so easy to track down her acquaintances and probe into their private lives. Within minutes I had discovered where she lived, her place of work, the bars and clubs she frequents on a regular basis, and the fact she had recently become single.

The process begins by tracking them from a distance, observing their routine, taking notes of any patterns, boyfriends, girlfriends, getting intimate with their monotonous daily routines, the times they attend work, lunch breaks, days off. I live their life alongside them, searching for the ideal opportunity to execute my trap, waiting for the optimum time to enact each phase in my meticulous fashion.

The first phase is the chase, the thrill of the hunt, the initial contact, giving them a welcoming smile or a prolonged glance, awaiting the reward of a positive reaction.

Second, breaking the ice, befriending the woman, working on her trust with a bucket full of fabricated stories and empty promises, all the time with one objective in mind: seduction.

Next, the indulgence of the flesh – fucking them, boning, shagging, making love, however you want to sugar coat the act of fornication. Sometimes this takes months, but seldom; most women, granted not all, will give up their dignity for a slutty one-night stand, which leads on to the final stage, the glorious ending when my angels take to the skies and fly to a better place.

The seduction process has become effortless. An abundance of women are willing to assist my games – it's boring, like shooting fish in a barrel. If you pick your time and place, moral standards seldom exist within the contemporary woman. You make them appear empowered and wanted, or ply them with alcohol, drugs, whatever floats their boat. The new age woman doesn't care so much about their reputation: *"We're not in the bloody 1940s you know, we ladies crave sex as much as you men, any woman telling you any different is simply lying,"* a female work colleague kindly informs me with regularity, which is obviously a subconscious attempt to justify her own lack of ethical values.

With some women you can sense their desperation to be wanted, like they need to prove their worth to the entire world. A driven desire to be categorised as successful and popular in every aspect of life, to impress the unimpressed members of society. Popularity has never been a concern for me; in my experience, a friend in need is a pain in the arse, a drain on your soul, always wanting, sticking a nose in when not required. I enjoy my own company, fuck friendship and adulation, none of that can give me that for which I hanker. My friends are loyal to the end, never questioning my integrity, asking where I've been, why I'm late in or what I've been doing. They show unconditional love with a wag of the tail, a wet nose and an enthusiastic greeting at the door.

The more avaricious women are preferred for my project. Ones where to gain their undivided attention all it takes is a flash of cash, or a fabricated tale regarding the affluent lonely lifestyle I tolerate within my four-bedroom detached half-a-million-pound house, with a drive and double garage. The heart-breaking dear John demolishes any resistance, tugging on their heart strings, playing for the sympathy vote. The luxurious car I possess, Jaguar, BMW or Lexus, also plays out the desired effect, alongside the overpaid job, of which I am of course so passionate. My roles include doctor, solicitor, airline pilot, CEO of a fashionable women's clothes brand – the world is my oyster, I can be whoever and whatever I choose. But you must be realistic, and prepared. With each character I portray, a backup plan is necessary. Forged ID cards are straightforward to produce on a laptop with a decent printer and laminator. A few fake photos stored on my phone taken days before of a random house and other people's flash cars, they never question me, never think 'this guy is too good to be true'. Natural defences can be broken down by materialistic greed. On occasion, to show an interest in my life, they may query my role or pry into what is involved, but this is part of the plan, and the internet provides me with the abundance of information I require to authenticate my concocted existence. Bullshit obviously does baffle simplistic brains.

This woman I am watching took little persuading before providing me with her confident and generous offer, desperate to be liked and wanted. A superficial compliment and two expensive bottles of plonk induced the first stages of inebriation, accompanied by a cheeky line of coke; a gut-full of shots was all it took to persuade her of my trustworthiness. Nothing complicated and she became mine for the evening. Taxi to her home, sex, and gone out the door, never to be seen again.

Her story continues, there is still one more craving to appease, one which gnaws away at my bones. This is nothing to do with sexual impulses – the stable door is shut, been there, done that and got the fucking t-shirt. No, this is something sinister, something dark, a niggling urge, an itch which requires scratching – or is it a scratch needing itching? An overwhelming sensation coursing through my veins and refusing to be ignored, like the smack rat rattling for his hit or an alcoholic's shaking hand awaiting the first calming splash of scotch of the day. I will need to put an end to this appetite, to nullify this addiction, it will not miraculously vanish or fade over time into insignificance. But these feelings are put to the back of my mind, nothing will happen tonight, I'm not ready, this is not the right time yet – excellence must be achieved, no mistakes, she deserves perfection. Before long, I will make Becky Holt a shining star and present her with the centre of attention status she desires, the special one, my angel.

For a time, I monitored her from the cavernous darkness of my dripping leafy hide as she waited for her bus, the number nineteen, which would deliver her to the relative safety of her small but extortionate chic luxury flat. She wouldn't need to wait long, the buses are generally reliable; she stood glum faced, engrossed by a handful of modern technology, with the icy rain continuing its barrage, and the gusting wind toying once again with her umbrella. A gathering crowd joined from their sheltered spots, awaiting the imminent arrival of the public transport.

CHAPTER 7

The office appeared silent for a pleasant change. Sally and Jordan were mobile questioning in and around the St Mary's area in a bid to unearth any possible witnesses. DS Turner busied himself tapping away on his keyboard with one hand, whilst spinning a pen between the fingers of the other. His obsession with this case had started to manifest itself from the initial stages; Gary dedicated too much of his life to his work, a fact sad but true. Two years ago, his loyal wife decided she couldn't cope with being a police force widow any longer, with the extended hours required, the distinct lack of attention, all those anxious nights at home with only the TV for company wondering if some nutter had exercised their psychopathic tendencies upon her husband. It was bearable for a certain time, exciting at the start I supposed. But in the end, the pressure, boredom and numerous instances of disappointment build to breaking point, and the hardiest of human beings fold.

I leaned back in my battered old red chair, a pencil in my mouth and coffee mug in my hand, a well-versed situation which I find helps me think. Although the blank notepad in front of me told an altogether different story. I mulled the new case over and over, but nothing sprang to mind or smacked me around the head, no gut feeling followed. An alternative plan would have to be devised. My phone rang, saving me from a morning of unproductive failure. Jenny flashed up on the screen.

"Hi, what you got for me?"

"Well, some significant findings following the initial post-mortem result, how much will become relevant will be down to you."

"I see, hit me with whatever info you've got."

"Judging by the stage of rigour mortis, Ms Hannah Craven's death occurred twenty-four to thirty-six hours before the discovery of the body, sometime Saturday night or early Sunday morning. Whilst conducting the examination of the young lady's body, it was established that the trauma injury to the base of the skull, a depressed fracture, was indeed the cause of death. Such was the severity of the impact, fragments of her bone were lodged deep within her brain matter, brought about by two or more separate blows both measuring between forty and sixty millimetres in size. I would assume a hammer head or similar implement, which in turn induced a colossal haemorrhage rendering death almost instantaneous."

"No noise? No screaming? No shouting? Bang, bang on the head and goodnight princess?"

"Quite! We can also discount any sexual motive, as we are distinctly lacking rape evidence – no sign of forced penetration, vaginal or anal damage, internal lacerations, bruising, sperm deposits, nothing. None of the usual suspects linked with a sexually driven crime, she's all perfectly intact down below."

"Shit, the DNA profiling's fucked I guess?"

"The crime scene and body are spotless DNA wise, my team and I have conducted numerous scans of the area and taken hundreds of potential samples to analyse in a vain attempt to unearth anything out of the ordinary or any trace evidence, hair, bodily fluids, fingerprints, etc, etc. We did discover five foreign wool-based fibres on her blouse. Sadly, these are manufactured and used in vast quantities across numerous clothing industries, as well as for the internals for motor vehicles, furnishing, the list is endless."

"Bollox."

"Sorry but virtually nothing else from the scene came to light."

"Do we have anything at all?"

"Yes, the toxicology report revealed that Hannah had consumed a notable level of alcohol together with a small dose of Midazolam, both were found in blood samples. Not enough to render her unconscious by any means, but adequate to affect her actions for sure. Suggests planning and that he's competent with the administration of drugs."

"Midwhatzolam?"

"Midazolam, a common anaesthesia and widely used drug which can be administered orally, intramuscular, intravenously or even as a nasal spray, a diverse product hence its popularity within the medical trades. A measured quantity consumed with alcohol can induce an enhanced drunkenness or drowsiness. As I said, not a significant amount that would cause unconsciousness but enough to subdue a person in the right hands without a doubt. Which accounts for the fact that Hannah Craven's body revealed no signs of struggle, no defence trauma bruising or cuts to the forearms and hands which we would normally associate with a violent attack of this type. A small blood spatter pattern was present on plant fauna which would back up our theory of limited blows, unfortunately the blood was from the victim herself. Again, all I can say is, as predicted, whoever carried out this act of violence took their time to plan and execute the attack, covering all angles prior to the incident, which is scary, because this becomes a calculated individual."

"To make sure she did what he wanted and didn't create a fuss in the process."

"Precisely Kell. Ponder this from the killer's point of view, if she walked in a contained manner to the chosen spot, not only would it reduce the chance of being caught in the act, but he wouldn't need to consider the inconvenience or risks involved with the disposal of a body. I mean why would he want anything to spoil his perfect crime?"

"So, you think this was a man?"

"Well this is a notion I've mulled over in my mind. There's no proof you understand but, considering the callous brutality of this murder, the angle of impact and the force required to inflict an injury of this magnitude, I would question how many women are tall enough and capable of mustering the strength to deliver such a devastating wound in only a couple of blows."

"My gut feeling swayed towards a male too, but you never know these days do you? Anything else while you're on?"

"Yeah, we did find another hair on her clothing, which we can confirm is not hers."

"Halle-fucking-lujah, why didn't you mention this snippet of information earlier?"

"Don't get over excited Kelly, this is a canine hair not human, but I'm led to believe from the statements gathered to date that Hannah doesn't own a dog, nor do friends or immediate family who she had seen recently."

"Well finally we have something I suppose – a dog-loving psychopath, which narrows it down to about eight million people across the country," I said trying to lighten the situation a tad.

"Yeah, this is a line of enquiry to pursue albeit a long shot. And last but by no means least, and I suspect the most significant piece of evidence we obtained."

"Go on please Jen."

"The entire dorsum has been carved with gruesome wings, in conjunction with ligature contusions on the wrists and ankles and what we believe to be a halo."

"I've seen the halo, or crown or whatever it is. Enlighten me on these wounds."

"Well remember the photographs I took of the corpse at the scene, showing the blood staining on her intact blouse?"

"You said you suspected she may have been subject to some sort of injuries prior to death."

"Yeah, wings."

"What?"

"Angel wings my dear Kell, carved into her back from the centre of her spine, commencing at the T1 and T2 area, up over both scapulars, continuing down through the rib cage to the top of her pelvic girdle, covering her entire back in precise detail. The incisions are definite and clean with no serrations, indicating the implement used was indeed sharp and surgical, clarifying our initial prognosis at the scene with reference to the use of a scalpel or similar blade. But this hasn't just been hacked willy nilly, time has been taken over this – let me tell you, if this wasn't so brutal, the artistic content would almost be admirable. All I can say is she must have been in excruciating pain."

"Jesus, poor woman, so you definitely think she was alive when she received her artwork?"

"Oh yes, the wounds were beginning to heal, a clear indication these incisions were already present before her death, two to three hours prior to her demise, which may also account for the contusions on both her wrists and ankles."

"So, at some point this woman was restrained? I'm guessing whilst receiving the gruesome artwork?"

"Yes, the bruising on both her wrists and ankles is approximately thirty millimetres wide, but lacking flesh penetration. I would guess this was some type of strap, possibly leather, samples from her skin have been sent for analysis. But you can rule out chains, handcuffs or ropes which tend to penetrate deeper into the soft tissue and often through the epidermic layers. Now strangely, there are no other injuries, none of the bruising around the neck, face or body that usually accompanies an investigation of this type. Another topic of interest, when we removed her grotesque halo to DNA test it before cleaning the mud off for examining the details, we found the words '*MY ANGEL*' had been elegantly scribed into the ornate decoration. And whilst we are on the subject, again the décor on this thing is incredible, believe me when I say a lot of time and effort went into creating this masterpiece, but it's clean – no fingerprints, DNA, sweet fuck all apart from the victim's."

"A thought, you don't think this was a cult sacrifice or some weird shit like that do you?"

"No, I don't. Think logically – surely if this were a religious-based martyr killing like the ones witnessed in the past, we would be overwhelmed with DNA, footprints, hair samples, etc, etc. An incident of that type is more often than not a shared experience for all involved to worship in their own particular manner, but we have nothing apart from a bloody dog hair and some mass-produced fibres – not a single muddy boot print, smudged fingerprint or drop of DNA barring the victim's."

"Yeah, I think you're right. Thanks for the update Jenny, can you send me the reports over please? I'll pass them on to the team for perusal."

"Not a problem, enjoy your weekend, let's hope for no more bodies ay?"

"Are we still on for a night out soon, work allowing Jen?"

"Definitely, Harry went out last night for a couple at the local and came home absolutely bladdered again. Therefore, I do believe it's my turn to make a fool of myself."

"Brilliant, I can help you with that."

CHAPTER 8

The itch is scratched, an element of relief from my pain provided for the time being. I've scored my drug but it's unlike heroin or coke, nothing as run-of-the-mill as that. This is a much greater high than any narcotic can provide. Hannah has fluttered away to the heavens to complete her quest. No struggle was given, no argument offered – she sacrificed herself to my cause, my perfect beauty and now she's gone.

To keep the cogs turning, a new search has started, this thirst for violence won't stay quenched for long, the demanding nature increases with each day. This person haunting me is starting to announce himself with more frequency. For decades, it used to be years before he raised his ugly head, then it became months, now only weeks. There is no control over him, I'm not allowed the privilege. Starting as a distant fluttering, a butterfly dancing in the pit of my stomach, building, surging through my body, overwhelming my being, eating me up from inside like a cancer until I'm engulfed.

A random name entered my head. I typed it into the search bar. *Gabby Lloyd*, half a dozen possibilities appeared. Two brunettes, an extremely pretty black woman, another attractive blonde – a *secretary from Birmingham, twenty-six, loves to be active, likes dogs, romantic comedies. Favourite music, the script, little mix and blue.* I'm not judgmental, but Blue? I don't think so, bin her straight away.

To continue, I rack my brains for another name before searching my friends list. What about Lizzy Forester, an old work colleague?

Her profile popped up and I perused it for several minutes, reminiscing on our time working together, the nights out, a shared passionate kiss leading to drunken sex before she moved north to marry her girlfriend much to the disapproval of her staunch Catholic parents. The screen revealed two others, only one of whom is a blondie. *An instructor at Forester Fitness,* original not, *lives in London, thirty-eight, likes athletics, rugby and dancing, loves banging tunes and socialising.* But there's a problem – she has a body from *Baywatch* but a face from *Crimewatch*; binned. My selections need to be perfect in every way.

Another name springs into my head, Helen Richardson, a former schoolteacher of mine, one for whom I held a schoolboy crush. Fuck me, there's an abundance – too old, dark-haired, ginger, a Scottish woman who is alluring, granted, but travel can introduce unwanted attention from the boys in blue. One stunner grabbed my attention, I stalked her profile and photos. Cool – limited privacy settings, wow, fantastic figure, extremely sexy, fabulous holiday bikini shots, she likes to party. More information is required – my women need to be the epiphany of perfection. She's single, only thirty-two years old and blonde. A barmaid at the King's Arms, which is workable, only a tube ride away. Hello, my next angel. My nerves leapt with excitement. The process can begin again – Ms Richardson, I can't wait to meet you.

*

"Please let me go whoever you are. I won't tell anyone about this, honest. What are you going to do to me? I don't want to die," bleated Janet yet again.

"Shut up will you. I'll get around to you when I'm ready, now BE QUIET UNTIL I HAVE FINISHED HERE."

"Let me go, I'm begging you."

"You will be liberated soon, I promise," I said with a smirk, but her incessant whining was starting to grate on me.

"What have I done to you?"

"Leave it Janet, he's not going to let us go, the man's fucking nuts."

"Nobody asked for your opinion Becky. Now shush."

"Where did Mr Nice Guy go?"

"He doesn't exist anymore."

"No fucking shit Sherlock."

"Please, spare us the profanities Becky, they are not an attractive trait for a young lady."

I noted the new woman's details on a sheet of A4 printer paper before placing it in my back pocket. The process can begin, stage one will be put into action ASAP.

"Right, all done now. The next woman is stunning too, like you my gorgeous." I crouched in front of Janet, lifting her head with a delicate hand under the chin, admiring her beautiful face; her Disney-like sky blue eyes sparkled with overflowing tears. Streaks of mascara-stained rivulets flowed down her cheeks and dark rings laid heavy under her eyes; only the leather restraints around her wrists held her upright. "Don't cry my sweetheart, you're special, in fact, extraordinary."

Janet struggled away from my attention, diverting her gaze and avoiding eye contact. I waited for her to calm; again, she slowly raised her head with a scrutinising gaze. A single tear overflowed down her cheek as I ripped the thin material of her blouse down the front; two buttons flew into the air, one narrowly missing my face. The remainder of the material I cut free and placed into a transparent plastic freezer bag. Only her underwear salvaged any form of dignity for her. Goose pimples appeared on her skin indicating the slight chill in the air. Again, she fought against my attentions whilst I caressed the marble smooth skin up and down her spine with soft fingertips.

"Don't worry my love, here's new clothes for you," I said popping her bra strap single-handedly with an element of expertise. All those months of practising with Kay Parker on the school field had finally come to fruition. Janet's breasts sat rounded and firm; a surge of testosterone tightened my balls, tempting me away from the task in hand, but I resisted, her nakedness raised no interest to me, my sexual urges suppressed for another time.

"Sweetheart, you do not possess any wings, do you? How do you expect to fly away to the stars and beyond to the kingdom above without your wings?" I asked whilst cutting the shoulder straps of her underwear with a pair of scissors and pulling her bra clear of her with a jiggle of breast, placing the item into the plastic bag alongside the sliced blouse for incineration.

"What are you doing? What are you going to do to me? Psycho bastard. Are you going to rape me?"

"No, no, no, please, rape is for the Neanderthals. I'm much more sophisticated than forcing myself upon you, as you have both already discovered, but if we were in a film right now, this might be where the tension music begins."

"Leave her alone you twat," screamed Becky, witnessing the donning of my surgical gloves and the removal of a small scalpel from its rightful antiseptic home.

"What the…?" her voice wobbled to breaking point before fading to nothing. From deep within she mustered an element of strength, fighting against her chains and leather straps. I took a moment to view her gorgeous blank canvas of skin and to find the perfect place to begin, assessing the curves of her hips and narrowing of her waist to ensure the work I completed would be of a high standard.

"Please stop, somebody help me!" The shrill scream which followed addled my head, ringing in my ears.

The scalpel blade cut through her soft bronze skin like a hot knife through butter, opening her up like a zip on a jacket. Blood pooled in the wounds before trickling down between her ribs. There is no requirement to cut any deeper than the epidermis, the artwork will get seen, and she will be welcomed into the heavens. Ear piercing shrieks continued to echo around the cellar as the bloodied angel wings began to take shape, awakening the one inside with bloodlust. Janet's claret tasted sweet and the metallic tang induced a ripple of adrenalin down my spine and through the hips, continuing its journey along my legs before it withered out to nothing at my toes. With a shake of the head, I brought myself back to earth with a bump, cleaning the blood from my fingertips, caressing her silky skin with a cooling wipe to calm her panic.

"You fucking animal, leave her!" Becky shrieked in a disgusted rage, rattling and banging her cage front.

"Manners young lady, your turn will come," I assured her with a calm poise.

"Please, please, please, my back, dear god, help me!" Janet screeched in between sobs.

"God will help you soon, as you approach those pearly gates he will take you in his arms and welcome you. Anyway, cease with the whinging, I distinctly remember my hands on your back when I took you from behind only weeks ago, you didn't mind me scratching you then."

"Help me someone, stop you bastard, stop!" she continued her exhausting fight against her shackles, bawling frantically, but the artwork must be finished.

"Screaming and shouting will not be of any assistance to you now, no one will hear down here. Now keep still, I'll soon be finished."

The blood continued to ooze from the wounds down her back like tributaries to a river flowing onto her short pencil skirt before dripping from the seams and pooling on the floor beneath her.

"Someone help me please, stop, stop, I'll do anything."

"I'm more than aware you'll do anything – remember our dirty night together in your flat? You were utter filth. You wouldn't take a break, wanting more and more of my cock, I was quite exhausted," I reminded her, taking a moment of contemplation towards the artwork, then crouching in front of my angel, peering deep into her submissive tear-filled eyes before returning to her back.

"I can't take much more."

"LEAVE HER YOU TWAT!"

"Shush Ms Holt, please be silent and let me concentrate. We're almost done here aren't we Janet?"

"You are a hateful bastard, I hope you burn in hell," Becky sneered towards me.

"I'll soon be done, and you'll be perfection won't you my beautiful? Now that's great news do you not think? Then your mission will be completed. There we go." I stood back and admired my bloodied artwork with an element of pride. Janet sobbed, her head slumped in a state of panicked exhaustion, her tears dried to nothingness.

"Your wings are stunning darling. Now you can fly my sweet angel." I returned the scalpel to its rightful receptacle, a jam jar containing sterilising fluid which turned scarlet in an instant. Janet's wounds were cleaned with disposable antibacterial wipes which I transferred to the plastic bag with her other items. The flow of blood slowed to a steady trickle, drip, drip, drip, to the white tiled floor. "Once she's gone, I'll clean up," I thought to myself.

"Please help me, please," her sobs faded to a whispered silence.

"You're a complete bastard. Let her go, you've broken her, are you satisfied now?" bellowed her roommate with a face of pure rage.

"She's not finished yet Becky my love, but it won't be long. Now, back in the cage please Janet. When the bleeding ceases, we can put your new blouse and jacket on. We don't want you catching your death of cold darling."

CHAPTER 9

"Fantastic timing boss, you've saved me a phone call," Jordan announced as DS Turner and I returned from pounding the streets.

"Go on, what you got?"

"It might be something or nothing, but my gut feeling is telling me this is too coincidental to be overlooked considering less than a week ago the body of a young woman was discovered."

"You never know, any info is better than none."

"This is a missing persons report sent to us this morning for a Becky Holt."

"And what's special about this one? A hundred and eighty thousand mispers are raised per year."

No answer was warranted – he held a photo of the woman aloft, a blonde-haired, blue-eyed stunner.

"Shit, spitting image of our dead woman."

"Precisely."

"Listen in please, it appears we've got another missing woman," I shouted across the open-plan office donated for the duration of the investigation, clapping my hands together to grasp the attention of the army of borrowed detectives from their PC screens.

"What we got on her Jordan?" asked Gaz pulling a chair closer.

"Guys and girls, this is Miss Becky Holt," he announced, dealing out copies of a mug shot. "I will email a copy to all later."

"Fucking Jesus, Hannah Craven's twin," Sally exclaimed.

"Exactly. So, after chatting to colleagues and friends, the story goes that Becky Holt turned into work Monday eighteenth of October at approximately eight am, as per usual, admitting to her bestie in the office to be hanging out of her arse. What's unusual about that you might think? It's not a bizarre concept to accept for a young single woman after a weekend on the tiles with her girlfriends. However, she went on to inform colleagues she'd been drowning her sorrows and by all accounts had made a fucking outstanding attempt at doing so. According to these work mates, our woman met a bloke Saturday night, which would have been the sixteenth; after several drinks, she decided to invite him home for coffee."

"Not being funny here, but in my long and illustrious experience, if a young lady invites you in for 'a coffee', it almost certainly means one thing – she's after sex. Every fucker knows that it's code for she wants to play the hide the sausage game," Gary kindly highlighted to a ripple of mostly male stifled laughter.

"Not always you idiot. A woman can invite a man in for coffee without it always ending between the sheets," Sally explained in defensive mode.

"Yeah, because you fuck them on the sofa before you reach the bed," Gary replied laughing.

"Rude," she said, presenting the one finger salute.

"Sal, you tell me this, how many times on a drunken night out before meeting Mr Glover did you invite a lad home *for coffee* with the sole intention of bedding him?" Gary posed, popping a pen into his mouth in a quizzical manner. The room fell silent awaiting the answer.

"Point taken but, in my defence…"

"Back to the investigation please, we can discuss Sally's former sordid sex life at another date. Please, carry on," I interrupted, gesturing towards DC Willis.

"It's not sordid, honest," she defended to the hoard of sniggering detectives.

"So, to continue," Jordan laughed under his breath at DC Glover's expense, "the gentleman in question met our woman on the Saturday night. This man epitomised Mr Perfect – suave, sophisticated, well-dressed, splashing the cash, treating her like a sort of goddess, allegedly managing to charm his way into her home, her bed, and then her knickers, our source revealed. After their one night of steamy passion, Mr Ideal proceeded to do a disappearing act, vanishing without a trace or a *'by the way thanks for the shag'*. Personal details were swapped. Unfortunately, when our woman tried to call mystery fellow, all she got was *'this number is no longer available'*. It transpires the woman in the image only finished a shitty relationship with her long-term boyfriend in recent weeks and, reading between the lines, I get the impression she was grateful for a bit of male attention."

"So, when was the missing persons filed?" I probed.

"Well she turned into work for the rest of the week, and the following Monday, Tuesday and Wednesday, although still pissed off with herself for being so gullible for sleeping with the sweet-talking stranger. Here's the twist – Thursday and Friday, she was a no-show at the office. No phone call to say she would be late, or that she was sick, nothing, all against any previous form, she's never wagged work before. In fact, she is the epitome of a model employee – punctual, dependable, well presented, and bloody excellent at her job. To date, she has not answered calls to her mobile or home number or taken leave to her parents which she often did at weekends. A colleague took it upon herself to visit her humble abode across town, a shared flat in Camden; she talked to her flatmate who insisted she hadn't seen her for days, presuming she was away at said parents. So, she decided to file a misper."

"Guys and girls, let's find out where this pair met, venues visited, bank transactions, public transport utilised on the evening in question, taxi, buses, considering the weather was fucking awful all night and she lives five miles away from the area marked on the map provided. Peruse CCTV to establish any possible ID on our Prince Charming or at least a description of possibilities; remember, view the footage in both forward and…"

"In reverse, we know Kell, it often reveals missed evidence taken for granted with natural orientation," Gaz interrupted.

"Thanks, am I that predictable?"

"Yes, but it's not a bad thing," he smiled, removing his pen from his mouth and scribbling notes on his pad.

"One more thing, locate the ex-boyfriend too, talk with him, determine the last time he saw her, spoke to her, or had any form of contact with this woman, you can never discount the jilted boyfriend. OK people, let's move fast on this for the sake of this young lady," I said, holding up the mug shot provided by Jordan. "Once the press gets hold of this it will spread like a dose of diarrhoea and questions will require answers."

"All over this boss. According to her mates, she started out in the trendy new gin bar the Limes, off the high street not far from her workplace. Our woman was scheduled to meet an ex-colleague outside, who cancelled due to a family crisis. I'm going down with a photo to jog memories and to check their CCTV, plus I've asked for anything from the ANPR or private cameras."

"Cool, carry on Jordan, and talk to this ex-colleague and her current work mates again, she may have revealed some details of our man. Start building an MO of this bastard, cross-reference previous offenders with a particular interest in carving women up and the three B's – blonde-haired, blue-eyed and beautiful. I think we have to assume these cases are linked, considering the uncanny similarities."

"I'll take that," Gaz said, propelling himself across the lino floor towards his workstation with one brisk flick of the legs.

"I'm on with the boyfriend boss, I found him on her Facebook profile. I'll check him out, also I'll contact the techies for her mobile phone activity," Sally confirmed, pushing her glasses back up her nose.

"Listen folks, let's not forget the victim we are currently investigating. For both these women, I want lifestyle indicators – any drug habits, alcohol addiction, sexual fetishes or orientation, her favourite chocolate if needs be. We need to understand every little detail of these women and their lives before," I said, addressing the entourage of mumbling detectives assigned to our team.

CHAPTER 10

A thick early morning mist cleared to reveal azure October skies speckled with cirrus clouds drifting effortlessly high above the dull grey concrete jungle. The mid-afternoon autumnal sunshine provided a pleasant warm glow on my broad shoulders, rejuvenating my body with a much-needed dose of vitamin D. Birds were perched high in the trees, singing out their joys to the skies. City folk enjoyed what might be the last credible signs of sunshine for the year, an enjoyable and much-needed respite from the previous week's horrendous weather of rain, rain and more fucking rain.

The usually bustling city roads were quiet with only light traffic and couriers cycling hard for an early finish. Obligatory black cabs raced unnecessarily through the sun-drenched streets, enacting a bizarre game of Mario kart whilst open-topped bus tours chugged along, allowing tourists to absorb the sights London has to offer. Occasional joggers pounded the almost deserted pavements, headphones banging music of choice into their empty skulls as they dodged families walking excited dogs towards the parks for a couple of hours of stick chasing and valuable time with loved ones. It was an ideal time for a leisurely stroll into town to partake of a cool refreshing pint or two, avoiding the madness which usually engulfed the streets through the working week, and to meet my next angel for the first time.

The King's Arms was a quaint 19th-century building with bright white rendered walls, black oak beams and an ornate porch entrance. It was the type of public house you would expect to find in some picturesque greenbelt village, with a duck pond and a kids' play area to the side, serving overpriced roast lunches to affluent country bumpkin farmers who visited once a week in their Range Rover Discoveries to catch up with their neighbours on the state of crops over a pint or two of the landlord's best hand-pulled real ales. Instead, this oasis of idyllic rustic charm appeared to have been unceremoniously dumped amongst a forest of skyscrapers, concrete, glass and tarmac, thus providing a much-required tranquil escape within a world of hustle and bustle.

Four benches along with brewery sponsored parasols populated the beer garden to the front of the building, occupied by weekend drinkers relaxing before re-joining the rat race which will be London in the morning. To blend in with members of the great unwashed I'd opted for a casual look of sports shoes, blue Levi jeans and a tight emerald polo shirt so as not to draw unwanted attention to myself. In general, my chosen attire would be more sophisticated and formal. The route to and from the establishment and the surrounding streets had been scrutinised daily prior to my visit, noting all the camera points. For peace of mind, I perused the location again, checking all the potential areas, commercial buildings, ANPR, lamp posts – there was nothing much to worry about on the street as per previous recces, but it's good practice to keep verifying.

The light traffic provided ample time to skip from kerb to kerb, noting a CCTV camera on the eaves of the porch, way above a classic style carriage lamp hung above the door. The spying eye will not be a problem, a plan will be actioned to avoid any incriminating photographic evidence.

A tinge of stale ale tainted the tepid air inside the dingy ye olde worlde King's Arms. My eyes struggled to adjust from the bright autumnal sunshine on the street to the near darkness inside. Two antique brass wall lamps sprayed a shroud of unimpressive artificial light from above a couple of cosy snugs; they were supported by a single ceiling fan/light combination in the lounge which stirred the warm air. Some modern LED spot lamps situated in and around the bar area provided the only form of acceptable illumination, a modern twist but completely out of place alongside the traditional Victorian stained-glass windows which blazed a rainbow of colour across the beaten-up wooden floor of the redundant smoke room.

A brace of locals no doubt considered part of the furniture were perched close to the bar. One, a younger gent with a mop of greasy ginger hair and matching week-old stubble, glanced up briefly; he revealed a smile containing only three teeth he could confidently claim as his own before returning to scrutinising the sporting press for racing tips. The other was a relic from World War Two, with leathery tanned skin pulled taut over bony features, and narrow sunken dark eyes that squinted to focus whilst checking me out. Placed firmly upon his head sat a grimy tweed flat cap, removed briefly to wipe his brow with a grubby blazer sleeve then quickly replaced to cover a receding silver hair line. He slurped his ale casually using both hands to steady his shakes. Immediately to his left, underneath a series of vacant coat hooks, leaned a walking stick decorated with a deer antler handle smoothed by years of use which he touched intermittently, I could only presume as an element of reassurance.

To the rear of the old timer was an open fireplace stocked with split logs either side which I imagined during winter months provided a welcoming glow to the establishment. Mounted above it in an equally spaced triangular formation, in pride of place on the chimney breast, hung three coats of arms claiming to be those of various historic English monarchs.

"Hi, can I help you sir?" a friendly Helen Richardson asked, taking a break from drying glasses with a small towel before replacing them in their rightful place on the shelfing. She is ignorant to the fact that I am familiar with her and her mundane life. For weeks I've followed this woman, establishing her routines, friends and homelife. Now is the time to execute stage one – make her acquaintance and establish trust, a huge risk on my behalf but one I'm willing to take for this beauty.

"Hi, lager please," I replied with a cheerful charisma whilst casing the joint for additional cameras, examining each room for button devices, which can be difficult to locate, but there's nothing glaringly obvious. Ms Richardson was no disappointment – as attractive in the flesh as she appeared in her holiday snaps. I gazed her way whilst she replaced the drying cloth over the handle of the dishwasher, admiring the way her jeans clung to her shapely thighs and backside.

"Any particular kind sir, we have Carling, Fosters, Coors light, Birra Moretti?"

"Anything to quench a thirst, Carling will do thanks."

"Had a busy day sir?"

"Yeah, sort of, unpacking boxes. How do we manage to accumulate such vast amounts of nothing important? In fact, some of which I didn't realise I still owned, unseen for years, hidden under a blanket of dust in the attic."

"You just moved in around here?"

"Earls Avenue, around the corner," I lied. I had observed the sold sign being erected several weeks ago.

"Impressive, I love those old houses, they are huge though. I wouldn't want to clean one – or pay the bills for that matter."

"I know what you're saying, but I like it. The old girl needs a bit of knocking about to make it mine, but I'm in no rush."

"That will be £4.10 please sir." A gorgeous smile beamed across her stunning face as she placed the cool golden pint down on the bar in front of me; the condensation trickled down the outside of the glass. Yet again, my choice was outstanding, she shone like a new penny.

"It's Dave, if you don't mind. When you call me sir, I think my dad is standing behind me," I joked, giving her an approving smile, which Hannah reciprocated with sparkling blue eyes.

"Sorry, force of habit."

"Is the food menu still available?" I asked, pointing towards a chalk board on the wall advertising culinary delights of all tastes, ranging from a basket of fries plus cheese with a dip of choice to share platters feeding four, and every single dish imaginable in between.

"Sorry sir, I mean Dave, the service finished twenty minutes ago, but I can offer some bar snacks – sandwiches, pies and pasties?" she said, guiding my eyes to a two-tier heated display cabinet containing an abundance of pastry food items.

"Yeah, a pie please, I'm not bothered about the filling, anything will do, I'm too hungry to be fussy."

She finishes work at ten on a Sunday evening. I stayed all evening, acting Mr Nice Guy for the rest of her shift, making idle conversation, gaining her trust minute by minute and enjoying the cool refreshing beer. When the time was right, I introduced her to my fabricated life story – a tale of woe regarding my ex-wife's sordid affair with her much older boss, a man of extreme wealth, which drew her in for the sympathy vote. I took the time to describe a blossoming adulterous relationship which came unexpectedly after ten years of what I deemed a blissful marriage to my teenage sweetheart. I exaggerated the emotional journey experienced by myself and the overwhelming desire to evade my former shitty life with the shared friends, and our home sweet home, a fantastic detached house where we, in my mind, lived a happy and affluent life. I over-dramatised the scenario that, due to my own mental fragility, I dare not chance witnessing my wife and her lover together, a broken heart being enough to deal with without adding to my fragile emotional state. The new life meant I could relax more and avoid the chaos central London promotes. She listened to my every word, contemplating the story, absorbing it like a sympathetic sponge. I'm excellent at reading people, and her body language was all correct, reacting with an understanding smile. The seed was now sown, ready to grow and bloom into glorious colour. I was taking the ultimate gamble befriending her like this, chancing familiarisation with locals, but it gave me an opportunity to scout the premises, take note of friends who visit her on shift and decide whether the risk factor for this woman wavered upon precarious – if so, I walk.

Judging by her reaction, my chosen alter ego was acceptable – her ears pricked up in an instant as I introduced myself as Mr David Roe, a solicitor with his own company in Ealing, specialising in small injury claims and petty criminal cases. A business providing a generous turnover, not huge, but more than ample to maintain a comfortable living. A role researched prior, should she question the integrity of the story or intrude further. *David Roe Law, Ealing, established 1999, now employs two additional solicitors, Gareth Ross and William Smythe, alongside an accountant, Heather Giles, with part-time receptionists Maddie Wilson and Jayne Croft.* That should impress my new angel.

CHAPTER 11

"Helen darling, I think you've got an admirer," my colleague Candice Jackson whispered whilst walking by me with empty pint pots for the glass cleaner.

"What? Who? Me?"

"Yes you girl, Mr New Boy at the end of the bar, he can't keep his eyes off your assets. So, work it girl, tease a bit, work the angles."

"You need help. He is fit though I'll give you that, and single, a solicitor he told me earlier, but I don't need a fella in my life right now even though an element of male company would be nice from time to time."

"Yeah, I know the feeling chick, some attention other than these old drunken perverts here ogling yer tits and backside every time yer move."

"Too right, I do miss the electrifying touch of a man's hands all over me – being uncontrollably desired by another human being is exciting and I love the sense of satisfaction it produces."

"You need a shag for definite Helen my love."

"No, it's not only that, there's the aroma of a man in your bed and the warmth of his skin against yours. You feel safe with a man sleeping beside you as well as sharing your life and experiences with someone special."

"Yep, you definitely need a good seeing too sweetheart, some non-committal wild dirty sex, that would sort you out babe."

"I'm not sure, after all my escapades with the ex I'm not sure I'm ready for another relationship or anything else for that matter."

"Take a dribble of advice from a girl in the know. If you want him, he is yours – and remember one thing my lovely, your pussy is too far from the ground to feed itself, and at some point, it will get hungry."

"You are pure filth, Candice Jackson."

CHAPTER 12

"Jacob, it's nine o'clock, are you up and ready? Your bloody dad will be here soon, and I don't want to spend any more time than necessary in his presence."

"Chill DCI Lynch, attention," came my son's voice from upstairs.

"Cheeky, it's Mum to you, and I'm a copper not a drill sergeant in the army."

"That's not what Gary says," my son laughed.

"Oh, does he now? I'll speak to him later, now are you ready?"

"Yep. Why does Dad insist on picking me up at this ungodly hour? He's mental man, he knows school's out and I don't like getting up early."

"Let's be honest, this is not early to normal people."

"Do I have to go Mum? The man bores me to death, and I can't stand his stupid frigging slutty girlfriend."

"Yes you do, and language please, the neighbours will hear you."

"Sorry Mum."

The boy was right though, Fiona was a slut, as he so eloquently expressed. Which is a shame. As young girls, we were inseparable from primary school right through secondary and beyond, like sisters. Nobody, and I mean nobody, messed with either of us, they were all more than aware it meant double trouble if they did, not recommended. Fiona Frost had decided her destiny from an early age, unlike me – she only ever dreamt of being an A&E nurse, incessantly droning on over the years and boring me silly with her dreams of grandeur. The girl chose her path in life and stuck to her ambition like shit to a blanket.

Despite her desperate yearning to nurse, modelling could easily have been a career option should she have so desired, because she is stunning in every conceivable way: blonde, beautiful, tall, with long slender legs and fantastic tits to top everything off, not that I'm the jealous type. Instead, she achieved her ambition and, after years of working the wards, she met and soon married a paediatric surgeon, a lovely bloke by the name of Miles, an incredibly handsome man as you would expect, although quite a bit older than my mate.

And so began the euphoric life for which she had always hankered. The extravagant house and flash car were easy, but the two point four children eluded them; despite their efforts, the patter of tiny feet was still a distant sound. But apart from the pressure of conceiving, life was idyllic. Then came the black fly in her Chardonnay. Miles, her loving husband, had other ideas on life and decided to indulge himself in an affair with another much younger doctor from the hospital where they both worked. What is so significant about another affair you might ask – people conduct such activities constantly, trading in the beaten-up old banger for a modern model with less mileage on the clock. But this upgraded version was a male one. The concept totally blitzed Fiona's head. If his lover been female, I'm sure the impact wouldn't have been quite so devastating, but for her fella to leave for another man, well she could not compute that situation. After consulting with Darrell, my partner at the time and Jacob's father, I offered her the spare room at mine until she sorted her life out; the last thing she needed whilst dealing with a messy divorce and the associated stress and anxiety was to worry about where she might live.

My ex-fiancé Darrell Rogers is a forensic pathologist. We met at a grisly murder scene alongside the train tracks in Ilford on the banks of the river Roding where, despite the brutality of the situation, I found an instant attraction. Whether it was his sports model body which he obsessed over or the handsome knee trembling smile which charmed itself into my bed who knows, but the chemistry was evident from the first date. Before long, the relationship bloomed into a devoted couple of sixteen years managing to produce our only child Jacob, despite my heavy work schedule in combination with studying for promotion. Jacob and his father are chalk and cheese – my boy adores rugby, his dad loves football, our son follows boxing, my ex considers the sport pointless and barbaric; in fact, they possess nothing in common. If I didn't know better, I would question Darrell as his biological father, but there is no doubting the connection, they are almost twins despite the obvious difference in skin colour.

A few teething problems aside, our happy little household consisting of me, Darrell, Jacob and our lodger and my bestie ticked along with relative ease. Fiona mucked in with the housework, cooking and cleaning when I worked a late. She made Jacob's lunches and fitted into our life perfectly. Right until the day our son made an unscheduled visit home from school to fetch his footy boots for PE and caught his dad fucking Fiona on the kitchen table. From that moment on the relationship sort of spiralled downhill with drastic effect. Now the adulterous pair live together and are looking to marry. As if this twisted, fucked-up scenario of my best friend of more years than I care to remember and the man I'd devoted sixteen years of my life to being involved wasn't bad enough, both parties admitted their sordid affair had been conducted behind my back for months on end and I hadn't suspected a thing. It never once crossed my mind that the pair of them would stoop to those levels as human beings. Some detective I am – I couldn't see the wood for the trees under my own roof.

"Listen, you've got to go mate," I said, about to justify my reasoning as to why.

"Yeah Mum, I'm part of the deal and you don't want to appear like the shitty one in the situation, I get it," he replied as he descended the stairs, bag over one shoulder and rolling his eyes whilst reciting the all-too-familiar scripted words I must utter on a continual basis during these moments.

"Come here sunshine, your mummy needs a cuddle." He laughed and embraced me. I held him tight and took a lungful of his aroma, something which never changes, I love his smell.

"Come on, let go now, I'm fifteen."

"A few more seconds, what about a sloppy kiss for Mummy?"

"Leave off me you lunatic woman."

Both his smile and laugh are infectious, no wonder he's fighting girls off left, right and centre. A knock, knock on the front door echoed down the hallway and Jacob rolled his eyes for the second time in as many minutes.

"Try to enjoy yourself. Listen, we are investigating a major case at work, but if I get chance I'm out with Jenny over the weekend. I don't go out often, so please, don't fall out with your dad and Fiona again, because I won't be able to pick you up this time."

"I'll be a good little boy, promise," he said, pecking me on the cheek and striding towards the front door, showing me his crossed fingers and laughing.

"Hi son, go wait in the car mate, Fiona is waiting," Darrell uttered like a stuttering imbecile as his son acknowledged him with a cool nod and silently passed by and headed towards their vile rusty brick coloured Audi A5.

"What time do you want him back on Sunday Kelly?"

"Whenever is convenient I suppose but make an attempt to do something different with him this weekend, he's saying you're boring."

"Right, we'll take him somewhere decent, the football or something."

"You do that, spend some quality time with him as his dad. Oh, by the way, for your information, he fucking hates football, just throwing it out there, goodbye," I said with a satisfying slam of the door before any response could be given.

CHAPTER 13

For weeks I have frequented the King's Arms on a regular basis, making conversation with Helen Richardson, gaining her trust. A joke shared together induced an infectious smile; her sky-blue eyes glisten like crystals when she's happy. Once more my choice is exemplary, this woman will be a perfect Angel.

"Another one David?"

"Yeah, why not, one more, no more. I was contemplating a walk home, but you've talked me into it."

"Didn't take much arm twisting," Helen laughed, already re-filling my glass.

"What's your name by the way? You know mine and everything about me apart from my inside leg measurement, and I don't recall you telling me yours," I asked, more than aware of the answer.

"I'm Helen."

"Well Helen, I'm pleased to meet you," I replied, shaking her hand mockingly as if we were new acquaintances.

"So, are you enjoying living around here David?"

"Yeah I am. This is a pleasant area with decent people, an excellent boozer down the road, the barmaids are a bit ropey, but the beer and food are decent."

"Cheeky, here you go, £4.10." An attempted slap was evaded with a laugh and an impertinent wink.

"No, I'm enjoying my new life, I'm considering getting a dog to give me something to do and help meet more people."

"Well good for you."

"Listen Helen, please don't take this the wrong way, but do you fancy grabbing a drink or something to eat at some point? As friends, nothing else you understand. I could do with a tour guide and an introduction to new circles," I asked, holding my hands up to emphasise the innocence of my question.

"Well I'm not sure I am the right person for that, and I work most of the time to make ends meet if I'm honest."

"No pressure, I don't get offended easily, but if you say no you'll never set eyes on me again," I joked over dramatically. "Sincerely, it was only a thought, I need a bit of help to find my feet around the area. Old George is a top bloke, but he's not much of a mover and his conversation is somewhat limited to World War II. Don't get me wrong, I consider the sacrifices veterans like him made during those times admirable and I take my hat off to those brave young men to whom we'll be for ever indebted for the life they have provided for our generation, but I feel like I served with him. I'm positive I could recite his stories word for word," I paused for effect as she laughed. "Hey, you can invite your boyfriend or some mates?"

"I'll tell you what, yeah, why not. I've not been on a night out in ages. Problem though – my only time off is today. So, we can do tonight, unless it's too short notice?"

"Well I will check my remarkably busy diary. I am in demand to make you aware. No, you're lucky, I'm free, old George will need to find someone else to bore to death this evening."

"Poor old sod, he'll be more than happy ogling Candice and I'm relatively positive it won't take him long to trap another unsuspecting victim instead of you sat at the bar."

"Listen, like I say, please bring your partner and some friends, we can make it a proper night out," I suggested, knowing full well she's single and most of her friends reside miles away in Leicester or are married with kids. I've done my homework, I know her life almost as well as she does.

"I only moved here six months ago so I don't have many people I consider mates down here, apart from the girls I work with, and if I'm not on shift they'll be working. And as for men, I don't do boyfriends at the minute, bad experience, you are more than aware of that sentiment."

"Well, we can still make a night of it. Seven o'clock in here?"

"Yeah, I finish at half four, which should give me more than enough time to put my face on and dig out some glad rags. Thanks Dave, seven it is."

"And don't be late," I said wagging my finger like a schoolteacher.

"It's a date. Purely platonic."

"Platonic is fine for me. Please don't be overly disappointed but women and relationships aren't number one on my agenda right now," I assured her. *But making you my angel is,* I thought to myself as I eyed her stunning figure whilst she shelved the clean glasses.

CHAPTER 14

"Hello team, have we come up with any additional info we haven't already been over twenty times?" I addressed the office with only a scattering of bodies left.

"No Kell, I'm conducting a search on the ECRIS. I've also emailed a mate in Europe who's helped us before with snippets of information regarding alike crimes across the continent; it's a shot in the dark and as you are aware it could take some time," Sally replied.

"Excellent, thinking out of the box. Not strictly by the book but brilliant all the same. Keep me informed if we get any feedback at all."

"Will do."

"Nothing from us at the moment I'm afraid Kelly," said Gary. "We appear to have hit the proverbial brick wall – no CCTV footage, well, I say no footage, nothing incriminating. We did obtain a snapshot of Hannah Craven in a bar surrounded by drinkers but nothing definitive of who she was with, and the bars were shoulder to shoulder busy on the night in question. There was any number of males in the vicinity of our woman but no one suspicious. One of the staff did mention he thought he recognised the victim's mugshot but couldn't say for definite. He described her as the one woman who stood out above the others because she was dressed to the nines, long blonde hair and stunning. Now this might have been our Hannah with a fella described as a body builder type, but again, he couldn't be sure and wouldn't be able to give me an accurate description having only glanced briefly whilst another member of staff served them. We don't possess anything else to go on so we are pretty fooked at the minute," Gary explained.

"Jordan?"

"Same boss, nothing as yet, sweet FA. Waiting on missing persons to return my email with a broader report of women matching our description from further afield."

"Right, it's getting late, and I don't think we can do much more tonight. Dr McCabe is going to ring me if anything develops their side, but as we don't have a lot to go on, I suggest we all go home, shower, rest our brains and replenish ourselves, watch the footy, play with the kids, drink wine, and Sally, you do whatever it is you do to relax. Let's go again in the morning. We'll hit the streets, talk to Hannah's friends, family and any other associates again. I know we've already been over this, but I want to pinpoint her lifestyle indicators, professional contacts, drug habits, alcohol consumption, sexuality, relationships past and present, sexual fetishes, hobbies, interests, leisure activities, anything at all we can nail down to propel the case forward. This killer has left us with zero from the scene to assist our enquiries, we need something and soon. Gaz, anything on Danny Walker and friend yet?"

"No, I'm afraid both did a disappearing act, but I'm sure it won't be long before they show up," Gaz suggested as he pushed another chocolate biscuit into his mouth washed down with a gulp of coffee from his oversized mug.

"What about the media, boss? They've been snooping about as usual, wanting details concerning 'the beauty in the bushes', as the headline reads." Sally pointed to the front page of the evening rag.

"Yeah, I'll deal with them Monday. Using them to help us cover a larger field may be advantageous to the investigation, providing we don't scare the killer into hiding. I'll ring media liaison first thing and give them their story. The press might do us a favour."

CHAPTER 15

The plan was running without a hitch – stage one was complete, and had taken only weeks. Step two was set in motion – the woman was beginning to trust me and consider me a friend. She had recently revealed a previous shitty life with her obsessive control freak boyfriend. A tale of a jealous, controlling, violent wanker. Helen had poured her heart out whilst cleaning glasses and placing them back on the shelf one by one with the advertising slogans facing towards their public.

"Wow, what a complete twat."

"My ex promised the slap was a one off, sobbing his heart out at the kitchen table, pleading forgiveness, which I stupidly gave him. Months passed before another incident occurred, but soon this escalated to weekly, then daily occurrences. The violence became normality, never damaging my face you understand, or areas where people might see and raise a question. Always the torso or legs, places which are normally covered. This man found a way to enforce his control over me, rendering me a prisoner in my own home, afraid to step outside."

"I don't know what to say, Helen."

"Considering he professed an enduring love towards me, he presented his affection in the most peculiar fashion. Thankfully, something inside me clicked, and finally I managed to pluck up the courage to call my brother – he's an ex Royal Marine and Mr Grant Holmes received some of his own medicine. In fact, he ended up in hospital with a broken jaw and numerous other minor injuries and abrasions."

"I'd like to shake your brother's hand, the bastard got what he deserved."

"But that's when the real battle began with a barrage of endless text messages, phone calls and Facebook posts. All of which followed the same tone. His utter regret for the beatings. An enduring love for me and how he couldn't live without me, and my living hell began. The violence and abuse I could cope with to a degree, but the incessant contact every minute of the day and night started to drive me quite mad."

"Couldn't you block him or call the coppers to do anything? There are laws in place to protect victims of domestic violence."

"I blocked him a number of times, changed my phone number, but he always found a way around it and as per usual the police were unable to help. After a long day at work, I arrived back to my new flat to find he'd broken in and was waiting in the kitchen with a carving knife, threatening to kill himself if I didn't take him back. Hence why I'm living down here now, giving up my job, my career, family and friends simply to escape that fucking idiot or I'm convinced he might have done something to harm me on a more permanent basis."

Why the fuck would anybody want to spoil the gorgeous perfection of this lady? What a twat you must be Mr Holmes. Perhaps I should pay you a visit and put a hammer in the back of your FUCKING skull. A deep breath supressed a building inner rage, you'll keep for another time Grant Holmes. For now, though, I focused on the task in hand – emptying the sob stories from my head. There is no room in my world for sympathetic tendencies, they make you weak.

Tonight, I will attempt to execute stage three and claim my prize – a steamy night of passion. I pride myself on my expertise between the sheets, and will give her what she requires first before I relieve my pent-up sexual desires. If not this evening, I suspect the wait won't be long. My cock starts to tingle and my balls tighten as I think about performing in bed for this angel. I need to fuck her soon – this part of the process has to be executed before I can concentrate on the glorious ending, a role my inner self craves more than anything, the priceless finale when she becomes a special angel. The pub door opens behind me blasting my body with a gust of wintery air as the stale warm of the bar fights for freedom.

"Hi Dave, you been here long?" Helen appeared at my shoulder, pulling my thoughts away from the darkness of my subconscious.

"No, sorry. Wow, you look amazing," I stuttered, my privates stirring again. No false bravado, she was gorgeous. Her hair and face were immaculate, and not too extravagant. I despise when women plaster themselves in make-up, with unrealistic bright orange faces and drag queen eyes, it's not an attractive look. Helen's face was perfection. An ivory silk blouse revealed enough cleavage to tease but not enough to appear slutty. A short denim skirt was the cream on the cake, those legs were so shapely and almost endless. I'm looking forward to being between those at some point – and I will be, I'm confident of that.

"Thank you, all compliments are gratefully received. I thought I'd better make the effort; I don't venture out often," she beamed, taking the stool next to me and placing her handbag on the bar.

"Go girl, shake your booty tonight, you look gorge," said Candice whilst serving other customers.

"Thanks babe."

"You got your work cut out this evening Davey boy, you'll be fighting men off this girl with a shitty stick."

"I know, she's stunning, in fact she doesn't scrub up bad at all. Drink Helen?"

"G and T please, Dave, you're a cheeky shit."

"No problem, Candice – gin and tonic for the gorgeous lady please."

CHAPTER 16

A couple more drinks were consumed in the King's Arms while we mocked Candice and her new multicoloured talon-like fingernails, suggesting if she did happen to ensnare some prey tonight, she'd require her quarry to don PPE before any acts of fornication took place. We left in the direction of the Red Lion, a small but homely public house with a blazing log fire and comfy side saddle seating traditionally upholstered in claret paisley. It's an establishment renowned for producing excellent classic home cooked food and tantalising bar snacks, which we indulged in and washed down with a few more drinks before moving on again to the Limes, a trendy gin emporium full to the rafters with inebriated punters.

Prior to the evening I had established a strategic route between all prospective venues, noting the camera points and other devices which may provide incriminating evidence on each of our short journeys. A lively nightlife would help to conceal me amongst the crowds and addle memories. I chuckled within at the ironic situation – the very city hustle and bustle I so despise was now providing me with the curtain of protection I desired.

The evil feelings started to rise with the increased level of alcohol. I contained myself, nullifying the soaring testosterone coursing through my veins; *self-control* I kept repeating within the confines of my skull. Helen was becoming more flirtatious with every drop of alcohol she consumed; touching me not in an intimate fashion, she exuded an air of class unlike the street corner monstrosities observed from my hideouts performing oral sex on unsuspecting young lads, in the vain hope they might be treated to a sordid knee trembler down a back alley for twenty quids' worth of their precious time.

On more than one occasion I glimpsed her silky thighs in combination with a flash of lacey black knickers as her inhibitions began to fade and the effects of the multiple gins engulfed her body. The element of self-control kicked into action, a mindset I'd improved over the years to allow me to control my overwhelming lust for flesh until the perfect moment. I'd mastered the art of body language, playing it cool and minimising the risks of unnerving my angels when nearing the finish line.

Her hand caressed my leg uncomfortably close to my groin and she asked me to dance. I'm no John Travolta but how could I refuse this gorgeous creature? An upbeat track for which I had no recognition thumped out of wardrobe-sized speakers; disregarding the tempo we opted to slow dance together. She placed her slender arms around my neck, pulling me in and nuzzling into my chest, warm breath causing a shiver to ripple down my spine. I was in a world of my own, ignorant to the music which blared out and the array of flailing arms and legs classed as dancing surrounding us. My mind focused on the woman in front of me, and the warmth of her skin rubbing against mine, plump breasts pushed into my pectorals; her crotch grinding against me induced a surge of hormones. My penis reacted – a full erection would be an embarrassment at this point.

Jesus, I wanted to fuck her there and then, but I kept myself calm with controlled breathing, slowly easing all the cravings, awaiting Helen's lead. Her body language screamed that she wanted me as much as I wanted her. Patience was needed. The other feeling was also rising and an image of the dark one passed through my brain, smiling sadistically before he faded back into the abyss in my soul. It was not his time. I won't allow myself to be rushed, I'm not prepared –

not for her anyway. Statistics show that incidental memories, such as events, facial features and situations, dwindle over several weeks which is drastically increased by the consumption of alcohol. I'll bide my time before the rest of the plan is executed. The last thing I needed was half of London giving a convincing description of a man witnessed with Helen Richardson in a bar before she becomes the next.

"Dave do you want to come back to my place for a bit of a night cap? It's only down the road," she sprang upon me.

"Well, I suppose, if you want?"

"Yeah I would like that," my angel smiled sweetly, her ocean blue eyes sparkling as the stars.

"As long as you don't try and take advantage of my good nature," I joked back, thinking *fucking bingo*.

"I can't promise anything," she beamed, oblivious to the consequences of her words.

CHAPTER 17

The walk to Helen's flat was about thirty minutes of drunken swaggering. My selection appeared happy as we ambled along, talking and joking, acting the fool and taking in the sobering effects of the cool winter air, our breath billowing into the clear night sky.

Helen clambered onto my back in a vain attempt to rest her weary feet from her crippling heeled black leather ankle boots, her long legs clamped tightly around my body. The little denim number she'd chosen for the evening's attire rode high around her silky thighs, the warmth of her skin evident through my shirt. A joke was made regarding her weight and she jumped down, resetting the length of her skirt over the top of her tanned legs and producing a feeble attempt at a punch on the arm with a heart-melting smile.

"Cheeky shit."

Continuing down the road home, she took hold of my hand and squeezed tight as we passed a busy venue called the Shining. Dance music throbbed from the door, thudding beats loud in the still night. The doormen dressed in full bib and tucker glared with a nonchalance towards us from either side of the flashing neon entrance, like book ends questioning our audacity to pass their precious club without sampling their wares first.

I'd walked the route to her flat numerous times prior to our date, using my dog to camouflage me amongst the busy streets as I scouted for surrounding cameras. Face facts, who would take a second look at a white man enthusiastically walking a dog down a populated road or sitting on a bench petting man's best friend? This surveillance strategy had allowed me to establish the exact location of all the CCTV cameras along the route, especially those facing the direction of the pavements and scanning the roads which would provide the local plod with a gifted mugshot. All these danger spots were imprinted in my photographic memory and their prying eyes were evaded by walking strategic routes in between trees, bus stops, shop fronts and advertising boards or by turning my back towards them during the half hour stagger to Helen's.

The reason for her generous invite was apparent, the woman wanted my company and the elation within was overwhelming. I tried to hide my euphoria, but who am I to deny this gorgeous creature a basic human sexual need? Everything was in place for this scenario – condoms in my pocket, genital and body hair removed to reduce the deposit of evidence about her bed. Most women will wash their bedding after a disgusting one-night stand, perceiving themselves dirty and used by the act, therefore destroying DNA. But to minimise the risks further, I delay the final part of my plan for at least a fortnight after any contact with my angels. According to a professional, fluids and skin samples deteriorate by drastic proportions after several days, hence the period between the sex and her ending.

"Here we are Mr Roe, my humble abode."

"Genuinely nice, I like it."

"Don't feel obliged to be polite; I know this is nothing special, but it's mine."

"No, I love it. The place possesses character, unlike most of the portentous monstrosities they throw up nowadays," I assured her.

"Do you still want to come in for a night cap?"

"Yes, I do."

Helen ran her soft elegant fingers down my face, glaring into my eyes intensely and kissing me gently before dragging me into her ground floor flat by a handful of jacket and pinning me to the wall in a passionate embrace. The heavy fire door closed with a slam under the strong spring tension behind our entangled bodies; the situation was becoming intense quickly. Blatantly, the promise of a late-night tipple was, as I suspected, but a young woman's ploy to woo me back to her place for the sole purpose of sexual sin. Her hands strayed inside my open shirt, caressing my gym-toned body, stroking my neck and shoulders, over my pecs and sensitive nipples. Her breathing intensified with the passion before her focus switched down below to my enlarging manhood, fondling him through my slim fit jeans. The sensation pulsed through my tingling balls as she dropped to her knees, opened my belt and tugged on the buttons to release my sprung-loaded penis; with an air of expertise, she fondled my genitalia.

Oh, fuck me, that's intense, Helen knows what she's doing. The pleasure pulsated through my body, but I needed to make her happy first. She didn't understand that it was part of the process to be completed before I could move on to the next stage – treat her first, before I indulge myself. This angel deserved satisfaction. Although, to be polite, I think I'll enjoy her attentions for a while longer, fuck me, she is well practised.

"Hey, let's take this to the bedroom," I suggested in between breaths of growing excitement.

The seduction process began by slowly stripping her naked, item by item, removing her blouse, denim skirt, lacey black bra and matching knickers, then kissing, caressing each millimetre of her newly exposed gorgeous body and marble smooth skin. Groans of pleasure were emitted whilst she enjoyed my every touch. Jesus, she is outstanding, with perfectly rounded and plump, ample breasts. Her curves flowed down her body in an elegant stream and my penis twitched in anticipation. Diverting my thoughts from my erection I started to work my way from her ankles to her groin, licking, kissing, nibbling each glorious inch, parting her thighs gently, giving her the attention she deserved. Her back arched and she grasped at the floral bedding, digging her fingernails into the soft mattress, knuckles whitening, weaving her hips and covering her face with a pillow to muffle her screams of sexual ecstasy from the neighbours as a climax convulsed through her entire being.

"Oh god Dave."

Time to pull on a condom before the abundance of hormonal demands addled my brain into an act of stupidity. Since the day in my cellar when her selection was complete, I've been aching with anticipation for this moment. The vast quantity of alcohol consumed was playing into my favour, prolonging my sexual stamina, like a fucking porn star. The moans of pleasure increased and she raked her manicured nails into the flesh of my back. How much longer could I hold off? The sensitivity of my manhood was increased, she told me not to stop, but as much as I tried, I could not control my orgasm any longer and it exploded like thunder through every sinew in my body. Stage three was now complete.

CHAPTER 18

Sometime during the early hours of the morning, I awoke from my alcohol-induced slumber. Blurred eyes cleared and focused on the house phone docking station shining a red LED time of 08:37. For a short while I lay motionless, gathering fuzzy thoughts from the depths of my mind before realising my brain was attempting to thump its way from my skull and my bladder was at bursting point. A slither of morning light cut the velvet darkness of the bedroom through the gap in the curtains dazzling a bright beam of floating dust particles. The tut, tut of a blackbird on the cold streets of London voiced its morning discontent towards one of the local feral cats which populate the area. A sudden flood of the previous night's memories entered my head, and a contented smile crossed my face. What a night! Booze, food, dancing, more drinking followed by mind-blowing sex. With this image in tow, I rolled to cuddle into Dave, the thought being that a morning romp might improve my hangover, but the bed was cold to the back of my hand. I sat bolt upright and listened for movement in the flat, any signs of life, but nothing.

"Hello? Dave?" I quizzed in a curious heightened whisper, but was met by silence.

"Dave?" I probed again, an octave louder, whilst climbing out of bed with a spinning head; a wave of nausea washed over me, causing me to steady myself with one hand on the chest of drawers. I grabbed my ivory silk dressing gown from the hook on the door to cover my nakedness; still no answer.

"Dave are you here?" The florescent kitchen tube flickered into life. I squinted until my eyes adjusted to the blaze of artificial light, but the silence told the story. The bastard had gone. Wait, was he forced to leave for a dawn appointment, some petty criminal banged up in a cell awaiting his legal expertise, and he would contact me later to apologise for his impolite exit? Considering today is Saturday, I don't think so. Is it possible he's embarrassed by the evening's events? Perhaps he considered he'd exploited my drunken state. Or alternatively I'd been taken for a fool and a quick screw. I'd thought this man would at least respect me enough to stay the night, share a morning brew or breakfast. Fuck – I checked my valuables; I didn't know this man until a few weeks ago when he started frequenting the King's. He was nothing but a stranger off the street to me, a face amongst the many. I only had his word for his identity. Thank God, all was present and correct, my money, phone and credit cards were all still safe and sound in my handbag. I'll ring him later, I'm sure there's a simple explanation, he's a great guy right, I hope.

CHAPTER 19

"Hi guys, sorry I'm late, Jacob requested I drop off his iPad at his dad's, according to him, he's bored. He's only been there a day. Although I did call into the bakery and pick up pastries for breakfast, tuck in, there's plenty."

"Cheers I'm starving, the posh coffee's in the pot."

"Thanks Gaz. Right guys, today's plan."

"Can I muscle in here? I'm hoping this is important – I've got something back from my little friend in Europe."

"Carry on Sal," I say, attentive in an instant.

"My little foreign mate informs me…"

"Sorry to interrupt but when you say mate, do you mean the married French copper you made an acquaintance of several years ago at the European police congress? Proceeding to drink him to a point of 'extreme intoxication' followed by shagging the poor bloke to sexual oblivion?" Gary joked.

"Obviously I can't divulge my sources, sorry you idiot. And for your information, jealousy is not an attractive trait," Sal replied, birding Gaz. "So as I was saying, before being so rudely interrupted, my informant reveals that between 1996 and 2001 three unresolved murder cases were raised across Europe, two in Spain, an Isabella Perez and an Elena Martinez, another in the south of France, an Aude Boucher. All three with similarities to our killing and almost an identical profile to that of our victim and missing woman."

"Carry on," I instructed taking a notepad and pen left out on a desk and slurping some much-needed strong coffee.

"The reports received all present similar MOs, which I will pass on for perusal at your leisure. Witnesses suggest a similar story, these women were befriended by a young man either in bars or cafes, who presented as charming, handsome with a fit, well-toned, tanned body, blonde crew-cut hair and blue eyes – he sounds totally irresistible, don't you think?"

"Not my type," Jordan joked.

"Are you sure?" said Gaz, blowing a kiss whilst receiving the bird for the second time in the morning.

"Boys behave yourselves," Sally scoffed. "This man lured the women in with tales of an affluent lifestyle as a pilot for a prestigious airline and on another occasion a surgeon for a private health care company, flashing the cash, treating the young women to a different life experience. Eventually, he dated each briefly and managed to have sex with at least two of them, confirmed by friends, only to disappear off the face of the earth. Sounds familiar doesn't it? Again, after a few weeks, each victim vanished and was unfortunately discovered sometime later brutally murdered with their skulls battered in."

"What information can we obtain from the investigations at this time, Sally?"

"Not a lot. Colleagues and friends remembered him as English, claiming his name was Nathan James which of course in all three cases turned out to be false – it was confirmed by the airlines which could not confirm any employees going by this name, and the only surgeon who existed with said name was sixty years old and retired. No DNA was discovered at the scenes apart from the final recorded murder in France, that of Aude Boucher, where the body was disposed of deep in a thorny shrub, revealing several droplets of blood exiting the scene which didn't match the profile of the victim. The database drew a blank."

"Shit, start a search on the suspect name, though I'm not holding out any hope Nathan James will appear. If this is our man, I think he's too shrewd to present us an easy exit but you never can be sure. What about wings or any other similar mutilations Sally?"

"Yes, small wings, nothing like the ones we've witnessed, but get this, no halos, instead all victims had MY ANGEL carved into their foreheads. All injuries were believed to have been inflicted prior to death."

"It's him, this is our killer, he's developed his technique, become more elaborate and confident in what he does."

"And another bombshell – all three women were blonde, late twenties, early thirties and extremely attractive like our dead woman Hannah and the absent Becky Holt."

"You're right boss, this is our man, I'd put my mortgage on it. Now all we have to do is catch the bastard," Gary agreed.

"Kell, I've got something back on the misper – it transpires we might have another one."

"Go on Jordan."

"A Ms Janet Storer, disappeared three weeks ago from Croydon, south London; reported by her parents after neighbours contacted them raising concerns their daughter had not returned to her home for two days and her cat was at the door trying to get in. She attended her job on the Monday morning, but no one has seen her since."

"Change of plan guys, let's raise the bar – these women are now high-risk missing persons. Make some calls Jordan, get more arses on seats please. Sally, Gaz, talk to the neighbours, parents and work colleagues, find out if she dated a Casanova before disappearing. If so, I want a where, when and any other details we can squeeze out of people. We'll concentrate on these missing women until anything else manifests. Let's find these young ladies before they appear face down in some bush with their heads bashed in."

CHAPTER 20

"Come on then Hel babe, give us all the juicy gossip – did you have a fab night?" asked Candace as I propped up the bar, studying my diet Coke, ice and a slice.

"Yeah, we did. Has he been in?"

"No darling, why?"

"We had a great night, plenty of drink, a bit of dancing. I laughed until my cheeks ached, which is what I needed, and…"

"And what? Don't tell me you slept with him? Fucking hell girl, tell me all about it. Did he rock your boat?" My friend began to pry like some excited schoolgirl.

"Yes, and yes, he was exceptional in fact." My face glowed crimson with embarrassment. "Only when I woke this morning he was gone."

"Well where's your problem girl? An unconditional night of passion, no ties or awkward silences in the morning when neither of you is sure if a night of pump and grind was the right move, and you're left with a glow of satisfaction. Now, turn that frown upside down my lovely, you got your sex on, he got his rocks off, it's a win for both parties involved. And let's be perfectly honest here, the pair of you needed to relieve the sexual tension, it was becoming unbearable."

Candace is a remarkable person, she possesses an uncanny knack of taking a dire situation, scooping up all the elements in the equation, processing them through her sick perverse brain and spitting out a positive outcome. Even if that extravagant result is not one you would necessarily contemplate yourself. Prime example – the circumstances presenting themselves with David Roe. We have mind-blowing passionate intercourse, only for him to vanish before sunrise. To me, this is a massive negative. To Candice, I had a night of sex which she, devoid of compassion, described in her usual blunt manner as desperately needed – therefore, it's a win in her world.

"I really don't know what came over me, I've not known him that long. Jesus, I almost frigging raped him. Maybe I came across too desperate and frightened him off."

"Honey, I doubt that. Take a glance in the mirror, you are stunning. He'll be back for definite my girl."

"But why did he piss off in the early hours then? And why can't I get hold of him?" A dilemma I posed, trying not to sound obsessive. "I was gonna walk down his street to see if he was at home, but I thought that might be stalkerish."

"Yeah, don't turn up at his house girl, it stinks of desperation. There'll be some simple explanation, you'll see. To be honest, he seems a proper genuine guy and you know I don't like or trust many men, especially not after some of the shit relationships I've experienced. What you find is most blokes are only after one thing, that little damp piece of paradise we have between our legs and that's it. Don't get me wrong girl, men do have their uses – well for a start, a dildo has many satisfying qualities, but it can't buy you drinks or provide a warming cuddle in the morning can it? This Dave seems sincere."

"Yeah, I suppose. I just can't help feeling something is not quite right with the whole scenario."

"Don't worry babe, life's too short, it'll be fine. Right, don't you move from that spot, I'll serve George. The dirty old bastard keeps looking at my tits when I'm pulling his pint, you watch him. Then I want all the juicy details about last night and don't miss anything out, I sort of get off on it."

"You need help."

"No, I need sex, and fucking knee-knocking, long, hard, filthy, sweaty sex too, but your lust-filled stories will suffice for now," she said, pulling a pint and nodding towards old George who was obviously hypnotised by the amount of cleavage on show. "Don't even think about it George my love, I'd eat you alive and spit you out in bubbles."

"What a way to die though, you'd make an old man very happy," he replied with a grin, baring teeth resembling a burnt down fence before shuffling off to his table with his pint of best bitter in hand.

CHAPTER 21

"Hi Jenny, so sorry, I'm running late. I've just finished recapping the details of this case for the umpteenth time having received another misper matching the description of our dead woman. Additionally, information regarding similar cases on the continent has transpired. I'll be with you in about quarter of an hour, honest," I promised over the hands-free in my car.

"Kelly, I've come to expect nothing else nowadays. Do you think our man has got another?"

"We hope not. You know the score – we've been questioning everyone involved in her life, except her work partner at the hairdressers they own between them, she's away in Lanzarote until Tuesday."

"Hopefully she can shed some light on the situation. I'll get the G and Ts in shall I?"

"Yes please, where are you gonna be?"

"The Royal Oak. I like the snugs here and you'll be at home – it's full of present and ex-coppers, all talking bravado and perusing the scenery. Although, from a female perspective there appears to be a vast array of eye candy on show."

"Keep my seat warm, I'll be fifteen minutes."

"You said that five minutes ago."

As of this morning, new data had come to light in the form of three unsolved murders from the sunny climes of France and Spain. Young, talented, bright and beautiful women who had been dazzled, used, abused and discarded like a dirty tissue, replicating the MO of our lady, Hannah Craven, along with another missing woman indiscriminately thrown into the mix. Apart from this possible link to murders across the continent, the LSCIU had retrieved no incriminating evidence as such thus far. The St Mary's murder scene had provided nil on the DNA front, all CCTV footage collated to date was somewhat limited with little chance of offering any credible images which would satisfy the CPS, and we had zero plausible witness statements from the evening on the town. Although, scrutinising my own rare nights frequenting London's busy trendy bars, (A) under the influence of alcohol, would I be capable of accurately recollecting any moment of the evening's events? and (B) even if I was able to remember any details, the chances of facial recall amongst a plethora of drinkers would be improbable.

It was not uncommon for cases with similar profiles to initially progress at an annoyingly slow pace. Calculated killers tend to be cautious in the beginning, like an actor giving their first recital. Their lines are practised to perfection at first and they execute the ultimate performance, but as belief builds, the entertainer relaxes and makes errors, covering each ad lib with consummate ease, assuming the majority of the baying crowd will never notice the faux pas, blinded by the talents of the performer, continuing to provide a ripple of appreciative applause for the entertainment provided before returning home, none the wiser to their ignorance. But the more attentive and familiar members of their audience note the flaws, they will critique the performance, pick at every miniscule point, exposing the inaccuracies of the act – on the streets of London, my team are those people, awaiting the mistakes, oversights and the lack of concentration that is bred from arrogance. The LSCIU exploits these blunders, and this is when cases escalate and all those jumbled jigsaw pieces fly into place.

For most of the week, my notes have been scrutinised as I attempted to think like the murderer, contemplating his characteristics in my head, concluding again the gender of the killer to be male. A man who is a meticulous narcissist, obsessive in every way, shape and form with his exploits and the impact manifested upon the public, thriving on the attention which emanates through the media. Now in my experience, even the best of criminals will leave a fingerprint, some DNA or make one tiny mistake – but not this guy, not yet. If I was a betting woman, I would take an educated guess that our man is of high intelligence as well as charming, charismatic, pleasant on the eye, according to the reports from Europe, disciplined and collected. I am merely speculating but I anticipate him to be a person of extreme confidence, able to engineer the characters he portrays to impress the ladies, allowing him to influence the emotional state of intelligent young women into his web of deceit and to manipulate these respectable women into bed before conducting their murders without a single plausible witness or piece of evidence. The intelligence factor causes us problems. Especially when you take into consideration that most of the country's prolific serial killers all have one thing in common – a higher-than-average level of intellect; this makes my job vastly more difficult, and this person is going to be no exception to the rule.

CHAPTER 22

Dr Jenny McCabe is one of my best friends although I cannot understand why because I always let her down in one way or another, much the same as any other relationship in my sad, twisted life. Considering the job she performs, with an air of professional competence unlike any I have ever witnessed before, her patience for intolerable idiots like me is second to none. On our rare nights out, we adopt an unwritten rule not to discuss aspects of work, enforcing a pleasant well-earned break from the continual brain strain and the pressures which accompany an investigation of violent crime. Instead, we focus on Jenny's incessant quest to marry me off or at least get me laid, although this always ends in disappointment for both goals. Despite all our good intentions, nine times out of ten we succumb to our obsessive natures and lapse into a drunken police-based discussion. Although unprofessional, this has often been an advantageous practice, resulting in the solving of some of the most testing of cases when several gin and tonics have lubricated the tonsils and started to work their way between the ears and into the grey matter.

"About bloody time, I'm half pissed already," my bestie kindly informed me as I entered the Oak like a whirlwind, discarding my coat and matching hat and scarf combo in one movement.

"Jen, I am so sorry, AGAIN. Thanks for the drink."

"To be honest I've come to except it now. I've taken to adapting my regime by calculating the estimated time of arrival from any giving arranged rendezvous. On this occasion, my maths was out by a considerable margin. By the way, before you clamp your eyes on him, I've spied the fit black bloke at the bar while sitting here on my own for what appeared to be an eternity."

"Piss off, you're married; do you need a dirty one-night stand?"

"Don't be presumptuous on that subject. Anyway, that aside, the gent with the curtain blonde hair, briefcase and pinstripe suit is yours. I earwigged his conversation earlier and he sounds like a total bore, so you're welcome. But the hunk in the corner reading the sports news is mine," Jenny suggested, floating a seductive smile in the direction of a blond-haired, square-jawed Adonis across the room.

"As I've mentioned, you are married. I'll give you a full and concise report after the goods have been sampled, I promise. Allowing you to fantasise to your heart's content when your Harry fancies a bit of leg over."

"Bitch, a single desperate bitch, but all the same."

"That's life. By the way, how's your mundane two point four child lifestyle?"

"Boring conversation with my hubby and meaningless two-minute sex once a month whether I need it or not. The twins are adopting an untapped wealth of attitude because they're eight going on eighteen and are explicitly more experienced in life than myself, and we have a dog who won't stop chewing the fucking furniture. Not the cheap crap we bought years ago, oh no, the best antique table and chairs in the dining room which, incidentally, I paid a fortune for. It would appear our pooch inherited expensive taste. Otherwise, life is fantastic."

"Yes, apart from the sex and canine elements of your tedious marital being, which I would frankly class as a bonus, my life is similar, so let's drink to celebrate our monotonous existence."

"Chink, chink to that my girl." With a clash of my glass, Jenny disposed of her beverage without so much as a breath.

"Bloody hell, you're on a mission. I'll go for refills, shall I? Gin and tonic?"

"Yes please. PS, the bloke relaxing on a tall stool in the corner with the wonderfully toned and tattooed arms checked your arse out earlier before you sat down. I'm positive I witnessed drool."

"Evidently he possesses excellent taste." I made accidental eye contact with my admirer, and a flush of embarrassment reddened my cheeks on approach to the bar.

"Hi," the gentleman said, confidence presented in a deep baritone voice as I awaited service.

"Hello," I reciprocated with a nervous glance into his ocean blue eyes, gaining an instant attraction for him. I glared at my hands performing nervously with a bar towel before raising my head and smiling again to share my interest. He replied with a handsome broad grin and returned to the rugby page of the evening newspaper.

"What did he say?" my mate pounced upon my return like some over-enthusiastic teenager rather than the consummate professional she portrays during work hours.

"Hi."

"You are getting some action tonight let me tell you. He's looking again."

"And you can tell his sexual intentions because he was polite?"

"Yeah, good god girl, don't you know anything? If a guy says hi like that he wants to fuck you, that's the rules, like women asking a fellow back for coffee."

"How much do you sound like your brother right now? He produced those exact words to Sally a few days ago."

"Great minds think alike, and as much as it pains me to admit it, he does possess an intelligent mind, despite the rest of his endearing flaws."

"Changing the subject, how are you and Harry getting on now?"

"We still argue a lot if I'm honest. I don't think he appreciates the fact I'm the major breadwinner in the house, which, believe me, doesn't sit well with the male macho chauvinistic concept adopted by my husband, and his irrational need to bang his chest with the misconceived expectation females will fall at his feet. Well sorry, not this girl, I enjoy what I do in a sadistic way."

"Well he's a prat. I would love the chance to be a kept woman for a while, to sit and relax for a month or two without a stream of emails or my phone ringing on a constant basis. What about the barmaid at your local?"

"Yes, the young bar wench Vicky is still around unfortunately. I don't suspect any foul play yet, but then again it wouldn't surprise me if he had made a move. After all, he did profess to being a womanising pervert recently, and she appears receptive to his flirtatious advances despite my presence. To be fair, his infidelity wouldn't prey too heavy on my mind. I suppose it would give me the excuse I've been searching for to end the charade our marriage has become. But in all honesty, do I want to be drawn into what would be a messy and painful separation for all involved right now? I'm not sure. Somewhere in the depths of my heart I still love him I guess, additionally I don't want to distort the twins' concept of idyllic family life, you know?"

"Yeah, not an ideal situation for you or the girls. Whilst on the subject of men, the ex informed me that he and Fiona are thinking about getting married. The cheeky bastard asked for my blessing."

"What a twat! Throughout the whole of your relationship he treated you like something he'd step in on the pavement, and if that didn't try your sanity enough, he fucks your bestie in your marital home – and he still possesses the audacity to question you on his life decisions. What did you say?"

"After quickly bringing myself to a calm and collected poise I said, '*I couldn't give a toss what you two do any more, so fuck off and leave me alone,*" followed by slamming the door shut in his rather shocked face."

"Well done Kelly, stay strong. I personally can't believe what a dick he's become." Somewhere in the vicinity a mobile sounded with an annoying tone.

"It appears he takes considerable pleasure in rendering misery upon my life in any form possible. I think your crappy message tone just pinged."

"Yes it would appear so. Speak of the devil, Harry – *please ring me.* For god's sake, can I not do anything without bloody interruption," she groaned standing up with her phone already stuck to her ear and exiting the pub for privacy while mouthing "back soon".

A hum of conversation filled the room. I attempted to relax into my chair, surveying the room but avoiding eye contact while trying in desperation not to appear like the jilted best friend pretending not to be the jilted bestie but failing. The blond man sat alone, relaxed and casual; he never raised his eyes from the sports pages, but took a drink of his pint every now and again, savouring every drop, raising his glass towards a light and examining the clear golden liquid before replacing his prized possession in its rightful position directly in front of him. Butterflies rippled in my stomach momentarily as I admired his handsome, rugged face. This man obviously looked after himself;

his arms were lush, muscular and strong, decorated with dense Japanese artwork containing various swirls, curls, dragons, elaborate koi fish and cherry blossoms all intermingled with outstanding professionalism to create a single beautiful piece of artistry. Tattoos are my thing; I love tattooed men which is handy at present considering half the country are adorned with varying amounts of ink. Balls, he must have a sixth sense or something – he just looked straight at me and smiled; he bloody knew I was eying him up. "Smile Kelly," I said to myself, trying to exude sexy and confident as opposed to shitting myself.

"Sorry, am I interrupting something here?" Jenny reappeared.

"No, no, I was…"

"Save the excuses for another date Kell, I've got to dash. Tash and Lizzy are, and I quote, 'So ill'. They're throwing up all over the place and Harry is not brilliant with sick. You don't need to say it – my job is all about dealing with dead bodies, blood, gore and god knows what else on a daily basis and he can't manage a bit of vomit and diarrhoea from his own children. I married an utter wimp."

"How shit, literally, and I only arrived quarter of an hour ago; well I suppose it can't be helped, serves me right for being five minutes late."

"You were forty-three minutes late to be precise but by the by. I'll phone you tomorrow. Let's hope no more dead women appear. Bye babe and good luck with you know who." Jenny climbed into her coat, wrapped a thick knit striped scarf around her neck and, indicating towards the fit bloke we had discussed, made her swift exit to the nearby taxi rank.

Now I was the jilted best friend trying hopelessly not to resemble Billy no mates, sitting with two gin and tonics like some old alcoholic spinster. What a fantastic night this had turned out to be and it wasn't like I could go home and chat to Jacob. I texted him.

"How was your day with your dad matey? Xxx."

A reply bleeped back immediately, which meant he was bored or pissed off.

"Gud I suppose. We went to footy which wer shit but some fans wer scrapping outside, dad said we had to split though."

"And quite right, what's up with your spelling and mind your language."

"This is called texting slang mum, god, der."

"Good evening, sorry, I hope I'm not interrupting?" the handsome blond tattooed hunk said, his paper tucked under his arm breaking my casual poise approach.

"No, no, only messaging my son. He's at his dad's for the weekend."

"Well, that answers one question, you're not in a relationship I assume."

"No, I'm not married, or otherwise engaged at the moment."

"Do you mind if I join you? I'm assuming your friend won't be reappearing considering the hurry she left in."

"No, she has child issues, vomit and other nasties which tend to manifest themselves within young children. All the glorious aspects of parenthood. Please, sit down, I might be here a while." I gestured towards the two double gins which I had purchased for Jenny and myself before our night was rudely interrupted by the sickness bug.

"Before you take a seat though, I must warn you I am a copper, which tends to terminate any further advances at this stage, tagging me in a category along with politicians and traffic wardens as one of the most hated people on the planet."

"Well I'm sorry to disappoint you Mrs Police Lady but I'm afraid I hold the prestigious mantle of most loathed profession on the planet."

"Oh really, I'm intrigued, please enlighten me."

"Basically, I cause people unquestionable levels of pain, intoxicate them with various drugs and then have the audacity to charge them extortionate amounts of money for the pleasure," he replied, holding his hands aloft for me to guess his secret. "No?"

"No, not a clue," I shrugged with utter confusion.

"I'm a dentist."

"You win!" I said laughing. "So Mr most hated man in the world, what do we call you?"

"James Harrison," he said, holding out a large hand to shake. "And I won't be on the police database, I'm a good boy. Although I was reprimanded by our local plod for nicking pick and mix from the village corner shop when I was seven."

"Well Mr Harrison, I'm pleased you put my mind at rest concerning your illustrious chequered past. Sweets? Really?"

"Guilty as charged. I'd spent my pocket money and the temptation of jelly tots and pink shrimps proved overwhelming. My dad went nuts which was enough to deter me from further developing my criminal empire."

A newfound friendship flourished quickly. We chatted for hours, laughing together like old friends at a school reunion, becoming extremely intoxicated along the way. This was followed by a disgusting garlic laced greasy kebab after which I took him home and shagged him all over my house, like you do. Classy, but I couldn't help myself. On a personal note, I don't make a habit of sleeping with strangers, but this was on a whole different level. This seemed right at the time and I needed an element of male company and some sexual relief – desperate is a strong word but...

"Morning, how are you?" came a whispered voice from my side as I woke from my sordid night of passion to the unfamiliar sense of warm skin upon mine. With tiredness still present in my heavy eyes, I squinted against the morning sun beaming through a gap in the curtains.

"Fine thanks, you?"

"Yeah, a little bit fuzzy, but on the whole pretty sound considering we drank enough alcohol to sink the Titanic. So, what do we do now? I'm not well versed in this sort of situation."

"Nor me. Believe it or not, but I don't make a habit of jumping into bed with men I've been conversant with for only five minutes. I usually wait at least a day. On a positive note, at least I can remember your name which is a good thing, right?"

"I suppose so Jane." I glared towards him with daggers.

"Whoa, whoa, I'm only joking – DCI Kelly Lynch, right?" He sat laughing at my expense, his fantastically toned tattooed body causing me a second glance and a coy smile, appearing fresh and handsome even with bed hair. "Listen, if you want me to leave I will, but can I jump in the shower first please? Or suggestion deux, I could take you for breakfast. If you fancy of course?"

"Yeah, food would be lovely, fresh towels are in the airing cupboard."

"Thank you," he placed a lingering kiss on my cheek before

turning for the door revealing a sandwich of white arse cheeks between his tanned legs and torso.

"Wow, stunning tattoos by the way."

"Oh, thanks, I like being inked."

"No shit – they're huge."

"Yeah, when I was a teenager I suffered with chronic acne, which enveloped my entire back leaving me with hefty scars. So, I decided to cover them up. A lad up north is the artist, he's an excellent tattooist."

"They are so cool; and must have cost a fortune."

"Can you put a price on art?" he laughed, hands aloft, exaggerating his nakedness to my eye.

"You're an idiot, aren't you?"

"I hope so, being normal is so overrated. Right, shower."

The soft plump pillow engulfed my face as I nestled back into bed, pulling the quilt around my neck for comfort instead of any requirement for warmth, watching this relative stranger take his gym-toned body out and onto the landing. He turned and smiled towards me before disappearing around the door and heading the wrong way for the bathroom.

"James?" He reappeared in the doorway smiling. "The bathroom's that way." I pointed a finger indicating the correct route, giggling like a schoolgirl to his reaction.

"Thanks, I knew that," he joked, pointing in the same direction.

A contented, satisfied, warm sensation washed over my entire body; my nerve endings tingled and the hair on my arms stood on end, mixed with an overwhelming sluttish guilt vibe, but I can handle that to be honest. My eyes shut out the bright morning glow and images of the previous night returned to my foggy brain. The sex started down in the kitchen against the cupboard, where an innocent kiss exploded into a full-on passionate embrace; he'd removed my skimpy knickers, and lifted my short burgundy leather skirt before moving me to the breakfast bar, scattering the stools and the rack of condiments in all directions. Moments later our frantic passion took us to the stairs, discarding any remaining items of clothing before the grand finale, an orgasmic crescendo in the bedroom. Sex with my ex Darrell was dull, unlike last night which was on a whole different level of electrifying and exciting. I pitied Fiona – was she aware she was accepting a life of boring mundane sex with a man who has the sexual prowess of a chair leg? Listening to James bellowing out a tune in the shower I laughed to myself, thanking god in heaven that he was better between the sheets than at singing.

My phone rang close to my head, vibrating across the bedside cabinet and breaking the stream of delightful thoughts. "Shit!"

"Hi Sally, what can I do for you this morning?"

"Sorry to bother you Ma'am, we've got another dead woman."

"Bollox, where?"

"Hampstead Heath, not a million miles away from the East Heath carpark, past the picnic area and towards the viaduct bridge. An old dear walking her dog found her."

"Do you think it's him again?"

"From what the old girl told uniform, the similarities are more than coincidental."

"And description, do we know her?"

"I'm not sure yet. I'm about to consult with the officer who secured the scene; she's had chance to scope the body and took a statement from the witness."

"Good work. Ensure the whole area is secure please Sally, and will you make all the relevant parties aware, including the rest of our team. I'm on my way."

"It's done Kell, SOCO are en route. Gaz and Jordan are making their way. I'll meet you at the scene."

"What's up Kelly?" came a question from the other side of the room; water was rolling down his gorgeous, chiselled chest as he stood there with only a white towel around his waist to cover his modesty.

"I'm afraid I'm going to have to take a rain check on breakfast, something's come up at work."

"Oh well, it can't be helped I suppose. So, what we are going to do, us I mean? Did you want to meet up again?" He scanned the room for items of his clothing.

"Yeah, I think I do, and if you're looking for your clothes, they're downstairs in the kitchen," I smiled back.

"Cool, thanks, I'll take your number," he said, dropping the towel with a grin as I tried to divert my eyes from his manhood.

CHAPTER 23

The East Heath carpark was a hive of activity for such an hour. The press had already swooped like vultures awaiting a snippet of a story to enhance the standing of their insignificant publication. Four squad cars occupied a series of spaces towards a grassed area close to the entrance, blocking access to the area. Half a dozen uniformed officers had taken up residence, one with a clipboard acting as gate control, the others dispatched by a plump ruddy faced sergeant to patrol the border along East Heath Road. The forensic team had already arrived and, judging by the state of their parking, they were in a hurry. The young officer entrusted with the clipboard approached my car.

"Morning Ma'am."

"Good morning officer, where do you want me?" I asked, flashing my warrant card out of habit rather than necessity.

"Thank you, Ma'am, you can park near your colleague just to the left," he said, pointing in the general direction with the aid of the clipboard before noting the relevant details.

Spotting Sally's black Mondeo I pulled alongside as instructed, retrieving my phone from my handbag before placing it in the passenger footwell out of sight. I don't know why – it wasn't like anyone was going to break into my car with half the Kentish Town police station here.

"Good morning sergeant, what have we got and where?"

"A young lady Ma'am. Down this track, past the picnic benches on your left, follow the arrow for the nature walk for about a hundred yards towards the viaduct bridge, you can't miss her Ma'am."

"Thank you."

"Excuse me Ma'am, can I suggest you may need alternative footwear – the ground gets a bit boggy down there to say the least."

"I'll change, thanks for the heads up," I replied, examining my heeled tan suede ankle boots before switching them for the more sensible walking boot option from the rear of my motor.

The five-minute stroll down the gravelled pathway would be a pleasant and serene walk in normal circumstances. Morning dew glistened diamond like as the sun blazed between the remaining autumnal hues of the shedding trees, their branches a stage for performing birds singing out a morning chorus above me whilst others bobbed along the ground on an endless quest for sustenance to survive the winter period. A picnic spot opened out in front of me, with an overflowing rubbish bin central to the utopian parkland and surrounded by a series of randomly placed wooden benches. Adjacent to them, I imagined wild daffodils and tulips would provide a blaze of colour throughout the early spring months. A popular place with city dwellers who come to escape the rat race and find their little jot of tranquillity away from the hustle and bustle of the London streets.

To the left of me, three tracks meandered their way into distant woodland with red dog waste bins acting as sentries on each pathway. To the right of me, an expanse of overgrown briar, grass scrub and hawthorn bushes mingled together with swathes of knee-high sedge invading the deciduous tree line. Beyond that, barely visible through the thicket of trees, was Hamstead Ponds which played host to an array of breeding waterfowl and cold-water swimmers.

The blue and white police incident tape became visible in the distance, guarded by more uniforms. DC Glover stood in idle chatter with two young officers, drawing long and hard on an early morning cigarette, which she extinguished as soon as I approached.

"Good morning governor."

"Morning, I thought you'd given up with the fags?"

"Well I did, but I got pissed last week and without realising I started again, as you do." I raised a single eyebrow to mock her lack of self-discipline.

"Right, where is she?"

"This way boss." She indicated with a nod of her head to follow.

An old dear sat in the rear of an open panda car, drinking a warming sweet cuppa for medicinal purposes provided by a uniformed officer's flask. She was well-prepared for the outdoors considering the winter sun was warming up, with a rouge quilted jacket and fur-lined hood, jeans, green Hunter wellingtons and thick insulated gloves. Her springer spaniel milled in circles amongst the legs of several young coppers, its tail wagging ten to the dozen, appreciating the abundance of fuss available.

"Is this the lady who found her?"

"Yeah, bless her, Mrs Sandra Drake, a widower. She's in somewhat of a state to be honest. The dog located the body. Having failed to return to her owner's calls, which is uncharacteristic, Mrs Drake went to investigate why, and the rest is history."

A taped expanse and white tarpaulin loomed directly in front of us. As predicted, the ground beneath my feet was indeed a quagmire due to the persistent heavy rain received by the country's capital for the last few months. Jenny appeared from the entrance of the crime scene tent behind a small copse of naked trees, donned in the usual attire of hooded overalls, facemask, medical grade disposable gloves and welly boots; her cursory examination was already in progress. A waving arm indicated the direction I should walk to enter the cordon.

"Get a full statement from Mrs Drake ASAP and have someone take the old girl home, make sure she's OK." Sally nodded an acknowledgement, diverting her attention back to the old dear.

"This way DCI Lynch," shouted Jenny from the forensic works.

"Long time no see, how's the kids?"

"Unpleasant, the bedding is in the wash as we speak," she informed me with an expression of disgust on her face.

"Tell me we've got something please."

"Have you got something to tell me first? Come on, how did last night pan out after I left?" she asked, walking towards the entrance of the crime scene.

"Very well thanks Dr McCabe, very well indeed," I replied with flush-reddened cheeks.

"Oh my god, you didn't!"

"Shush, we can talk later," I whispered with a glance towards DC Glover, instantly informing Jenny I didn't want the whole department familiar with aspects of my private life.

"Understood, sorry. Down to business. From our initial examination, we have discovered a partial boot print situated adjacent to the body, estimated at a size ten or eleven, a cast is being taken as we speak. But otherwise, as per previous, he's left little in the way of evidence. The young woman of course fits the MO of our previous cases, including the European sector – she's blonde, beautiful, approximately five feet seven. Again, presenting a circular blunt trauma compression wound at the base of her skull and, corresponding with the Hannah Craven murder, the back of her blouse is stained with blood, indicating similar mutilations. As per protocol, samples have been taken from under her fingernails and are on the way to the lab. I'm expecting the results within twenty-four hours. I thought I'd mention that, in my humble opinion, this clever bastard is playing games with us."

"Why?"

"Yet again, the victim's handbag was placed beside her body. This prat wants us to know who she is. It's almost like he doesn't want us wasting time trying to identify the victim."

"Who is she?"

"A Ms Janet Storer," Jenny said, looking at the corpse at the centre of the scene with sympathy written across her face. "ID was found in her purse, which is bagged and boxed."

"The misper who came in last night," I sighed, recognising the young woman's name and face from the photograph emailed by her hopeful parents. "DC Glover, contact the FLOs please. I can confirm this is one of our missing women. They'll need to inform her next of kin that a body has been discovered. Don't relay any further details as yet, and remember a formal ID will be required once the forensic investigators complete their work here and her body can be removed."

"No problem boss."

"Dr McCabe, can we analyse this together please?"

"Of course, I'll instruct my minions to continue scrubbing the site." She handed me the usual overalls and a pair of new gleaming white welly boots which were two sizes too big and flopped back and forth on my feet.

Pausing for a moment, I scanned the tranquil landscape, searching mindfully for something which may present as out of place – a broken twig, scrap of material, spatter of blood. The birds in the background sounded out nature's choir, oblivious to the carnage which had ensued in their usually idyllic home. At least she died in a lovely place, but what a shame no one else will ever view these woods as a peaceful haven again. For years to come this will be known as the place where the body of a golden-haired beauty was discovered, or a gorgeous fun-loving daughter met her fate with an unnecessary brutality to appease the psychopathic animalistic tendencies of an extremely sick individual. Parkland where an innocent old lady walking her dog had her life changed forever.

The pity rose within me for the parents, brothers, sisters, friends – for the heartache and extreme sorrow they were about to experience. As upstanding members of society, we cannot begin to imagine the pain they will go through in the days, weeks and years to come after losing someone they loved in this manner. The unrelenting, desperate sadness, enhanced by simple elements of life once taken for granted – a glance towards a photograph which always brought happiness, birthdays, Christmases, all endless reminders of their lost loved one. I couldn't honestly say for sure, but I could imagine if a fatal disease such as cancer or a car accident had deprived her of life, over time you may learn to accept her death, adapt to live with the fact, but a murder is an altogether different type of beast to contemplate. One can only envisage the flood of emotional pain I would personally experience if it were my son laid out in the wild fauna, battered, bloodied and lifeless. The thought was unbearable and my heart started to thump in my chest, a sickening nausea erupted in my stomach and tears manifested themselves in my eyes, but I fought them back; for a person in my position, emotion is not an option, deemed not professional. Whether he likes it or not, my Jacob will receive a cuddle when he gets home.

"I'm ready, let's do this. Are you good DCI?"

"I'm fine," I replied, turning to face my friend. "Having perused the site, I can only determine one point of entry to the scene, that being the path running alongside the benches, passing where we are standing and continuing into the bushes to the body. In my opinion, this is the only realistic entrance to the location unless you fancy wading through six feet of brambles or a thicket of hawthorn, which is not a practical approach for a calculated killer who doesn't want to leave any calling cards to condemn him."

"Correct Kelly, and another aspect which sprang to mind whilst talking to my team – study the grass around the body."

Examining the vicinity where the body lay, nothing appeared out of the ordinary. The woman, again dressed in a blouse and pencil skirt, lay peacefully, her eyes closed tight, legs akimbo, any thoughts concerning the preservation of dignity long gone. A matted clump of blood-stained hair imposed itself upon a head of natural blonde, resembling the Japanese flag, and flashes of claret streaked across her ivory white shirt. All aspects of this death were similar to the last; nothing stood out to me.

"Please elaborate, I'm missing something Jen."

"The grass surrounding the body? Only a limited area is flattened, and considering the drenched conditions of the entire heath, there are no drag marks – which means?"

"She walked in under her own steam and the murder took place here on this exact spot, as per our first woman," I interrupted as the penny dropped.

"Precisely."

"In that case, we need to cordon off the whole park – from this point up to and inclusive of the carpark, and conduct a complete and comprehensive search."

"Without any doubt, and now as opposed to later. We don't want to miss clues because the evidence has deteriorated or been disturbed. I'll call a dog team to locate any further blood and the path taken."

"Let's get it done. Sally!" I shouted her across to the scene where she stopped behind the temporary barrier erected by the forensic team. "Can you organise a squad of uniforms ASAP to secure a perimeter from this point and all the way back down the pathway, inclusive of the entire carpark please."

"Of course, Kelly. For my brain to compute, can I ask why?"

"Because our collective opinion is that the victim walked here under her own steam, there's no trace of drag marks or flattened plant life. This bastard made our poor woman walk to her death."

Sal took a deep breath and raised her eyebrows. "Got it boss. I'm on it now. Jordan arrived a few minutes ago, I'll have him take charge at the other end."

"Good thinking Sal, and contact Gaz before he leaves the office, because we will need feet on the ground for a search area of this magnitude."

CHAPTER 24

The darkness down here is blinding. The chill in the air has raised bumps on my skin, sending a resentful shiver down my spine. A familiar aroma induced a moment of pleasant recollection. My grandma owned a house with a cellar and on occasions we would venture through her kitchen door. "Stay close Becky," she would say as we made our way down the creaky wooden stairs and into the dark abyss, utilising the scant light scavenged from the door above. I would cling to Gran's skirt until she illuminated the place with a single bulb covered in dust and cobwebs to reveal her treasure trove of historical artefacts. We would then spend hours perched on old sheet-covered dining room chairs reminiscing over wartime memorabilia. Albums of old black and white family photographs revealed distant relatives, stern in appearance and dressed in immaculate army uniforms with a proud chest full of medals awarded for various conflicts. Another battered cardboard box contained trinkets of gold and silver jewellery and old pennies worn smooth over years of use which were left to me when she passed.

I remembered the summer holidays I spent with her when my parents worked city jobs, and Gran's immaculate garden with its bowling green lawn surrounded by flower beds providing a rich tapestry of colour buzzing with a cacophony of insect life. What I would give to be there right now and not in this freezing dark hole. A tsunami of unprovoked thoughts began to meander through my head, one of which returned constantly – the number of women he's imprisoned down here before me, scared, lonely, desperate, stripped to their underwear, all possessions missing, handbag, mobile phone, before they disappear never to return for a member of the unsuspecting public to discover, battered, face down in a ditch.

My cage provided little or no comfort. A postage stamp blanket and grubby pillow aided me through the chilliest nights. Most nights though, sleep and relaxation were a distant memory considering the dilemma of being caged like an animal in what I can only presume is the basement of some psychopathic weirdo's house. A man who, in recent days, I'd witnessed slash brutal angel wings into the back of another young woman using a scalpel without a second thought to the pain he caused her or presenting any signs of sympathy for his actions.

In the initial days of my captivity, I managed to engage the other woman in conversation regarding aspects of her life, albeit resentful and in broken sentences, but she talked before becoming withdrawn from any manner of communication, petrified and submissive to her fate, a quivering emotional wreck, rocking back and forth in the corner of her cage. Then the man I know as Nathan came and allowed her to wash, dress fashionably and sit at his table for food. That was the last time I laid eyes on Janet.

I try not to cry, not wanting him to think I'm weak. He enjoys being the dominant force so to combat his bravado I've taken to engaging him in idle chatter, a ploy which makes him physically uncomfortable. This person wants to treat me as an object, it's easier for him. Another shiver rippled throughout my body; I pulled the small woollen blanket so kindly provided by my captor tight around my neck and sealed the edge with my legs to hinder the cool breeze. A narrow beam of light crept under the large oak door at the top of the stairs, penetrating the pitch darkness. It amazes me the level of visibility present once your eyes adjust to the gloom. Nothing stands out clearly, as you might expect, but silhouetted shapes are noticeable, in conjunction with the maps constructed within my memory of the room layout during the limited occasions he allows any form of illumination in this place.

In the house above me, movement was prevalent throughout the day. I listened and took notice of his routines. Doors opened and closed with a slam, followed by a car engine starting and the familiar sound of tyres on gravel. More movement upstairs, an accomplice, pets or both. Hours passed, how many I cannot say for sure, then the vehicle returned, the front door opened and he talked to someone or something. I'm now guessing a dog unless he has a friend who would like his dinner, a walk later and gets called good boy.

The now familiar grind of the three bolts on the cellar door jolted my attention from a plethora of emotional contemplation ranging from raging anger to total demoralisation. Each bolt slides with a thud to finish, one, two, three, the heavy lock clunks twice. A sequence memorised with detail should I find myself presented with an opportunity to escape my prison. The hefty wooden door swung open with an eerie creak, illuminating the gloom with a shaft of blinding bright light cascading across the room, causing me to squint and blink my night vision aside, emphasised when he flicked the switch on the landing above the stairway, awakening the two fluorescent strip lights which flickered with a reluctance before bursting into life with a low hum.

"Hi honey, I'm home, did you enjoy your day?" he shouted in comedic fashion, which of course was a total waste on me in this situation.

My eyes started to ease to the dazzling brightness of my usually dark, damp prison. The man named Nathan in my world emerged from the light, pausing briefly before his smiling face appeared as he trudged down the creaky wooden steps. The door – a mistake, he had left it ajar, it was an opportunistic chance, his concentration was starting to lapse. The stringent OCD routine he adopted religiously was showing cracks. In passing, he pushed the on/off button on his desktop computer, springing it to life, before continuing towards me.

"I brought Maccy D's, quarter pounder cheeseburger meal and a chocolate shake."

"Thanks so much, you're so kind. Where's Janet gone?" I asked as he leaned in towards me, placing the food near my cell.

"That doesn't concern you. She's gone which is all you need to know. Oh dear, I never thought, how inconsiderate of me, are you lonely? Don't worry too much, someone will be joining you soon."

"Is she dead, you bastard? When the cops catch you, I hope they string you up by your balls you fucking psycho."

"Now now Becky, why all the animosity? Don't be jealous, you will be elevated to stardom as a glorious angel all in good time, which is what you want isn't it? Popularity and fame? I'm going to give you both," he explained with exaggerated arm movements towards the ceiling and the heavens above.

"Do you realise this isn't normal? You're a fucked-up nutter."

"AND WHO THE FUCK ARE YOU TO TELL ME WHAT IS NORMAL BECKY?" he screamed, his face pressed against the bars of my coop, total rage written across his face as the spittle flew from his lips and dribbled down his chin, before calming in an instant, the rage passing as quickly as it had appeared. He wiped his face dry with his woollen sleeve and his voice died to a whisper. "What do you know about normal? What is normality to you isn't necessarily so to the rest of the population. Our God kills indiscriminately, do you not perceive his actions as normal? Here, eat your food before it gets cold."

"Are you going to let me out to enjoy my dinner? I need a wash, this place is filthy. A shower would be lovely, maybe you might entertain me soaping myself as you did with Janet?"

"Don't waste your time trying to distract my mind in a vain attempt to corrupt my thoughts with the sins of the flesh. Do you honestly think I am that gullible? As I recall, we've ridden that train, but if it's any consolation, you rode fantastic that night Becky. I particularly enjoyed you sucking my cock – you were so greedy you almost induced orgasm. Which couldn't happen, you do understand that, don't you? Providing evidence of my being present in your flat wasn't an option, far too much chance of Mr Plod discovering it. The highlight for me though was you fucking me until you convulsed in orgasmic ecstasy, soaking me as I exploded inside you. What a stupendous experience you were, Becky. But all that is done with now, we move on – sexual desire is no longer on my agenda."

The memory of our night together raced through my head – this man who had seemed so gentle, respectful and sensitive to my womanly needs; it was sickening to think I had been so receptive to his advances without questioning his intentions. Rising emotions were quickly dispersed to continue the engagement of conversation. "What is on your agenda Nathan or whatever you're fucking called? Because I'm guessing that's not your real name."

"No, but what I'm called is irrelevant don't you think? An endearing title forced upon us by loving parents to a bundle of joy. Who, incidentally, possessed no input or control over the situation, so names are meaningless to me. In years to come, no one will celebrate our legacy on this planet, we will all become nothing but a carved scripture in a piece of stone, resting in some idyllic overgrown graveyard, succumbing to decades of weathering, erosion and deterioration before collapsing into a pile of unrecognisable nothingness. No one will recall whether Nathan, Becky or Elvis fucking Presley is buried beneath the soil, becoming a speck of dust in a vast desert of insignificant life within the world's perpetual chronicle. Now eat, I'll leave the light on and bring you some water to wash."

"How many women have you murdered?"

"Do you really want to know that?"

"Yes, I want to know."

"Do you need this?"

"Yes, I need this please."

"Nine or more, some not discovered yet. When the sixteen steps to heaven are filled it will all end. And for your information, I don't class my actions as murder, thank you. The process is much more refined than premeditated killing. I'm releasing those women to the heavens and a better existence."

"You are fucked up aren't you? What the fuck happened to you? Jesus!"

"I don't like to discuss my former life, that life doesn't exist anymore. I am carrying out what is required by a higher being to complete my mission."

"And what is the mission – to kill every blonde in the fucking country?"

"I tire of your incessant garble, which is the problem with the female of the species. All you want to do is gossip. My patience for your idle chit chat is limited. I'll bring some warm water for you to wash, now eat your lunch," he snarled before turning to climb the stairs three at a time. He slammed and locked the door above me, missing the three bolts – another unfamiliar error on his behalf. His routine was usually stringent, regimental; perhaps my line of questioning had rattled his emotional state, diminishing his levels of concentration.

Silence again hit the dank cellar. I reached for the food, needing the sustenance; I was becoming light-headed, although I was cautious of eating or drinking anything he provided as in previous times his kind donations had been laced with drugs or something which rendered me useless. Recollection regarding the evening of my arrival to my living hell is vague, the fact that I walked down to this hellhole is only provided by the odd hallucinogenic flashback.

The computer flashed into life, demanding a password to proceed with the booting up process. My mind exploded into overdrive – if I could escape my cell and get to the desktop. If I could find his password, I could raise the alarm.

CHAPTER 25

"Can someone please enlighten me as to how the fucking hell the media found all the details about our case," I burst through the office door bellowing.

"People, does anyone here possess a single iota of an idea what the boss is on about?" Gaz said, scanning the room which remained silent.

"Look at this headline in the paper – 'The blonde angel killer'," I retorted, throwing the local rag across the desk.

"Oh shit," he replied.

"Yeah, oh shit. *'An anonymous source has revealed the brutal murders of two women on the streets of London over the last few weeks. Details regarding the incidents are yet to be disclosed, with no official clarification concerning the stories from the Police department. The women, believed to be in their late twenties or early thirties, are described as beautiful blonde angels. According to witnesses, friends and work colleagues, both victims had been in the company of an unknown male only weeks before the gruesome discovery of their bodies. However, we believe this may be the tip of a grisly iceberg as information from the continent describes three similar open murder cases, along with additional reports of other missing women. Whilst these cases remain unsolved, we recommend vigilance. Avoid nights out and travelling alone, if possible.'* How come the press collated all this information, including the fact other females are absent without leave? Come on guys, detectives – the fucking clue is in the name. Would anyone like to explain to me why? Someone, please?" I quizzed the team as my blood boiled under my skin.

"The info detailing the possibility of the other women was only relayed to us by email hours prior to this meeting," Jordan said. "And believe me, after analysing the reports, none of these women match the MO of our two dead females. The three new mispers the press are referring to are sex workers. Yes, they display similarities to the description of our victims, but our young ladies are well educated, from respectable backgrounds, with prosperous jobs and bright futures, not smack heads who will perform sex acts on anyone willing to pay enough for their next score. In my professional opinion, the facts didn't ring true. Also, in our defence, prostitutes disappear and re-emerge on a continual basis – it's part of the job description, you're aware of this Kelly. One minute they're working a particular set of streets then something panics them – threats from rival ladies of the night, a client becoming over-enthusiastic with them, or they owe drug money to dealers who will cut them up if they can't pay – and they move on to the next red-light district," Jordan explained.

"As I said, any detail, and this goes out to all of you, we mark it up on the board, whether we think it is relevant at the time, any little item at all. Jesus, how long have we been working together as a team? This is how we do things, the whiteboard," I said, emphasising the words as a desk phone started to ring in the corner of the room.

"These items were next on the agenda, honest – your last instruction was to investigate the most recent missing persons reports and expand further if needed, which is what we've done. All three women came to light this morning, disappearing within a month of each other over a year ago."

"Point taken Jordan. However, I still want to find out how the press got hold of the story. Gary, can you sort this? You've got connections at the local rag, let's use and abuse him, find out where all the details came from. I don't care what it takes. And will somebody please answer that fucking phone."

"Got it gov," Sal said, jumping to her feet to end the incessant ringing which had been annoyingly sounding out for what seemed like an eternity.

"Morning DC Glover, serious crimes speaking, how can I help you?"

"I want to speak with the SIO," a distorted electronic voice spoke.

"Sorry, she's busy in a meeting at this moment in time. I'll take your name, number and message and she will return your call at a more convenient time if that's OK?" Sal replied, waving her left arm to quiet the room.

"No DC Glover, call over Detective Chief Inspector Kelly Lynch RIGHT FUCKING NOW, and believe me when I say she will want to speak with me. PS, I presume you've taken the time to peruse the morning papers – 'Blonde bombshell killer'."

"Boss you ought to take this," Sally suggested with an urgent tone.

"Make them disappear please. I haven't got the time or patience for the press or idiot crank callers today."

"No, you need to talk with this person, he will only speak with you, he's mentioned the killings."

"Right, if this is that twat Danny Walker I won't be impressed." I took the handset off Sally. "DCI Lynch."

"Hello Kelly, can I address you as Kelly? DCI is so authoritative."

"Who is this please?"

"No formal introductions required, but I am more than aware who you are and of your impressive policing abilities. Have you read the papers today? Interesting reading, aren't they? Oh, do refrain from reprimanding your colleagues over a potential leak because there wasn't one. I tipped a journalist all the details concerning the cases and I'm more than qualified to do so considering the liberations of these angels to a more desirable life was actioned by myself," the shocking electronic voice boomed across the phone line.

"Sorry I didn't catch your name, Mr...? Let me get this straight in my head, are you saying you are the killer of the two women involved in our recent investigation?" I tried to reply calmly while also waving my arms like a lunatic to emphasise the fact that I may well be in conversation with our man and that we needed to instigate a trace on the line.

"Do you think I'm stupid Kelly? Why would I divulge my name? And do I need to spell this out? I alone helped the angels flutter away to the heavens and I will continue until I complete my mission."

"Listen to me whoever you are..."

"No, you listen DCI Lynch. Please don't try interrupting me again in a pathetic attempt to prolong the conversation so this call can be traced or triangulated. You amuse me – I can imagine you waving your arms about, trying to grab the attention of the office to fix the call, but you're wasting your time. I'll be long gone before you can begin a trace. Which incidentally would only lead you to the disappointment of a nondescript pay-as-you-go mobile in the middle of nowhere – no cameras DCI Lynch, no witnesses. As I've said, I'm not fucking stupid, please do not consider me to be so."

"I appreciate you're no idiot sir, you've been leading us a proper merry dance over the last few months – limited evidence at the scenes, no CCTV footage. You've really done your homework. So why call us now?"

"I'm calling to assist you. As you and your squad don't appear to be making any headway or excelling yourselves as detectives at the minute, I'm sure any help will be appreciated. There are three more women for you to locate. These filthy whores are sleeping in a derelict warehouse on the outskirts of London, East Grange Industrial Estate off the North Circular. I released them from their dire life of drug addiction, prostitution and poverty quite a while ago. Is it not a sad predicament we find ourselves in when women such as these are forced into lives of such debauchery when the abundant affluence in the world could be shared out to resolve such a humanitarian crisis? But I digress – I wish you luck with these angels," he informed me before the line went dead.

"Shit, that was him, the killer. The bastard's toying with us – it was him who contacted the papers. The fucker's playing games with us." Silence hit the office as the entire room went into a spin, attempting to contemplate the next practical move. My mind kicked into overdrive.

"Right, we need all the phones in here tapped ASAP, I want to be ready if he decides to call again. And how the fuck did he find the number for a private line? We'll think about that later. Gaz, continue with the local rag, find out when he contacted them, how, where – anything you can squeeze from the bastard. If he doesn't squeal, arrest his ass for perverting the course of justice."

"Got it boss," he said, standing and leaving his desk.

"Persevere with the mispers please Jordan, build a profile regarding the prostitutes – former lives, parents, boyfriends, pimps, dealers, everything. Find something apart from the sex game which might link these women."

"In progress Kell, and one more item to bring to your attention," he said, presenting photographs of the three missing prostitutes –

blonde and, considering their arduous lifestyle of addiction, still beautiful for all to appreciate.

"Wow he likes his blondes. What's their names?"

"Cath Hart, Isabelle Clarke and Fran Kirkby."

"Thanks, we can consider these as people now not mere mispers – or bodies if these are our victims. Last but by no means least, Sal, can you organise a team of uniforms please. You're coming with me – there's a possibility that more bodies will be on our hands."

"Sounds pleasant, not."

"It certainly won't be – all indications point to the fact they have been dead for sometime," I confirmed as the nerves and adrenalin started to kick in.

"Have we got any Vicks? To mask the odour of rotting flesh Boss."

"Yes, in the glove box of my car, I always have a tub."

CHAPTER 26

An hour from the office, situated half a mile off the A406 and through a series of terraced streets, sat East Grange Industrial Estate, a place I'd driven past hundreds of times this year without a thought. The estate, a relic from the Industrial Revolution, displayed brick-built buildings along with the surrounding area reclaimed by mother nature, with invading brambles and pockets of elderberry and hawthorn rendering parts of the site impassable by vehicles. A plot like this is not only a goldmine but a rarity in London suburbs, where any pockets of unemployed land are eaten up in an instant by new business parks or greed-driven property developers throwing cheap housing together to extort huge sums of money from Mr and Mrs Jones.

Each of the five remaining buildings portrayed themselves in various states of disrepair. Some sat with parts of their tiled roof missing, exposing a series of naked roof trusses and broken windows, clearly once a game for kids from the terraced streets down the road. Others were a crumbled mess, sporting heaps of brick and mortar rather than the sturdy walls they were supposed to be. The first two weather-beaten factories were small, compact units which proved fruitless to our search, but the next was a more imposing building.

Once a thriving family business, indicated by a dilapidated rotting sign amongst a bed of nettles – "B.R, Downs & Sons, Sheet metal work specialist" – it was now a crumbling shell on the verge of collapse, which provided a more encouraging prospect. The traditional pan tiled roof had morphed into a frame for climbing deciduous plants and a roost for local pigeons judging by the piles of excrement scattered across the floor. Vast openings revealed natural skylights, the missing tiles smashed to smithereens on the ground below. Nettles, brambles and moss covered much of the flooring, engulfing everything in their path with a tsunami of green. Sparse self-seeded elderberry bushes popped up, dotting the emerald carpet and finding purchase with miraculous ease between the narrowest of cracks in the concrete base. Swathes of ivy sprawled their way skyward utilising the eroded brick walls, ripping at the mortar with spiny penetrating green fingers. A pair of magpies, perched in a mountainous sycamore tree that was visible through a gaping hole among the eaves, sounded out their discontent to others – "strangers are present".

"One for sorrow two for joy," I thought to myself, as we continued our precarious examination through the old building – but there'll be no elation here today. The voice on the phone proved correct with his brutal confession – after searching the two other derelict buildings on the old industrial estate, the third revealed the hidden quarry. All the women lay together in a shallow grave covered by a dusting of soil, twigs, leaves and sheets of rusty corrugated steel weighed down with a ballast chock of wood.

Their prostrate bodies presented their emaciated faces, mottled blue and waxy in appearance, lifelessly staring into space. An overwhelming and unmistakable stench of death filled the air as we approached the temporary resting place.

This time, the killer had taken the time to place their arms across their chests as if praying, each one attired with the obligatory intricate halo, 'MY ANGEL' scribed across the front of the thin silver band. The odour from the decaying remains was horrendous, prompting gagging amongst the less hardened of our party.

There are several stages of putrefaction, all dependent on

environmental aspects such as temperature, humidity, pH and whether the victim is in water. Instantaneous after death, the blood settles out within the body and the internal organs begin to release enzymes inducing bacteria to initiate the breakdown of muscle and skin. Gases form within the body, and liquids ooze from every conceivable orifice – it's completely gross. The corpse will soon become infested with invading insect larvae on the hunt for an opportunistic meal, rendering a body back to life with millions of ravenous maggots. This is the point when the aroma is at its worst, becoming an overpowering stench which will make you gag – hence the Vicks to mask the smell, though in general, this is only a token gesture as nothing on this mortal planet appears to quash the god-awful hum. It's an odour which taints your being for hours after – your clothes, your hair, the pores of your skin become contaminated, it's almost impossible to rid yourself of the vile stench, shampoo, deodorants, gallons of perfume or aftershave, nothing helps. The bodies lay, a motionless buffet for an infestation of bugs, devouring them inch by inch, bones stripped bare, assisted in their mission by numerous forms of wildlife, until all that's left is skeletal and the only remnants that signify that this was once a person with friends, family and a social life are the blood-stained bones indicating a human was taken away in one moment of enraged sadistic madness.

"Ring forensics Sal and secure the whole area with a perimeter cordon. And one more thing, locate a building surveyor – I want professional clarification we are safe to be operating within this building. The last thing we need is the walls falling in on us before we remove the ladies," I said, glancing around the dilapidated remains.

"No problem, Ma'am. Right, you lot, you heard what the DCI said, and be careful, we have no idea of the structural integrity of the buildings. Secure and step away, awaiting further instruction, these women won't be going anywhere," Sally ordered with an authoritative manner.

A small clearing beyond my car was where I stood to clear my head and process the images I had witnessed. A robin bobbed around in front of me, hopping from branch to branch, cocking his head and puffing out a vermilion chest, showing no obvious signs of fear. My nan used to say when a red breast appeared close to people, someone from the other side was trying to communicate with us. I wondered if this little guy was someone attempting to tell me something.

"Hey little mate, what about telling me the name of the arsehole who is killing beautiful women?" I whispered to the busy robin before he took flight towards a thicker, more protective hedgerow.

The works phone vibrated in my pocket. Initially I ignored it, not wanting to be interrupted by any of the team, or by members of our ever-sympathetic press, whilst I thought the case through, searching the grey matter for leads, pointers, hints or similarities to provide a link to any previous or open cases.

Finally, curiosity overwhelmed me, and I decided to take a glance at the screen, justified in my head by the prospect Jacob could be trying to contact me, but it was the guy from the other week, James, he'd messaged or called me every day since our night together.

"Hi it's me James Harrison wondering if you'd like to meet up again tonight for some food. I can pick you up at seven if you'd like?" the text read, finished off with a happy emoji face. A smile formed in the corner of my mouth.

"That would be brilliant, I should be done by then, I'm having a busy day though so you may have to be flexible."

"Yeah me too, I wish people would take better care of their teeth. I don't like this work lark, and I can be as flexible as you like, as you've experienced ha-ha."

"Lazy git and thank you."

The industrious red breast returned, on the hunt for a juicy morsel to appease his appetite.

"Ha-ha see you around seven ish."

A vehicle pulled into the clearing behind me; the robin flew off into the distance, chirping his disapproval at the intrusion into his day. Jenny and one of her colleagues stepped out of the dark blue Ford Mondeo Titanium.

"Well, this bastard is keeping us busy," she exclaimed, wrapped in a thigh-length black woollen coat sporting large golden buttons and a bright red scarf.

"You're not bloody kidding."

"Are these women more angels?"

"Oh yeah," I said, walking to my car and retrieving the info regarding the prostitutes before passing the buff A4 file to Dr McCabe to peruse whilst her colleague joined the team of uniforms for a chat.

"Get this Jenny, the bastard only had the audacity to give me a call this morning to inform us what a crap performance he considers we're putting up solving the case. And to add insult to injury, he briefed us with the details regarding these three, and blabbed to the press."

"Do we have anything on them?"

"All working girls, ladies of the night, whores, whatever title you want to assign them, reported to missing persons within a month of each other approximately a year ago."

"The cheeky shit. His approach surprises me though, with the occupations of the women. Wouldn't you suppose if these female victims are to replicate angels in his mind, he'd want them perfect in every way? Take this one for example, Ellie Clarke, a dedicated heroin addict with a list of convictions for prostitution and theft as long as your arm, not to mention the two arrests for violent conduct. Not exactly the gleaming angelic type you'd expect."

"He's developed better taste since the three whores."

"Or these were practice for the real thing, his first kills to hone his skills with an opportunistic trait, picking women off the street rather than taking the time to seduce," Jenny replied.

"I see your point, but we don't think these were his first. We think he may be linked to three other murders carried out on the continent, in Spain and France, which display similar MOs, all more than coincidental to our killings."

"OK, why?"

"A friend of Sally's passed on some information regarding three unsolved murder cases across Europe, the three are again blonde beauties. Each received a fatal wound at the base of the skull, only small wings were carved into their backs and no halo, but they displayed 'My Angel' sliced into their foreheads. And as with the women we are investigating, they were befriended by a young man months before they vanished."

"Interesting – he's developing as a killer, he's growing up, becoming more sophisticated in his approach and confident in his abilities to perform these gruesome acts of violence. That will be his downfall – over-confidence, we've come across this before."

"Yeah, I know, but this one is different. He's professional for want of a better word."

"Send me the details of the foreign cases – if he does slip up at some point, I can cross-reference any evidence which comes to light."

"Will do, as soon as I get back to the office," I confirmed as the late afternoon sun started to fade and drop below the tree line, along with the temperature.

"Right, where are the new women?"

"You can't go in yet Jenny, we're waiting for some clarification on the state of the building – the fucking thing looks like it will collapse at any time."

"So, while we have time to kill, how's your love life going?"

CHAPTER 27

As per usual, I was running late for my dinner date with James but managed to message him in time to inform him of the change in ETA, with plans altered accordingly. The remaining daylight we wasted awaiting the structural engineer who decided within minutes the building integrity was in fact safe to proceed.

The forensic team estimated from the state of decay that each of the bodies in the shallow grave had been there between six and nine months. Each woman was now subject to individual examinations and swept for hair, fibres and DNA before being taken away for further intrusion, allowing a more intensive exploration of the site. The victims all possessed the obligatory fatal circular compression wound at the base of the skull, and a halo fitted to all three bodies, decorated with meticulous intent and displaying the words 'My Angel' branded across the metallic band, was clear to the eye. What remained of the decaying flesh and skin on their backs displayed the habitual brutal wings, these examples covering the entire back.

Thoughts raced around my head on the laborious journey back into town. This case was fast becoming a stalemate, a situation I would be scrutinised for whilst chairing a press conference in the morning, an experience which is never pleasant. I had attempted to back hand the job to DS Turner, but my shoulders were obviously not sloped enough to reassign my responsibilities as the gaffer had insisted on my presence as the lead investigator.

The radio was playing the Oasis tune 'All around the world', one of my favourite tracks, and I bellowed out a sing along on the strict basis that no other human was within the immediate vicinity. I'm not one for stage performances or karaoke, and public speaking fills me with utter dread, unfortunately, as the latter is a necessity for a person in my position. The music silenced in my car, and 'incoming call Gary Turner' flashed on the screen in front of me.

"Hi Gaz, what can I do you for?"

"Hello boss, good news, Danny Walker plus accompanying mate are in custody. Uniform picked them up for lifting in the Kingsland shopping centre, the one near Ridley Road market. Considering the thick bastards wanted to stay inconspicuous, nicking a tracksuit in a place with more cameras and security guards than Hollywood was not one of their smartest moves," he informed me, laughing at their stupidity.

"Keep hold of the idiots, I'm on my way."

The next left took me onto a side street and into a council estate not dissimilar to the one across town where I grew up. A gang of youths occupied a street corner, intently watching my car, scanning for potential danger from rival gang members. Their body language eased when they saw a single woman turning the car before heading back in the direction of the station through the now easing traffic. This was the last thing I needed tonight – for the first time in recorded history, after a slight timing adjustment, I was going to be on time for a date before our old friend Mr Walker and his partner in crime decided to throw a spanner in the works by insisting on partaking in a spell of retail therapy whilst lacking one vital commodity – the finances. This is what happens with murders cases, your own life is put on hold often for months on end.

CHAPTER 28

"Evening boss, dumb and dumber are in interview room two, and not particularly interested in being cooperative," Gaz informed me, a broad grin flashing across his face before stuffing a Penguin biscuit down his throat.

"Right, let's go make their day shall we," I replied with gleeful anticipation.

The door creaked as we entered the interview room, alerting the two would-be shoplifters of our presence. Walker stood in a flash. I held my hand up immediately to silence any opportunity to inform me of wrongful arrest or police brutality, or to spout the compulsive verbal diarrhoea he generally adopts.

"Shut up before you start. Seriously I'm not in the mood for any more of your bullshit stories, so, fucking sit," I said glaring towards the pair of them over the top of my glasses like some headmistress about to dish out detentions. Both sat abruptly like a pair of loyal dogs. Danny flashed a resentful look to his obedience.

Gary and I took our seats in front of the two street kids, both of us well versed with the routine we adopt for interview situations. We began by flicking through some paperwork in silence; unbeknown to the two idiots opposite us, those notes were completely irrelevant to this case, mere emails sent from the boss regarding an up-and-coming charity sports event to be held by the station. We find this strategy adds an element of tension and apprehension while additionally giving us time to gather our thoughts and judge their mood and assess their state of mind. Out of the two, Danny appeared relaxed as if waiting for a bus or having a pint, well-practised with the routine, but the other kid was rigid and tense – his body language screamed fear. He projected youthful, in fact he looked about twelve if I'm going to be honest, spotty, gaunt-faced, crew-cut hair, straggly stubbled beard, shifty nervous eyes and, judging by the state of him, beginning to suffer cold turkey – all the symptoms were evident, beads of sweat forming on his forehead before trickling down his face to be mopped away by a grubby coat sleeve, a gifted bargaining tool if required.

"Let's get down to business shall we? I'm DS Turner and this is DCI Lynch, you are here under caution and not arrest, which means unless you so desire, legal representation is not required and both of you can leave at any point during the interview. Although such an act may imply you are more involved in these murders than only finding a body at which point, we may consider arresting you on suspicion of murder rather than nicking a crappy tracksuit. Are we clear?"

Both nodded their consent.

"Full names please, we'll start with you Danny." Gary twiddled a pen through his finger which he placed into his mouth while awaiting an answer.

"Brought the big wigs out today man, fuck me," Danny joked.

"Name, now!" the DS repeated, unamused by the attempted humour.

"Daniel Giles Walker, no fixed abode, but I don't need to tell you."

"Thank you, and you sir?" he continued, probing the twelve-year-old look alike.

"Why do you want his name?"

"Oh no reason Mr Walker, apart from the fact your friend here found a dead woman under a bush in St Mary's. So we've deemed it kind of important as I'm sure you can appreciate," Gary uttered calmly whilst I remained silent, analysing the kid.

"Mrs Lynch, we've spoken about this man."

"No we didn't Danny. We could have talked about the situation before it got to this, but you put the phone down on me. So, a name please," I replied, diverting my attention to the ailing drug addict.

"Na name sorry Mrs. Tae mony skeletons in mah closet tae be giein mah name oot. Tae mony tap profile crims ur oan th'hunt fur me Mrs, bit ah will tell ye whit a've seen." The kid spoke for the first time in a deep Scottish accent which stunned me momentarily. I'd been expecting a squeaky high-pitched teeny boy's voice, but instead a tone resembling a sixty-year-old Jockanese gangster who's smoked forty fags a day bellowed out of the man with kid-like features facing me.

To emphasise my building frustration, I leaned back in my chair, shooting my eyes skyward towards the ceiling before listing forward with my elbows on the desk, crossing my arms, taking time to inspect my nails for an instant before making full eye contact with the young Jock, which obviously made him uncomfortable. His gaze deviated away within a split second, focusing on his grubby hands placed on the graffiti-ed table-top.

"Right young man," I spoke with my best authoritative tone. "You can be as awkward as you like, we are here all night if required. While I'm sure your former criminal life is a dark yet compelling read, I am not interested in one single word of it. I genuinely do not give a monkey's fuck what's happened to you during a previous life. I'm only concerned with the here and now. Let me assure you that what is said within the confines of these four walls will remain here. Do we understand each other?" The Scot acknowledged my question with a slow but deliberate nod, prompted by a nudge in the ribs and a reassuring toothless smile from Danny Walker.

"Whilst I have your undivided attention can I take the opportunity to emphasise the severity of your predicament. Should you continue with your plea for anonymity, and considering we are at this moment in time investigating several brutal mindless killings of beautiful young women, for which, to jog your memory, prior to this conversation, you have already placed yourself at the scene of one such murder, you will leave us no other choice than to presume you are withholding vital evidence and, as DS Turner insinuated earlier, you will be considered a suspect in this case. To a degree harsh you may think until you take into account our point of view, being, you are at present the only person connected with these murders. All we would require is a link to any of the dead women and hey presto you will be banged up on multiple murder charges in an establishment of her majesty's pleasure for an extremely long time. Incidentally, a place where I'm relatively positive associates of those high-profile criminals you described will also reside." I smiled sweetly towards him and relaxed, satisfied he would break in front of my eyes. "The ball is now in your court boys."

"Declan Aikin, no fixed abode."

"Well done, now that wasn't so bad was it?" I gloated, scribbling his name down for future reference.

"Let's git oan wi'it," he grimaced through rotting teeth, his discontent apparent.

"Right, tell us what you can," I said, slumping back into my not-so-comfortable plastic chair.

"Aboot a year 'n' hauf ago ah made pals wi' some girls aff th' street.

Bella used tae let me stoap in her flat fae time tae time sleeping oan th' flair especially in winter whin nights oan th' pavements ur chankin."

"Are these girlfriends?" Gaz enquired.

"Na wey, na nae in a sexual wey. Ah wouldn't gang thare wi' yer boaby pal. They young ladies hae hud mair pricks than a second-hand dartboard, bit thay did whit thay wantit tae survive. Ah guss ye wilnae ken, bit thay wur pleasant tae me, and shered gear wi'me if ah rattled."

"So where does this fit in?" I probed.

"These girls hud umpteen clients, bit yin staun oot ower thaim aw. A huge bloke, Nathan, aw muscles, tattoos 'n' wit. Ye see he became a bawherr o' a regular, bit ainlie wi' blondies. Th' man is loaded, thay rallied fur his cock 'n' th' rewards, i.e., dosh 'n' gear he served up oan a platter, whilk is whin thay became generous tae me. Bit thay soon began tae jook him, th' lassies hated him fur o' his requirements, he's intae some vile mingin' pure weird shite. Bit as a've said he paid weel 'n' provided thaim wi' smack tae, bags o' th' feckin stuff."

"Right, this is helpful. Declan – elaborate on his sexual preferences," I prompted, head cocked to one side, simultaneously peering over the top of my glasses.

"Yeah, he used tae insist oan taking thaim tae his hame, some mansion farmhouse in th' sticks bit whaur, ah dinnae hae a scooby. They girls ah hung aroond wi' prefer tae stay local if thay kin, tis fur protection, owt cuid feckin happen tae thaim otherwise."

"One of the hazards of their trade I suppose. Elaborate – what type of kinky sex is he into?" DS Turner continued.

"The girls talked aboot a place he cald th' special room. Stowed oot tae th' rafters wi' various contraptions, frames wi' chains 'n' leather straps, cages, whips, dildos, anither contraption wi' a lever 'n' restraints whilk he bound thaim tae, cranking open thair legs, sae he cuid dae anythin he wished wi' thaim. Some he made wear pvc outfits hoaching with spikes, he does some wally fookin shite tae them."

"Like what?"

"Do ah honestly need tae elaborate further? He wis thrawn end of."

"Every detail is required, it is important – thrawn?" I quizzed.

"Yrah thrawn, twisted, sick. Ramming stuff in thaim 'n' up their erse, wi' god knows whitevur he cuid fin'. Oan occasion git aff oan slapping thaim aboot or choking thaim oot whin he fooked thaim. Whin Bella git back fae a visit tae his she cuid barely walk th' wee lassie. Ano' th' young lassie tellt me aboot a time she git tied doon tae a cross, he cut her up wi' a stanley blade whilst he shagged her, sae thay refused tae gang wi' him again."

Alarm bells rung in my head. Declan was unaware of the gruesome angel wings carved into our dead females, so was oblivious to the importance of the last few words he uttered.

"Again, to highlight DCI Lynch's point, where does this fit in with the investigation? It's not uncommon for street workers to service the odd client who will pay substantially more than the average for ladies of the night to take a slap or two, or perform sex acts out of the ordinary shall we say," Turner continued.

"The headline in th' newspaper, 'The blonde angel killer' – this bloke wid insist oan cawin th' girls as his angels, 'n' whin ah fun th' lassie under th' bushes ah thought she wis Bella, she wis spitting image."

The excitement started to rise inside me, shortly followed by a surge of adrenalin. Was this the first breakthrough? A lead on this monster at last? A man into kinky shit – our victims had been restrained at some point, and for this Nathan fellow to cut one of them up and insist on calling them angels – come on, give us more.

"Are you able to provide a description of this man?"

"Probably nae a've ainlie witnessed th' man a few times bit thro' th' motor windae, he ne'er git oot, a posh as fuck black beamer."

"Can you divulge anything else regarding this man or his car – any distinguishing features?" I pushed, sensing we may be close to a viable development.

"As a've said, muscled up, short blond locks, ah didnae pay much attention tae his boat race. Ah waved cheerio the nou hoping thay wid be back in yin piece," he lied as his head dropped to avert his eyes from my gaze, but too late – I clocked the deceit he was trying to hide.

People, particularly witnesses or suspects, are a speciality of mine. I analyse them – not to be intimidating by any means, but the eyes are the first parts of the body to give away lies, experience teaches you this. The rest of the traits associated with bullshit will soon follow, such as their body language, including turning their head away when talking to avoid eye contact, jiggling legs and continually running hands through hair. The attitude can change rapidly – criminals can go from confident bravado, cocksure dick heads, to an emotional wreck in seconds when the reality of their circumstance becomes apparent. Some become over cooperative, or frustratingly go to the other extreme and answer an entire interview with 'no comment'. On occasion, the aggressor appears to think intimidation and violence will inhibit us from discovering the hidden truths. All situations subconsciously promoted from the depths of the mind in the vain attempt to prevent us from revealing a bite of information they are desperate to keep under wraps. But the eyes – they never lie, whatever the emotional state.

"Is your friend's given name Bella?" Gaz quizzed.

"Who kens. A've nae seen her aboot fur months whilk is common amongst thae girls, happily some thay reconcile wi' parents or loved one's 'n' gang back tae thair lee afore th' crappy streets 'n' addiction strangles thaim. Mair often than nae they'll shift onto a freish feck zone, workin' a different area 'n' an alternative client base, generally whin thay owe dosh tae dealers or pimps, they'll reappear again oot th' blue wi' a slap fur thair troubles, bit a'm sure Bella is ainlie her street name, a dinnae ken her real name."

"How long have you been on the streets Declan?" I asked with genuine sympathy, the years of hardship easy to appreciate.

"A lang time, years."

"How old are you?"

"Twenty."

The answer shocked me. I scribbled a note on my pad for Gaz to leave the room and return with the misper photos of the dead working girls.

"Shall we take a break? DS Turner will fetch a brew, how do you have your tea boys?"

"However it comes if it's free," Danny Walker answered. Gary nodded, shutting the door firmly behind him.

"So, while DS Turner is absent, would you be willing to come back tomorrow afternoon to study a few mugshots, help us find this Nathan guy? Should your busy schedule allow."

"Yeah but only if you feed us and there's cash involved, and both of us want the charges dropped for nicking," Declan negotiated for them.

"The only promise I can make is I'll see what I can do, how's that?"

The creak of the door alerted us to the DS returning. He dished out the steaming tea. The young Scot took his up like a prized possession, as if he thought we might rescind our kind offer, whereas Danny Walker relaxed back into his slumped position like a teenager in a school lesson which held no real interest to him.

"Right, we'll show you several photos of some women we would like you to peruse before you go. If you recognise them, simply answer yes." Gary revealed the unflattering photos one by one, placing them in sets of three on the graffiti-riddled desk in front of the boys.

"Never seen her, or her, nor this yin, hauld yer horses, aye, this is Coco," Declan confirmed, placing a confident nicotine-stained finger on the photo to the left under the first three.

"Are you sure Mr Aikin?"

"Defo man."

Gary continued to reveal two other women.

"Th' lassie in th' middle is Frankie, 'n' she's mah mukker Bella, bonnie int she? Ah dinnae ken how come she's oan th' streets, she cuid be a model in different world. I bet ye wouldn't ton ony o' thaim doon wid yer?

"I'm happily married thanks Declan," Gaz lied, scribbling the girls' street names on the snapshots.

"What about you, Mrs Lynch?" Walker asked with a cheeky wink.

"Sorry to disappoint you Danny, but they don't exactly float my boat."

"Ur th' girls in th' shite or sommat?" Declan asked us with genuine concern written across his gaunt drug-fuelled face.

"No, they're not in trouble, people are worried that's all. None of these women can be located, and we are trying to find them to ensure nothing is untoward, but having their street ID will help, thanks."

It came to light, sat in that interview room, that Coco was in fact Cath Hart, Fran Kirkby identified as Frankie, and Isabelle Clarke we established was Declan's beautiful Bella. I declined to inform him his three friends were all sadly victims of our man. It sounds callous but I'm hoping they might help more with mugshots of men who like to damage young women for thrills.

"Thanks Danny, Declan, you've been most helpful. Shall we say half two tomorrow and I'll sort something out I promise."

The boys left with their hot drinks, back to their unyielding street life. I glanced over towards my colleague.

"Fucking hell, it's our man Gaz."

"I'll arrange to get CCTV footage from the area and dates, and we'll start trawling through to find this posh-as-fuck beamer as he so eloquently described it. Sally is still here to help; you go home Ma'am."

"I can't Gaz, I need to be here."

"Go home Kelly, you're knackered, it's been a long day. I'll call you if anything develops, promise, scouts honour and all that bollox. Now go, you'll only distract me anyway."

CHAPTER 29

I reluctantly made my way towards the station exit as Gaz had so rudely insisted and left him to work his magic with Sally. The pair often work together, not because they particularly preferred each other's company but for the simple reason that Gary is obsessive and Sally is a whizz at research. The woman has a flair for finding obscure, relevant information on the internet, a talent for producing a dot of evidence from nothing.

The city's evening streets were bustling with commuters heading to public transport that would deliver them home to loved ones, where they'd discuss the day's events over their latest culinary masterpiece and a glass of chardonnay. Others were scuttling off to overpriced one-bed flats with an adjoining kitchen to watch the latest over-produced TV show starring talentless idiots talking about their favourite topic, themselves. A wintery chill bit in the air; the seasons had changed and not for the better.

I took a long deep breath before heading to my car and towards home. It was strange to think that the killer was out there somewhere on these streets. A crowd was gathered at one of the sets of endless traffic lights in anticipation of the green man so they could continue their quest for relaxation, their faces depicting a plethora of cultures and ages. Some were dressed for the city in business suits sporting raincoats with scarfs hanging across their shoulders as a fashion accessory rather than providing thermal qualities as per design. The majority adopted a more casual style of dress – jeans, tailored jackets or hoodies. One individual stood out from the crowd – his fashion sense remained stuck in the seventy's punk era, clad in Doc Martens boots with red laces, skin-tight jeans and a battered leather jacket advertising his taste in music, all brought to a crescendo with a huge black and green Mohican. I scanned all of them one by one, pausing momentarily to assess each. To think I could be looking straight into the killer's eyes right now, he could be laughing at my ignorance, planning his next humiliating phone call.

An impatient toot of a horn alerted me that the lights had changed to green, and I continued my drive down the dark damp city streets and home. My mind wondered to thoughts of James – would it honestly be fair to drag another person into my chaotic, fucked-up life and the job that goes with it? Could I realistically expect him to continually tolerate all the late nights, missed events and mood swings that are involuntarily inherited with my work? I mean I've only been seeing the poor bloke a few weeks and already I've had to let him down twice and now I was late again by over an hour. But he seemed at ease with my life and career presently. Of course, it was early days in the relationship, things still had time to go tits up and, in my experience, I wouldn't have to wait much longer for that to happen.

I trudged wearily up my garden path to the large fake wood-finish PVC door with its narrow flash of decorative glazing down the centre; the overgrown hydrangea which I have been meaning to prune for months wet my legs, causing a whispered curse. My breath billowed out in front of me against the chilly night air before floating up and out of sight into the dark cloudy evening sky. The door was unlocked which is against my strict instructions when Jacob is home alone. Entering the warm hallway, my heartbeat was raised in anticipation, but my fear was appeased when I heard laughter and chatter.

"Hi mate, I'm home, did you have tea? Because I'm supposed to be going out with James for food tonight and I'm running late," I shouted through to the kitchen diner, kicking off my sensible flats in the direction of the shoe rack and removing my coat simultaneously before hanging it on the stair banister as I passed.

"What's new and yeah I've eaten at my mates, his mum did pizza and chips. By the way, James is here."

"What, right now?"

"Yes, right now," James said appearing around the kitchen door with a tin of beer in hand and a sparkling smile.

"Do you want another beer, James?" Jacob asked, emerging from the living room.

"I'd better not Jacob. I've already had one and you know what these copper types are like."

"You're so funny, not. We all right here?"

"Yeah, fine Mum," Jacob replied beaming.

"That's good, I think. So where are you taking me James?"

"It's a secret for now, go get ready. There's no rush though, me and Jacob are on COD."

"Yeah, and I'm kicking arse."

"Cheers Jacob, you're supposed to keep that a secret, I'm trying to impress here."

"Mum, James has been telling me about his contacts at Saracens rugby club, he can get tickets for the next home game, can we go?"

"We'll see honey, I'm very busy at work at the minute."

"You're always busy. Well if you can't make it, me and James can go, that's ok, isn't it?"

"It's fine with me matey but it is totally up to your mother."

"Mum, please?"

"OK, OK, Jacob, you can go. Now where's my cuddle?"

"Yeah right, cheers Mum," he said darting off into the living room before I had time to ambush him for a snuggle in front of his new bestie.

"Wow, you've made quite the impression," I exclaimed, raising my eyebrows as James placed his beer on the worktop.

"Kell, he's a great kid, and it's no trouble. One of my victims so to speak at the dental practice works on the promotional team at the club, he's always offering me tickets. So it's not any hassle."

"Do you know how long he has been waiting to go to a rugby match? His dad the useless lump won't take him, and I rarely have the time."

"Hey, listen, I don't want to step on Dad's feet here," James said with a serious face for once.

"Really! His father is a knob, so don't worry about him. Anyway, sorry I'm late again, this case is proving to be a right bastard and then the two smack-head witnesses we've been looking for decided to show up. Meaning I had to deal with that first."

"It's fine, don't worry," he replied, giving me that smile I have already grown to love.

"Thanks," I said, stroking his huge hand and gazing into his gorgeous blue eyes.

"It's settled then. I'll sort out some tickets. Now you," he said, embracing me and pulling me in tight to his muscular torso which felt so good, "go and get ready while I get my arse kicked at COD again." He planted a prolonged kiss on my lips and then disappeared into the living room, retrieving his beer en route.

We headed across the city before jumping onto the A3 out of town towards the Putney Heath, Richmond Park vicinity, about three-quarters of an hour from my house. The further we ventured away from central London, the more open ground emerged along with the clearing night sky supporting a bright toenail moon and flickering stars. The city tends to engulf the night sky with a wall of concrete and glass hiding the natural diamond treasures of the midnight blue velvet heavens. Behind us the streetlights of London spread out like a vast glowing spider's web as we drove alongside the heath before turning left onto Robin Hood Way and Vale Crescent, lined with sentry trees standing bolt upright. The car stopped outside a large, impressive two-storey Victorian building with gardens to the front and rear and a gravel driveway, upon which stood a huge yellow skip full of brick rubble.

"Wow, dentistry must pay well," I commented, amazed at the size of the house and accompanying grounds which were visible in the darkness through a broken fence panel.

"Well, not bad, but to support my lavish lifestyle I do have to rob the odd bank or sell my body to older wealthy ladies."

"I bet you don't get much."

"Enough of the James bashing, let's go inside. I, madam, have cooked dinner for you."

"Now I am impressed, what is it?" My naturally inquisitive mind jumped into overdrive.

"Slow-cooked minted lamb, served with a rich homemade gravy, goose fat roast potatoes and caramelised veg washed down with a wine of the lady's choice," he beamed.

"But I'm a vegetarian."

"Bollox, really? I never even thought. Shit, well I can throw something else together quick and…"

"James, I'm shitting with you, get me in that house – lamb's one of my favourites," I gloated, taking hold of his hand.

He sighed. "Thank God for that, come on then. You will have to excuse the mess, I'm having some work done. And listen, before we go in…" His persona changed for the first time since we had met, and he looked almost serious. "There is someone else in my life that you don't know about yet, but I really want you to meet him because he's special to me. Be warned though he can get a little jealous."

"I'm sure I can handle any kids, I have a teenager remember," I said cautiously before entering his house only to be mobbed by his rather large golden Labrador. "Oh my god, you are a beautiful boy. What's his name?" I asked whilst receiving an affectionate saliva bath.

"Moody."

"Moody – what sort of a name's that?"

"He's named after one of my favourite rugby players – Lewis Moody, England star? World Cup winner? No, nothing?" I obviously, and disappointingly, didn't know of Mr Moody or his accomplishments playing the game. "Jesus DCI Lynch, you seriously need educating." James raised his arms, gesticulating his disgust towards my obvious ignorance before turning back to the hob, laughing to himself.

"Would madam like to take a seat? I'll just retrieve the wine from the cellar and then dish up."

"I'll get the wine if you like, just point me in the right direction," I suggested.

"No, no, seriously, it's fine," he said abruptly. "The renovations have started in there and it's like a building site at the minute."

"No problem," I said, retaking a seat, my enthusiasm to help quashed.

"Sod it. Come on then, I'll give you the guided tour. When it is complete, I can assure you that my man cave will be THE man cave of all time."

He took me by the hand, dragging me towards the cellar door and unlocking it with a clunk. Several fluorescent lights jumped into life as we descended the stairway and into a subterranean building site. Four brick pillars separated the large open room into three sections, two smaller side spaces and a larger open section central to the building.

"Kell, here there'll be a wide screen cinema system on the wall, games consoles, docking port for music and built-in sound bars," James explained, guiding me to the smaller left-hand section. "With a comfy sofa, coffee table and bean bags dotted about like a chill-out room."

"Cool."

"This side," he said, dragging me across the room to the other smaller section, "will be pinball and arcade games; a mate of mine can get them cheap."

"You're just a big kid, and what about this area, disco?" I said, spinning in circles in the larger section.

"No, no, no Kell. A pool table, a pool table will fit perfectly – with a beer fridge on the far side of course. It's hard to imagine now but it'll be well worth it in the end," he said, slightly too enthusiastically, like a kid telling Santa what they wanted for Christmas.

"I'm definitely in the wrong line of business."

"The bank of Mum and Dad. They died years ago in a car crash in the south of France, and I was the only child to inherit their estate. I didn't really want to live in their house, too many memories you know, so I rent it out for an obscenely extortionate amount of money," he laughed.

"Sorry about your parents."

"It's fine. So, what do you think?"

"It'll be so cool when it's finished," I assured him, thinking *child*.

The evening was great, lush food washed down with fantastic wine and topped off by the good company. I fell in love with Moody instantly and the feeling was mutual. James and I sat chatting about all manner of subjects, from dogs to politicians, although there's probably not much difference between the two subjects, which might be an injustice to dogs thinking about it. Fortunately, neither of us were in the mood to discuss anything work related. Then the atmosphere changed, we embraced, kissed and I found myself making love to him on the sofa, without Moody present of course because that would just be weird. We lay in a naked embrace, my head on his bare toned chest, watching TV while recovering from the sex, the incredibly good sex.

"Sorry to hear about your ex and your best mate, that must have been shit."

"Jacob has been talking I'm guessing."

"Yeah, I don't mean to drop him in the crap, and I wasn't probing or owt, it just came out in conversation."

"It's fine, I'm glad Jacob feels comfortable enough to talk about it eventually, it really fucked him up for a while."

"I can imagine, it must have turned his world upside down bless him. Kids tend to blame themselves in situations like that, they look at excuses for the adults."

"He didn't tell you, did he?"

"Tell me what?"

"Jacob caught them, his dad and my best mate, his godmother, he caught them fucking on the kitchen table, in full passionate motion – that's why he blames himself."

"Wow, poor kid!"

"Yeah, poor kid." I paused for a while. "I ought to be getting off soon Mr Harrison, it is a school night," I mentioned, sighing and tightening my embrace around his muscular body.

"I'll take you, it's no problem. I have trouble sleeping most nights anyway."

"Are you sure?"

"Of course. I need food for my boy anyway, don't we my mate," he say in a childish voice whilst petting Moody.

"Thank you, bye Moody, see you again, gorgeous boy," I said, passing through the kitchen diner to pet my new best friend and receiving another saliva bath before leaving into the icy night.

CHAPTER 30

Life on the streets at this time of year is arduous to say the least. For the last three nights, the temperature barely rose above the dizzy heights of freezing point with a biting icy wind which chills you to the marrow of your bone. A local flyover became our five-star accommodation for the evening; it's been nicknamed the spice rack due to the makeshift village being infested with abusers of synthetic cannabinoids, spice, K2, dream genie, skunk or whatever other title is gifted for promotional purposes. It's a favoured place for shelter and drug taking.

Although a high-risk place of residence where sleep is a bonus, it provides adequate cover from the elements and is a known point for street folk to find warm food and on occasions fresh clothing from a visiting charity for the homeless, hence the vast numbers who gather there through the winter months.

If honesty prevails, I don't particularly enjoy being around this area – the abundance of spice addicts is uncomfortable as the chemical-induced mayhem invades their bodies. This synthetic crap can affect an individual in numerous ways, including becoming euphoric, annoyingly friendly and over talkative, but most become zombie-like and statuesque, fixated on the same spot for hours on end in combination with the incessant chanting of utter bollox to themselves. The heart-stopping, ear-splitting screams as the hallucinogenic cocktail runs its course is too much for me as the overpowering chemical infusion engulfs their body, preventing brain function and mobility. But this shit they pump into themselves can deposit them to a darker side, depending on the mood of the addict. It can promote tremendous levels of paranoia, often leading to extreme acts of violence. All you can do in those cases is exit stage left as far away from the melee as possible, because the bare facts are that nothing you do or say will defuse the situation. Reasoning with them is a pointless exercise, normal rational human behaviour and morals diminish to zero, their drug-fuelled mind doesn't allow any form of intelligence to prevail. Eventually they return to our planet, or the local plod intervenes to escort them in a cattle wagon to the nearest station.

In previous winters I have been ignorant to this unearthly performance, but this is the first I have spent homeless, sober and clean. Over eight months have passed now and not a drop of alcohol has crossed my lips, or an ounce of Mr Brownstone coursed through my veins. How long it will last, I don't know. Every day I battle the demons, a fight which isn't made any easier living this life amongst all the carnage it provides.

My new mate Declan's stubbled pale face stirred under his filthy sleeping bag and cream blanket. The shakes were taking hold of his body, but it was not the bitter chill of the frosty morning causing him to convulse in this manner, this was different to the shivering caused by the hypothermic conditions; it was a condition familiar to me in recent times – he needed a hit and sooner rather than later.

"You good man? You look like shite mate."

"No, a'm needin' a scair mon. A've gotta drap some gear pronto a'm starting tae rattle lik' a bastad. Whit's the time?" Declan replied, beads of sweat forming on his forehead despite a night of freezing conditions.

"Half eight, what we gonna do man? No way can we go back to

the shopping centre any time soon, security will chuck us out before our feet touch the fucking floor."

"I need tae dae sommat Danny mon. Th' cramps ur comin' thick 'n' fest."

"Can you hang on until this aft? We'll go visit the black copper woman Mrs Lynch, do a few mugshots, baffle her with bullshit, take the cash and fuck off out of there to meet Izzy for a bag."

"Ah cannae dae Izzy. Aye owe him fae lest week. He'll click his finger 'n' his gorillas wull beat shite oot me again," he replied with concern etched across his grubby face, hollow eyes staring into space.

"Let's go to the refuge, beg a hot drink to pass some time and think what we're gonna do," I suggested.

"A'm needin' a hit man," he groaned as the lack of H started to gnaw at his bones. Such an excruciating suffering you can't describe, only those who have endured a body riddled with cramps will know what I'm talking about. Each agonising, muscle-tearing surge of pain screams heroin in your mind, at that point you will do anything for a fix, and I mean anything. All sense of morality vanishes out of the window at breakneck speed, you need skag before your body begins tying itself in violent knots. It becomes your sole purpose in life, the only thing you exist for, a precious bag of powder cooked up with water, lemon juice or whatever else you can lay your hands on and plunged into your veins to obtain the ecstatic feeling to satisfy the cravings.

"What about Nathan? You still got his number?"

"Yeah bit th' numpty scares th' shite oot o' me. He's nae richt in 'ere pal," Dec said, pointing to his head.

"Then go without Dec man because we don't have many more options left."

"Ah ring him noo if a've git enough credit," he agreed, taking to his feet wearily, ensuring his call was out of ear shot of other addicts who might overhear his score and contemplate commandeering it for themselves.

"He'll catch up wi' us at th' auld garages under th' railway at hauf eleven," he whispered upon his return.

"We better get a fucking move on lad while you can still walk."

CHAPTER 31

My experience of dealing with the press has never been a pleasant one. The only way to describe the whole charade is like having teeth pulled whilst attending a job interview but worse. Nerves jangled as I approached the allocated conference room where I was about to address the media alongside my chief superintendent Harry Thornton. His calming influence was reassuring beside me, the sort of man you never witness flustered or irate, his approach is authoritative but friendly.

"DCI Lynch, a word before we enter the melee."

"Yes sir."

"Remember, stick to the facts we discussed and don't give any details away unnecessarily. Use this media liaison to our advantage. Never let them assume they're doing us a favour because they'll simply take the piss."

"Got it sir."

The room presented at a low hum as we entered through the double glass doors which swung back into position obediently. To the centre and left, two TV cameras stood surrounded by a gaggle of photographers, who instantly jumped into action with a blaze of blinding flashes that left floating stars in my vision. The remainder of the room was a cacophony of suited reporters all vying for seats near the front of house in anticipation, readied with mobile phones, pencils, notepads and old school Dictaphones.

"Hello everybody and good morning, please can we have quiet," said the chief super. The buzz of chatter ebbed to silence until a ringtone sounded from the back of the room; numerous heads turned in the direction of the interruption where a red-faced young reporter dealt with the embarrassment pronto.

"Thank you. Our senior investigating officer DCI Kelly Lynch will now answer your questions regarding the cases which are currently under investigation. Can we conduct ourselves with decorum and order throughout. All present in this room are more than aware of how we manage press conferences and the principles I adopt. So, adhere to the rules, and make the event a much more amicable experience for everyone involved, thank you. DCI Lynch, the floor is yours."

"Sir. First on the agenda, I would like to take the opportunity to highlight this number displayed across the front of the desks. This is a direct line to the LSCIU specifically concerning all matters considered linked to these cases. It will be available on a twenty-four-hours-a-day, seven-days-a-week basis and I must encourage members of the public to come forward with any information, referencing the investigation code 9873. Please do not assume any matter insignificant, assume it may be relevant, many thanks. First question please." A dozen arms shot into the air like enthusiastic primary school kids vying to be the first to answer the teacher's question.

"Yes sir, with the orange tie."

"Good morning DCI Lynch, can you reveal how many lines of enquiry you are pursuing in respect to the man committing these murders, presuming this is a man of course?"

"At this moment in time we cannot accurately determine the number of murders this man has committed. For certain, the MOs in numerous investigations are extremely similar but as yet we have no rock-solid evidence to link said cases."

"So, you do consider the person in question is a male?"

"Yes, the prime suspect is a man."

"Can you provide us with a description, so we can release it to the public?" asked Mr orange tie.

"Unfortunately, no. We do not hold a definitive account of this individual as per this morning."

"Please forgive my ignorance DCI Lynch, but if you don't possess a portrayal of the killer, how can we conclude he's male?"

"That's an easy one – he kindly rang me and my team to inform us where the latest three bodies could be located." The crowd raised to a murmur inducing several camera flashes before order descended once again to an uncomfortable silence.

"So back to the original question DCI Lynch, how many killings are you considering?" asked a handsome young man from the back of the room.

"We are investigating numerous leads both here in the UK and in collaboration with colleagues on the continent for which we await further details, thank you. The young lady in the red top." I turned, pointing in the direction of an attractive young brunette, her scarlet lipstick matching the outfit.

"Thank you, DCI Lynch. Can you confirm whether the man has been called the angel killer because he disfigures the women with wings before killing them?"

"For obvious reasons, I cannot discuss the finer details whilst the case is in progress, and to broach the subject of nicknames or titles, I can't say I'm a fan. In my experience these elaborate pseudonyms tend to elevate the individual into the limelight, giving them almost pop stardom status. Which is often what this type of person desires, the attention."

"But do you think there's a religious link?"

"There is no evidence to associate these killings to any genre of religion."

"But they do have religious traits as in the wings of angels, do they not?"

"Some aspects of the cases could be deemed of a religious nature. However, this may also be an elaborate killer making his own individual mark on society in a manner which differs from previous murderers. I'm sorry, I can't comment further on the matter. Next, I'll take the guy in the cream blazer."

"Morning, can you release any details regarding the case – names, mugshots, any forensics which have come to light?"

"Not at this moment in time. Families have been informed and I ask for the press to respect their privacy. Regarding forensics, we are dealing with limited DNA evidence discovered from any of the scenes. As I mentioned with a previous question, there is a possible link to other open investigations but as yet no solid evidence to substantiate this theory has been established. I'll cover descriptions later in my concluding statement."

"So, nothing substantial to offer the public?"

"No, but the cases are still in the relatively early stages. Next please. Yes, madam," I said, pointing towards a red-headed Milf on the front row, dressed to impress in a charcoal pinstriped power suit, a pencil poised in her mouth.

"Hi, can I emphasise the fact that you've only answered a limited number of questions this morning. All of which you have managed to bat to the boundary like a politician at a public enquiry. So, are we expected to conclude that you and your LSCIU team do not possess a single thread of evidence from at least five bodies over three murder scenes? Furthermore, it is my understanding these young ladies may have been in the presence of a white male prior to their disappearance. Forgive me, I don't mean to be rude, but I, along with many others in the room today, find it difficult to comprehend that you cannot provide any details of this person – his height, build, hair colour, never mind a photo fit or anything similar, an aspect which I find incredible considering virtually every street in London possesses CCTV of some description, ANPR, security cameras and so on."

I attempted to answer but she shut me off. "To continue, you don't appear to have an inclination as to why he might be committing these horrendous crimes, and apparently, you are not able to divulge any details concerning the women or an MO, which additionally means the media are unable to provide specifics associated to these killings to the public in order to aid their safety or assist with the investigation. So is there anything at all you can divulge?" the woman said in such a condescending confident manner it instantly boiled my blood.

"Sorry, Mrs…?"

"Ms Belling, Charmaine Belling."

"Well to answer your question Ms Belling," I replied with a huge portion of sarcasm which brought about a ripple of giggles, "how could we, the police force, i.e. me in this case, release details related to a murder enquiry for which the evidence is either non-existent or at best circumstantial? We are not in the practice of fabricating stories to ensure people like yourself can dramatise every single detail we provide to scaremonger the community and aid your insignificant publication an increase in readers. The purpose of this press conference is to tell the truth and not to exaggerate or sugar coat. In my possession are details that I can release and I'm more than happy to go through those now. Is this acceptable to you Ms Belling?"

"Yes, thank you DCI Lynch," she replied, her confident bravado draining as she spoke.

"To begin, I'd like to put out an appeal for a missing woman. This is Becky Holt." I addressed the gaggle in front of me while an enlarged photograph of the woman in her full stunning glory was projected onto the screen behind me. "This young woman disappeared twelve days ago. She is thirty years of age and five foot seven, of average build with natural blonde hair and, as you can see from the picture, she's an attractive young woman. We are aware she either arranged drinks prior to or met with a man whilst out before her disappearance. Now of course this could be coincidental, an innocent night out with a friend or lover and not connected to this investigation, which is why we are appealing for this individual to come forward as soon as possible to eliminate themselves from our enquiries.

"This second slide is a vague hazy snapshot obtained from street cams showing a man who appears to be in the company of Ms Holt on said night. We believe this gentleman to be approximately six two or one meter eighty centimetres tall, well-built with a muscular physique, blond almost mousey cropped hair. As I expressed previously, this may be an innocent passer-by, but we do need to trace this reveller to eliminate him from our investigation.

"Regarding the killer himself, we are starting to build up a profile. Due to the lack of DNA evidence at the scene of the crimes we can conclude these were not opportunistic acts. We believe each case was planned to the last meticulous detail and a considerable time prior to the women's disappearance. Our prime suspect is a perfectionist to the point of obsessive, leaving nothing to chance. I'm guessing he's highly intelligent and extremely disciplined in his approach, which is why, extraordinarily, we possess little to no CCTV footage, and no witnesses, DNA, etc. To emphasise a point and make the media aware, all victims associated with this investigation, including the enquiries in Europe, are of a similar age, stature and hair colour and are single, but more significantly, they have recently separated from spouses or partners, so are probably vulnerable to attention."

"As per Becky Holt?" came a voice from the floor.

"Yes, like Becky." I paused as the room murmured. "To continue, work colleagues and friends of the victims describe similar stories – each of our young women befriended a man similar in description to my previous comments. Six two, well-built with a muscular frame and blond to mousey short hair. All were wined and dined before spending the night with a gentleman, not an uncommon weekend occurrence, I'm sure. Now obviously we cannot be certain if these events are connected or coincidental without establishing evidential links. But I would like to ask for vigilance amongst the public, particularly young ladies socialising alone. And I'm sure you can appreciate why we are anxious to locate the whereabouts of Becky Holt ASAP."

A hand shot up at the back of the room within the crowd of photographers.

"Yes sir," I acknowledged.

"If he had sex with them, one would assume traces of DNA, sperm, hair etc would be present."

"Yes, I agree, normally one or more of these contaminants would be discovered, but in all cases, none of the women when examined revealed any signs of recent sexual contact and their accommodation was devoid of unclassified DNA. As I have said, this man is meticulous in his approach and intelligent, I can only imagine he will have prior knowledge of or have researched the science behind DNA evidence."

The tooth-pulling press conference continued for another fifteen painful minutes before the chief super decided all aspects of the investigations which we were able to release had been covered several times over, and he concluded the whole charade, much to my relief.

"Well done DCI Lynch, I was particularly impressed with how you dealt with the rather obstreperous ginger-haired lady," the CS announced on the way back to the office.

"Thanks sir, she was a bit of a pain in the proverbial."

"Yes she was. Take my advice though, work on hiding your feelings towards these people. Try not to become aggressor or emotionally involved, it was so glaringly obvious the red head pissed you off, but well done anyway and keep me posted with any developments," he said, leaving stage right to his rather grand office before I had chance to defend myself.

CHAPTER 32

The two addicts arrived at eleven thirty-five, irritatingly late which was not unusual. I stood observing them through the old rotting door and a curtain of cobwebs of an abandoned storage unit built into a train line viaduct half obscured by a naked wild buddleia bush. Take nothing for granted with addicts, they are not trustworthy, and precautions were taken before I revealed myself. Cameras around here are in effect non-existent, and a security guard patrols only two to three times and day. The duo circled the small courtyard in front of me, nervous in appearance as they awaited my arrival, trudging amongst the obligatory London litter, far too close to my position to be comfortable.

The youth accompanying Declan was a stranger to me, so I retreated towards the rear of the old unit and into the safety of the darkness which I much prefer, brushing cobwebs from my face en route. The poisonous little Jock fucker had contacted me in desperation to fill his veins. He is the only human on this planet who could link me to the liberation of the street girls as the last person to be associated with the prostitutes, a fact he's used against me to subsidise his filthy habit, exploiting my situation into providing him with high-quality heroin. A ploy recently promoted by the infestation of missing persons posters in numerous areas around the city, all representing Bella prior to her addiction in her full stunning glory. A search financed by her affluent, concerned family who will never lay eyes on their inconvenient daughter again. A manufactured story eased the scrawny Scot's concerns, a tale regarding Isabel residing at my humble abode, emphasising the overriding fact that she doesn't possess any urgency to contact her family due to a previous abusive relationship involving her stepfather and his rather inappropriate obsession towards her. In addition, I also explained that the streets are now a high-risk distraction for Bella as she endeavours to free herself from the dragon she's been chasing for several years. Hopefully, this would be an adequate tale to ease his simplistic mind, although he's not entirely stupid, he is close but not totally devoid of grey matter, hence the occasional phone call for a bag of desperately needed brown.

The police are now aware of the situation regarding the liberations. I felt the need to assist their shabby investigation and enlighten them as to the location of the three fallen angels. Bella's family will soon discover the fate of their beloved daughter via the family liaison office, and heartache will ravage their bodies like some debilitating disease. The empathetic members of society will assume it is grief her parents are presenting, although an alternative theory could be that it is an overwhelming sense of guilt infesting their souls for abandoning a vulnerable young girl, their own flesh and blood, onto the filthy streets in her moment of need. Their paternal abilities would not or of course could not stretch to supporting their drug addict daughter. This scenario wasn't on the cards, not considered part of their idyllic picture-perfect lifestyle, a smack head in the family, oh no, not what the neighbours expect. Their photogenic precious little perfect daughter had become way too inconvenient for them to deal with, way too far off the scale, their support and love had been cut off at source, leaving her to face her affliction alone. But now they will shed a tear for their dearly departed, receive condolences from relatives and friends for their loss. I have no fucking empathy for the situation they find themselves in – it was their insensitive desire for the perfect urbanised lifestyle which gave rise to this occurrence, nothing else. No tears will flow from my eyes for those stuck-up materialistic bastards, not a single ounce of remorse will pass through my body for releasing their daughter to a better place than their affluence could provide. In fact, I will take an element of pride from the suffering her death will cause them. Only I was supportive to Bella and the other two whores when they needed assistance most, when they needed to flap their wings and fly like angels.

The little Scottish prick was rattling, the symptoms were clear. Sweat seeped from every conceivable pore, miraculous considering the winter air that morning was only managing the tropical heights of 4°C. The shakes were evident, meaning the nauseating cramps would follow soon, manifesting deep within the muscles and bone as his body vigorously disapproved of the lack of substance in his bloodstream.

This is the reason a huge number of addicts fail in their attempts to rid themselves of the sickening habit. The cold turkey starts off mild and bearable for a short while, but this doesn't last long as the body is starved of the evil of heroin, and soon the agonising spasms set in, contorting and disfiguring the soul with the agony of withdrawal. A pain which tears away at the muscle and penetrates deep into the bone marrow, screaming, suffering in a chemical induced torture chamber with only one cure – the ecstatic, euphoric easing effects of H as it pumps through their veins, satisfying the demands of their mind.

I left the little bastard for ten minutes or so, enjoying his rising agony as I contemplated a solution to my predicament.

"You were late," I shouted from the storage unit, satisfied they'd not been followed; his addiction pained him enough to quiet his loose jaw.

"Awright Nath. Ah didnae see y ower thare man, whin did ye

sneak in pal?" he replied, his over-enthusiastic smacked mind relieved by my presence.

"Come here and shut the fuck up. Who's this? I told you to come alone," I said pointing to the scrawny gaunt urchin at his side.

"Dinna fash yirsel. This is ma pal Danny, he's fookin' kosher bud honest." I eyed my disapproval in the direction of the other kid.

"What do you want Dec? I told you not to ring me anymore unless you hear anything on the streets about my angels vanishing." I glared again between both the scruffy looking smack heads who more than likely hadn't washed for weeks.

"Well that's it man. Ah fun a deid lassie under a hedge in St Mary's near th' bakers wha dish oot stale breid 'n' brose thro' winter. Th' coppers teuk us in fur a wee blether at th' station, thay brought some snaps oot o' Bella, Coco 'n' Frankie."

"And what did you tell them?" I said calmly, concealing the one inside me who was beginning to manifest himself.

"Bugger a' Nathan. Ainlie ah fun blonde lassie under th' bushes in th' chorch thingy oan th' high street. Ah didnae recognise her though."

"No, what did you tell them about me and the girls?"

"Naethin honest man."

"What did you tell them you fucking lying little ball bag?" I shouted, grasping his skinny neck with my leather-clad hand and pinning him against the wall with such force the back of his head crashed into the crumbling bricks and his sunken eyes almost popped out of his head.

"Get off him you fucker, he didn't tell them owt," the other bloke screamed, unsuccessfully trying to remove my hand from his mate's throat before the life drained from his deathly addict face.

"Calm down girls. Tell me the truth." I released Dec's neck. "I presume you are after some of this?" I said, waving a bag of skag in front of the two junkies. "If you want this, tell me the fucking truth regarding the police."

"Listen mate," the other urchin spoke.

"I'm sorry and who the fuck are you?" I turned menacingly in his direction.

"Danny, he told y, I'm no grass."

"Well Danny, you have no idea who I am, and I don't want to know you. Let's get one thing perfectly straight, you are not my mate. So be quiet until you are spoken to and maybe you can get your grubby junky mitts on this shit sooner than anticipated."

"I'm no smack head man. I'm clean, have been for yonks now," he replied with an element of pride.

"Oh! I do apologise for my ignorance, but you know the saying – once a thieving druggie etc, so shut up please." He nodded his reluctant consent.

"What did you tell the coppers Mr Aikin? Last chance or I'll walk with your prize."

"Nath pal, ah didnae tell thaim anythin' apairt fae a've nae seen they girls fur months. Ah tellt thaim wummin lik' thaim vanish intae tin air a' th' time oan th' streets 'n' reappear efter, thay believed me, ah swear." The little druggie squirmed, his eyes fixated on the magic powder in my hand which would take him to heaven and back and, more importantly, relieve him of his pain. But he was blatantly lying, that much was obvious.

"What else Dec?"

"Th' polis asked me tae gang in this efternoon 'n' scan thro' some mugshots tae see if ah recognised a'body wha wid visit th' girls. Th' DCI, a black lassie, says she's gonnae pay me, sae ah kin gie ye some dosh fur mah score."

"And that's all?"

"Aye man, promise, cross mah hert. Ah wouldn't tell thaim aboot ye Nath, we're mukkers."

"Yes, we are, aren't we Dec. Come in here, I don't want to risk prying eyes my Scottish brother." I escorted the boys inside the old storage unit. The friend appeared cautious and uneasy as we entered the darkness of the old dusty store.

"Here Dec, try before you buy boy," I said, tossing him the bag of precious dust. "This is the dogs' bollox of smack, I assure you." His eyes lit up like a kid with candy.

"Really Nath man?"

"Of course mate, fill your boots."

"Cheers mah mon, fook me."

The little Jock smack rat perched himself on a rickety, cobweb-infested wooden bench and removed all the paraphernalia associated with the administration of heroin from his backpack. With expertise, he cooked up his treasure, competent in dealing with the sobering shakes whilst completing his mission to escape his world of pain. Once satisfied with his efforts, the chemical soup was quaffed into a scummy syringe and a slim brown leather belt was applied to his bicep until the weak thready veins of his forearm become exposed. With meticulous ease he picked one not collapsed by years of abuse and pumped the lifesaving concoction into his arm, releasing the pressure of the tourniquet and allowing the chemically enhanced euphoria to engulf his entire body. The wave of blissful contentment hit him like a brick and the irritating Scot flew off to planet smack for the last time.

"Enjoy Dec, my wee man, this will be your last, you lying little prick," I whispered into his ear as he drifted away.

The fix I so generously provided would be sufficient to end this irritation. The young addict slithered down the bench to the ground and adopted the foetal position amongst the dirt, used condoms and old cardboard boxes full of newspaper cuttings while his body travelled to another world. A world where the heroin will block the signals from the brain to the receptors of his nervous system, causing a failure of lung function. With the diminishing levels of oxygen in his blood stream, vital organs would shut down, inducing his demise. A cold but calculated death, the beauty being the lethal OD he imposed upon himself.

The realisation of his dilemma hit the stranger in an instant and he darted in panic towards the rotting wooden door. In one movement I stopped him in his tracks before he made his bid for freedom, grabbing a handful of his jacket and yanking him back with such force he slammed into the floor amongst a cloud of dust, close to his dying friend. Only one punch was necessary from my leather-clad right hand to turn the lights off while I prepared for his exit.

CHAPTER 33

The throbbing pain in my jaw and the metallic taste of blood woke me from my induced slumber. A streak of sun cut the dust in front of my eyes and high above cobwebbed wooden beams spanned the roof. My fuzzy head began to clear and the rattling marbles in my skull settled only for the grim reality of my situation to strike me with a startling bound of the heart and a sharp inhalation of breath. Minutes previously I had witnessed some bloke I'd never met before kill my only mate in the entire world. Dec had drifted away on the hit of a lifetime, happy for the first time in days, never to awaken. A panic pulsed through my body, riding on a wave of adrenalin, but I remained motionless amongst the dust and debris, listening for incriminating signs of Nathan. The only noise was the sound of silence and the occasional car passing the courtyard entrance. All caution intact, I raised my head to check the area.

"Hello sleepy head, nice of you to join us again," came a sarcastic voice emerging from a gloomy corner of the unit into the shaft of light. A makeshift noose tightened across my windpipe, which looped over the rafters above me. The tension over my neck increased, causing me to rise to my knees and shortly after to my feet in combination with an involuntary desperate attempt to grasp the cord that was cutting painfully through my skin.

"On the bench boy," he ordered, one hand gripping the other end of the rope. My face turned crimson, and spittle flew from my mouth. Any words I tried to utter were near silent and tumbled away to insignificance. The ligature pulled tighter, slicing deeper. I caught a glimpse of Declan through bulging, watering eyes, statuesque in a pool of vomit, sleeping as a baby with his gods; his worldly problems would no longer cause him concern.

"Climb on the fucking bench Danny," he commanded again with increased assertion, tugging hard with leather-clad hands and causing my feet to leave the concrete floor. I flailed a well-worn Adidas trainer out to reach for the table behind me, the same table my buddy had used to cook up the deadly concoction; his backpack and belongings fell to the ground in a dust explosion. My weight was supported as the choker cut deeper into my throat, giving a moment's respite. The bench beneath me rocked back and forth but I steadied it with my right foot, gaining the balance required to alleviate the stretching of my neck. This was his cue for action – he pulled the opposite tether taut, securing it with a double knot around a rusting support girder.

"Sorry you've become embroiled in this young man, but I can't have you running around London putting my mission at risk, that wouldn't do, would it? Now you will fly with the angels like Dec and all my girls." He smiled sympathetically, then, with an almighty size ten, he rocked my life-saving platform backwards. I fought in desperation to gain control as the strangulating noose ripped and burned at my skin. The desk tippled forward and away from my panicked reach, hitting the floor in a puff of dust. An agonising jerk of the noose and my entire weight was supported through the vertebrae of my neck. Utter hysteria immediately set into my legs which defaulted to auto mode, frantically reaching out into thin air, trying to locate any sort of foot hold, while my fingers simultaneously attempted to prise the cord from my throat by digging underneath the slip knot to relieve the pressure being inflicted upon my oesophagus. Panic flashed over me like a tsunami as I realised the life was being strangled from my soul and no one was going to assist in my fight for survival. Soon my movements became laboured as my brain was starved of oxygen and, gradually, the involuntary kicking stopped. I could feel my life ebbing away.

This wasn't a perfect crime by any means, but almost. I mean, two street kid friends, one an addict with pin marks up his arms, the other recovering. The smack head ODs, the other is so distraught he cannot face life without his buddy after his long, hard fight to overcome his vile affliction so he takes the easy option and commits suicide. Nobody will think to question what's happened in this dusty old storage unit, it's almost an everyday occurrence with the druggies, death.

"Good night you boys, sleep well, fly away with my angels."

CHAPTER 34

"The two street rats are now three hours late, and I'm becoming more and more frustrated with each minute that passes," I said, doodling nondescript squiggles, triangles and circles across my notepad whilst taking another slurp of now tepid tea.

As promised, I'd arranged a bite to eat and a small but generous amount of cash to encourage compliance, considering we were aware this would only be spent on one thing, Dec's habit. When you're a junkie, food, water and shelter take a back seat, they are no longer the vital commodities necessary to sustain life, heroin claims that title, and nothing else in life matters apart from scoring a high.

"What did I tell you? I said the fuckers wouldn't turn up didn't I? We should have run a sweepstake," Gaz repeated for the hundredth time.

"You are boring me now, I'm going to watch the rain running down the windows, it's more interesting," DC Glover mocked.

"Well I did say not to trust them, but nobody listens to me."

I remained silent, continuing with the abstract art scribble.

"I'm with you love. He's tedious. Can I book a portion of window to peruse the weather too," DC Willis laughed, receiving a saluted V in his direction from the DS.

"Please don't bully him you two. The last thing I need is a workplace harassment charge to investigate. He can't help being right all the time. But on a serious note, while we are all here together and so as not to waste time while we await the hopefully imminent arrival of idiot number one from our extensive list of imbeciles, and his buddy a close second, let's brainstorm what facts we have in our possession."

"Well, he's done this before, given the professionalism with which he performs, and we have the DNA result from Dr McCabe which I'm confident will link him to the European killings," Sal stated, returning from the window and perching her somewhat pert arse on my desk.

"Yeah, then the blurred image of a mysterious man we glimpsed on CCTV who failed to come forward and clear himself, unlike the other three people present in the shot. From which we can conclude his stature and hair colour but nothing else I'm afraid, we don't possess a definitive ID," Jordan said, retaking a place at his desk and putting his brogue clad feet on the workspace.

"And to support the footage, we have Danny Walker's description, or rather his mate's, of this young man with blond hair, well-built, going by the name of Nathan. Apparently a wealthy bloke with a huge house and a black M3 as described by the Jock kid. A man who likes to use prostitutes, notably our three dead women, among many others of course, but these three being his favourites, and let's not forget his penchant for kinky sex in accordance with Mr Aikin's statement regarding the inflicting of pain and suffering during the sexual experiences, to a crescendo of slicing girls across the back with a blade. All the equations add up, now we need to find this man and his black beamer." Gary said, summarising the details from the interview the previous day.

"So, what else?" Sally asked, taking an office chair and crossing her long, elegant legs, flashing a generous glimpse of naked thigh.

"Fuck all regarding the victims – nothing from friends, family, old flames or the work colleague from the hair salon who was on holiday. Bugger all from the bars etc," Gaz replied.

"Kell, an idea to run past you. I might go spend some time on the streets tomorrow night, see if I can get into the heads of the girls, with an insight to pick up some info on this BMW driver. I'll tell them I'm doing an article about the alternative life in the city. They might let me probe deeper if I'm not a plod," Sal suggested.

"Go for it, Jordan do you want to accompany her?"

"Sure, no probs, it could be fun if Sal is probing prossies," he joked.

"You know what I mean dick head," she corrected.

"How about we locate any sellers of this perverse attire, so to speak. Try the adult shops within the area where the girls worked for a start, then move wider afield, internet deliveries."

"I can do that no problem," Gary confirmed.

A tap, tap on the door interrupted our chat. The front desk sergeant popped his head around the door.

"Ma'am a word please."

"Yes, carry on Stu," I said, ushering him inside.

"Only minutes ago we received a call from a security firm at some south Croydon storage units adjacent to the railway station. One of their operatives found a dangler on his rounds and what appears to be an overdose, there's drug paraphernalia laid about the place. I thought it might be of interest to your inquiry."

"OK, and?" I questioned as it's not an unusual discovery in regions of London in either case.

"One of the uniforms we sent down to secure the scene, PC Ross, recognised the lads – he nicked them for shoplifting. It's the two I processed in here yesterday, Dec Aikin and Danny Walker. Unfortunately they're both brown bread Ma'am." The bombshell dropped.

"Shit! And the officer is certain this is them?"

"Yes, he's one hundred percent positive."

"Thanks Stuart."

"No worries," he said, leaving the office.

"Fucking bollox, that's all we need."

"No wonder the poor bastards are late, and now we've lost our potential witnesses," Gaz commented, raising his eyebrows and throwing his pen across the desk.

"Kell, something isn't right about this," Jordan interjected, immediately standing from his chair.

"What are you thinking?"

"Well I perceive the situation like this. Mr Walker was a self-proclaimed former addict, and I emphasise the former. This kid buzzed with pride that he had exorcised his demons, to such a degree we overheard him stressing the fact to the custody sergeant. Sally made a comment to me."

"Yeah, I said if I got a quid for every time I heard that I'd be a rich woman."

"Fair point Sal," I agreed.

"Additionally, he continued to explain how he relished the prospect of making a new life away from living rough, having recently been allocated his own accommodation through a rehabilitation charity which in turn meant the possibility of a job and an opportunity to get back on his feet. Not only that, but he also implied that if the shoplifting charges stood, it might fuck his chance of receiving this charitable donation of a shitty one-bed flat. The sergeant assured him they only held incriminating evidence of Dec lifting gear from the shopping centre surveillance cameras, so he should only receive a slap on the wrist. The lad was ecstatic, like he'd won the lottery."

"What's your point?" Gaz questioned.

"Well it's crossed my mind, if our Mr Walker's life was almost back on track and his disposition was so obviously positive, why would he consider topping himself? Mull that one over while I continue with Declan. Right, prior to their arrest, Mr Aikin and companion were so wanting for money the anguish they had shown prior to the incident for liaising with the police in any way, shape or form diminished to such a point they chanced a day out of Christmas retail therapy, as we know distinctly lacking in monetary funding for an excursion of this type, risking being picked up by those very coppers they appeared so desperate to avoid. Upon their entrance to the department, Dec displayed all the symptoms associated with withdrawal – a deathly complexion, the shakes, profuse sweating, extreme agitation – but those agonising signs of cold turkey aside, he was still willing to await a small donation twenty-four hours later from the local constabulary for his assistance in their inquiries. People he hates by the way, correct?"

"Yes, perfectly."

"So, as a regular heroin abuser with an enormous addiction and therefore an overwhelming tolerance towards said chemical, ponder this. How did Dec manage to get hold of the vast amount of Mr Brownstone required to not only stop him rattling and to make him feel like a normal human being again, but to muster enough H to OD?

I mean, I'm no narcotics expert, but what are we looking at? Forty or fifty pounds for a gram? So, envisage the escalating cost to overdose a tolerant user of many years, taking into account the undeniable fact they didn't have a penny to scratch their arses between them."

"Are you implying this wasn't simply a case of a known addict scoring too much skag, and his mate killing himself because he couldn't help his one and only friend in existence?" Gaz posed.

"That's exactly what I'm saying. Contemplate this scenario from an addict's point of view – get into their head and their train of thought, don't think as a copper. Even considering Dec had miraculously obtained sufficient monetary funding to purchase a wrap so pure or vast to cause a fatality, surely he would regulate his use to maintain his habit over several days, by cutting his prize with other high-inducing substances to make it go further. Why the fuck would a person overwhelmingly reliant on drugs, and considered an expert in the application of them, blow his entire score in one hit of a lifetime not knowing when he might accumulate the finances for his next trip to whatever planet he ends up on? It doesn't make sense," Jordan explained.

"When you put it in that context, it makes sense. Give forensics a call, let them have a snoop around," I suggested, much to Jordan's satisfaction.

CHAPTER 35

The chilly night air bit at my face and I pulled my scarf up, bracing against the icy breeze during the twenty-minute walk home from the King's Arms to my flat. Old George and his pensioner crew had enjoyed their night, rattling the dominoes and ogling my tits, making cheap comments about my nipples protruding through my blouse thanks to me underestimating the chill in the air and leaving my jumper at home. As usual I tried my absolute best to accommodate and counteract their banter, but my heart wasn't in it today. In her customary blunt manner, Candice had endeavoured to console me over the Dave situation, or rather lack of him. Mr Roe has been the invisible man since our night out together on the town which resulted in drunken dirty sex in my bed. Each day I expect him to stroll through the doors of the King's and perch himself on a stool near the bar, but nothing, leading to a frustration building as to my predicament. I had sadly lowered myself to walking down his street, hoping he might be home. The house down Earls Avenue which he led me to believe was his humble abode on the first day he entered the King's Arms appeared empty. Realistically my only option is to face the fact that I'd been played like a puppet on a string, sleeping with a man I thought was a friend. A man I not only learned to trust, but someone I'd poured my entire life out to, and undeniably a person I had fallen for in a big way. To analyse the scenario further in my mind, I can only treat him as a total stranger, whom I knew absolutely Jack shit about, with me taken in by materialistic stories of affluence and heartache, to be used as a toy for his sexual pleasure and discarded like a whore from a red-light district.

A gust of the freezing north wind danced my hair across my face as I approached the one-bed flat I call home and contemplated the topic of my hunger. What did I have in the cupboards worth eating for supper? Probably bugger all, a pot noodle maybe. Thankfully a much-needed payday was imminent, and I could pick my wages up at dinner time the next day. Another fact I knew for certain was the flat would be a fridge when I got home, because I've started turning the heating off whilst out at work, to save on cash. Believe me when I say I'm not tight by any means, but I regard it utterly idiotic to waste money on soaring utility bills when I'm out on a desperate mission to earn enough of a wage to keep my head above water.

A sudden pulse of panic rose in my stomach as I saw movement in the shadows ahead. A stranger loomed from the darkness of a charity shop doorway, dressed in baggy blue jeans, an emerald hoody with gold script across the front which I couldn't make out. On his feet he wore a bright white pair of trainers which almost glowed in the dark with a scarlet Nike tick down the side. From the shop front, he loitered to the street corner below the amber glow of a lamppost, glancing both ways up and down the adjoining streets before spinning on a heel and meandering his way down the footpath towards me. The hood of the eerie figure was raised up over a lowered head obscuring all his face, with hands tucked firmly into the pockets of his jeans. Along with my heartbeat banging out like a big bass drum his stride quickened. This neighbourhood is not exactly Mayfair; it's a place renowned for numerous muggings, and in recent times two rapes and a stabbing. Cautiously I took a tight grip of my handbag strap, located my house keys and mobile phone should it be required, before glancing around the empty late-night streets on the off chance of another person in the vicinity, but the road was deserted. With this in mind I upped my pace, hoping to reach the relative safety of home before the stranger.

"Hello Helen," a man's voice sounded as he removed his hood.

The fact this person knew my name eased the butterflies in my stomach and actioned a cautious heads up towards the silhouette in the shadows to see Dave's handsome face beaming a smile back in my direction. *"Hold it together girl, don't let him think you're upset, be strong,"* I thought to myself.

"Oh, cool, how are you? Long time no see," I said with a calm persona, any previous anticipatory nerves switched to a simmering anger inside.

"I'm sorry I disappeared the other week, something came up that required my immediate attention. The ex is playing me up for more money."

"What, in the early hours of the morning? Do you honestly think I'm that stupid? And why would I be interested?" I tried to avoid any eye contact which might have revealed my true hidden feelings for him.

"I know you must think I'm a wanker right now but can we talk over a quick drink?"

"No, I don't *think* you're a wanker, I *know*. You've pissed me off Dave and I can do without this tonight. I've done a double shift and I'm cold, hungry and tired. All I want to do is go to bed, alone!"

"Please, half an hour. My car is around the corner, we could nip to the Fox and Hounds, they do food late, my treat. Give me an opportunity to explain why, where and what happened. Afterwards, if you still think I'm twat then so be it."

"Do you understand how much this hurt me? You left me feeling like a total slut, not a single text to say sorry or anything. For god's sake, we spent a night together and then you fuck off without a word, come on. You need to go now and please don't attempt to worm your way in again, it won't work," I said, my voice cracking with rising emotions which I fought back.

"Please Helen, let me offer an explanation. I will beg if needed," he replied, lowering himself to his knees on the damp cold paving slabs.

"Get up idiot, thirty minutes, that's your lot and I'm not promising anything. You hurt me Dave and I won't forget that in a hurry. I thought we were friends, I trusted you."

"We are friends, and I'm so sorry gorgeous, I am. I'll explain everything, cross my heart. You will understand and maybe excuse my unacceptable behaviour when you are more knowledgeable about my dilemma."

We walked to the end of my street as Dave quizzed me about my day, making awkward idle chit chat. As promised, his black BMW was parked in a residents' only space on the next road; the lights flashed and he held the passenger side door open for me before trotting around to the driver side.

"Bloody hell, it's a chilly one tonight. Here, take my coffee, you're shivering, it'll warm you through, I only bought it minutes ago."

He was right, the hot beverage did indeed provide the thermal qualities required, warming me through to my toes. Despite my condemnation of his unexpected appearance, he exuded confidence that I would forgive and forget, but he needed to kiss some major arse first and that's a fact. Annoyingly though, inside I developed an internal glow and not only from the coffee, secretly I was happy to be here with him, but there was no way I was showing him. I sat in the car with a face like a slapped backside and spoke only when necessary to escape appearing rude. The silent treatment was in full force. I decided to message Candice and inform her about the unexpected return of Mr Roe, also to exaggerate my diminishing interest in spending time in his company.

"Dave, we've gone past the Fox," I said with a hint of confusion evident in my voice. "I said you've missed the turn off, it's back there."

"My dear Helen, we are not going to the Fox, we are going somewhere of much higher standing."

"What the hell is going on? You're scaring me now, let me out of this fucking car," I screamed, yanking desperately at the handle and banging on the window.

"All in good time my angel, all in good time."

My head started to swirl, my eyes lost focus. A hot, nauseous state flooded over me. What's this bastard done to me? Then darkness.

CHAPTER 36

An all-too-familiar noise woke me from my broken slumber. Three metal door bolts ground to an open position and the heavy lock clunked twice. I had no idea what the time of day was, only that the mad one was back, a good thing considering my football-sized bladder was about to burst. On only three instances does he let us out of these cages – to relieve ourselves, to wash and the other instance which I don't want to contemplate. A time when the grotesque wings are brutally carved into the soft skin of your back, before being taken from this god forsaken place hours later, never to return, as with Janet. I wanted to keep my thoughts positive and with a focus – to target toilet or shower time for escape – and not think about an unsympathetic demise at the hands of this nutter in god knows where.

"Hi Becky, sorry to have woken you at such a late hour, but as promised I've brought you a little friend to keep you company, I do hope you two get along," he shouted cheerfully, like an excited kid; the fluorescent tubes above me buzzed and flickered before they flashed into action.

"Don't tell me you got me a puppy," I shouted back with a bucket full of sarcasm.

"That's not nice, I don't think she's a dog, far from it in fact," he beamed, descending to the cellar and assisting a slender figure to the side of him, her hands bound and head covered.

"Why are you doing this you sick bastard? Let her go before you destroy her life. I'll give you everything you want," I pleaded, rubbing the bright light from my tired eyes.

"I know you'll give me what I want, you have no option – you've been selected."

"By whom?" I quizzed, as he and the mystery person reached the base of the stairway.

"By me, Becky, by me. I chose you especially. This is not a random act of madness as you may conclude, no, no. I've planned this part of my life for years; this will complete me; you and all the angels will complete me."

"Why me? Of all the women in the fucking country, why me?"

"Because you matched all the criteria required to the last detail and you made the process so easy."

"Where did you search – idiots.com, freaky weird fuckingnutters.co.uk?"

"Please don't start being abusive towards me again. What sort of impression are you setting for our new guest? No, I found you on Facebook, you shouldn't share so many details about your life. Once I discovered you it became simple, you had all the endearing qualities required to be one of my angels. You are blonde, beautiful and possess fantastic statistics, like Helen here," he grinned, removing a tan hessian sack from the woman's head.

The new woman stood in front of my cage in a drug-induced state. She was a stunner too, long golden hair and an outstanding body – you cannot fault his excellent taste. Her face appeared gaunt and pale but still beautiful with ocean blue eyes and dilated pupils suggesting the influence of a substance of some kind. Her eyeshadow-coated lids drooped like lead weights on elastic bands as she fought to keep them open, eyeballs beneath absent of focusing ability, rolling in their sockets as if possessing a mind of their own. Her attempts to speak were slurred and non-decipherable, as if she'd drunk a skin-full of vodka. The poor woman possessed no clue where she was or what she was doing there.

One thing was for certain – she would awaken feeling like crap in the morning as I had some weeks ago. To emphasise her raging sickness and banging headache, she'd realise the desperation of her situation, caged like an animal in this dark hellhole world of shit. Utter confusion engulfs you in the beginning as your brain strives to compute your environment and recognises the magnitude of your dilemma. Once you ascertain you are in crap up to the neck and there's fuck all you can do about it, the panic hits you like a fucking brick in the face, adrenalin surges through every cell in your body, your heart attempts to beat out of your chest, and you begin to climb the fucking walls with anxiety, nausea rising from the pit of your stomach to your throat, causing you to gag on foul-tasting bile. This woman will wake tomorrow dazed, confused, a frightened girl, petrified in fact, and it will be down to me to reassure her and help as best I can.

CHAPTER 39

"Good morning, Ma'am, how are we doing this lovely winter day? Cuppa?" Sally shouted from the mess-room causing me to start as I expected to be alone.

"Good morning, a brew would be fantastic. You not been home yet?"

"Not for long. I took to the streets last night, some girls were pleased to talk but not many. As soon as I mentioned the names Frankie, Coco and Bella, the shutters came down and shtum. So, I came in early because my curiosity got the better of me after Jordan's outstanding dissection of the facts behind our boys' deaths. Sometimes his intelligence astounds me considering he's completely devoid of any common sense. At secondary school we had a phrase for people like him," she explained.

"Go on, enlighten me."

"Well, we described them as intelligent thick bastards, and Jordan is the epiphany of that saying. A moment of pure genius followed by another of complete and utter stupidity." Sal continued to pour steaming hot water into two coffee cups, one with the phrase 'Don't drink water, fish fuck in it' and the other indicating the owner to be the boss in exaggerated bold script.

"I understand what you mean," I chuckled.

"However, in the case of these street kids, I think he's flawless. Like he said in his analysis of the situation, the basic facts simply don't add up. So, I began trawling through the CCTV in and around the girls' described working area before and after the disappearance, and I can definitively inform you Declan Aikin was lying," she beamed, carrying the coffee to my desk.

"Now I'm intrigued, but not surprised."

"Perusing endless hours of footage I discovered what appears to be our former little Mr smack rat on more than one occasion approaching a black BMW, to score drugs I assume. But several times he was engaged in full conversation with the occupant of the car. He must have known this person, there's no other explanation, in fact I would put my mortgage on it, and a fucking huge one at that."

"Can you show me, because during the interview Gary and I conducted with the dynamic duo, Declan's eyes told me he was either holding information back or lying which was why I invited them back with a monetary incentive. I'd hoped that perhaps I might squeeze more detail out of them with the temptation of enough cash sat in front of them for a score."

"I like your thinking boss. Walk this way, the footage is saved on my PC. Now trust me when I say it is not the best, it would appear the camera upgrades haven't made their way to the red-light districts at this point. The quality is grainy at best, but I'm positive this is our man."

"Was our man."

"Yes, of course, sorry I forgot. Here's the first clip, showing a black BMW pulling up, several of the girls go over to meet and greet. The driver makes his choice of young lady for the day, Frankie in this case, and here she jumps into the passenger side without a care. Now forgive my ignorance but if these ladies hated this dude as per Aikin's allegation, she's doing a bloody excellent job of hiding her concerns, in fact I would say she's almost celebrating," Sal pointed out.

"I must agree, she doesn't appear pissed off does she? From what the former Mr Aikin told us, this client, although perverse with his sexual desires, was an excellent payer and sweetened them with copious amounts of high-quality drugs."

"This would be like a lottery win for these girls," Sal continued, "but here comes the scrawny Jock from the right-hand side of the shot. There we go, he ambles over to the motor and leans into the car window. Now I'm aware the picture quality isn't brilliant but watch this. Unless I'm much mistaken, our mystery man and Dec appear to be in deep conversation for several minutes before money changes hands along with something else, which I can only presume was drugs of some description."

"Rewind the film." The footage whizzed backwards in a blur and Sal replayed the scene. "That's definitely cash, you're right, and our dead smack rat is more than familiar with this bloke driving the BMW. The question is – was Dec dealing for our man or was the suspect paying Declan for female company?"

"That's something we can only surmise boss, but right now we need to find this dude," she said, ringing the computer cursor around the blurred driver. "I've run a check on said vehicle, but annoyingly on each appearance up to date, different plates are employed – and guess what?"

"None of them match the car in question."

"Correct," she confirmed. "I ran an examination of ANPR covering routes on major roads to the region, but he must have planned his route in via back streets. The other annoying factor is that on no occasion does the black beamer bloke show himself, never. The approach never differs from this direction," she pointed to the left of the monitor, "to his preferred parking space here," again using the cursor to highlight the area. "If his place is taken, he drives around until it is free, and not once does he get out of the motor, at no point do any of the cameras reveal him to us."

"The man has done his homework hasn't he? You're right, he's planned his drive and, I would hazard a guess, is aware of the exact positions of the CCTV in this area. He's calculated and intelligent as per the prime suspect in the murder cases – this is our killer, I'd bet my life on it."

"Yeah, I tend to agree, I also think Jordan was correct with his analogy of events yesterday. Those young men didn't die in unfortunate circumstances as uniform first concluded due to some accidental OD and depressive suicide. These boys were murdered for the simple reason that Dec knew too much, and poor Danny was basically an inconvenience."

CHAPTER 38

The cold darkness stiffened my aching bones. I sat wearily listening to the sound of silence broken only by the new woman's soft peaceful breathing whilst she slept off the effects of whichever chemical was contaminating her body, all in blissful ignorance of the chaos and sheer panic which was about to engulf her entire existence.

The small crack of light beneath the door was the only respite from the total darkness I've endured for weeks. A sudden abundance of pity for this poor woman overwhelmed my thoughts, knowing this will be the final time she sleeps soundly, the last decent night's rest she will enjoy. As a rule, you do nap on and off down here, your fatigued body and mind demands it, but it's never real sleep, not the full relaxed, rejuvenating, replenishing slumber we take for granted in everyday life. If you do manage forty winks, you wake with a start when the dark dreams begin and the stark realisation regarding your dire situation returns and hits you like a punch between the eyes.

The petrifying realisation that I might not ever return to my boring mundane life again flooded over me. A life I took for granted, moaned about, the meaningless existence I would give my right arm to be part of now. A fleeting glimpse of my family and friends entered the memory bank, loved ones I might never hug again; a tear rolled down my face, and my heartache returned. I cannot imagine what emotions my parents are going through right now. The worry and anguish they must be experiencing knowing their little girl and only child is out here somewhere, lost and alone. Another tear tumbled down my face, wiped away quickly with a grubby sleeve as the woman murmured.

As for the time of day, personally I have no clue whether we are in day, night or fucking Christmas. The perpetual gloom addles the brain and plays tricks on the mind. To keep me sane, I try my upmost to save a mental note of my captor's routine, when he leaves the house, when he returns, assuming this may indicate morning and evening for a nine to five job, although this concept is blown out of the water if he works shifts, or is simply out stalking his next victim. Movement stirred in the cage next door.

"Hello? Is anyone there? Answer me," came a groggy whisper of a voice close by.

"Hi, don't panic, I'm Becky."

"What the fuck is going on? Where's Dave? Is this some kind a sick prank? Because it is not fucking funny if it is."

"That was his name with you was it? He was Nathan for me and Matt for the last woman, and I'm sorry to be so blunt, but unfortunately this is no joke so get used to it."

"Let me out NOW!" the woman screamed, rattling the bars of her cage with a teeming rage, which would wilt and fade as the hours passed by.

"Save yourself love, trust me, there is no point in shouting and bawling. I managed to shout and scream for three days until I lost my voice and became exhausted. Nobody came. No one except him."

"Please, I can't stay here, there must be a way out. I can't just give up." She screamed again.

"Please don't misunderstand me, I'm not giving up, far from it. Believe me, I want to escape here more than you can imagine because if his routine continues along the lines I have witnessed, I will be the next one to become one of his angels."

"One of his what? I don't understand."

"Fuck me, must I spell it out? The women this animal kills are classified angels, a term of endearment."

"No, no, shit, I need to get out of here. LET ME OUT YOU FUCKING TWAT, CAN YOU HEAR ME DAVE? LET ME OUT!"

"Calm down for god's sake, he won't hear you, he went out hours ago."

"Listen, there's movement above us."

"Yes, I think he owns a dog, I've not actually seen the thing yet but I'm sure he talks to an animal of some sort."

"Hey boy, can you hear me boy?"

"Give it a rest, save your energy, you'll need it. What did you say your name was again?"

"I'm Helen."

"Hello Helen, I'm Becky."

"Hi Becky. How long have you been here?"

"I'm not a hundred percent sure, two weeks maybe, how are you feeling by the way?"

"Like shit."

"It will pass in a few hours like a hangover."

"Only a million times worse."

"Helen, listen to me please, you need to keep strong. Both of us will only have a chance of getting out of here if we stay strong together."

Silence descended as if Helen was trying to compute my words and her dreadful situation.

"How do you know you are the next one?"

"When he first brought me here another woman sat in your cage. She became a mess, I'm not sure how long she'd been down here, but her mind was broken – she wouldn't talk, eat or acknowledge my presence apart from telling me her name was Janet one time. The only time I witnessed any fight in her was when he came to take her away, and she fought like a street cat, all claws and teeth, her last stand I suppose." I paused to gather my emotions as they began to rise. "But she didn't come back." I finished the sentence to silence.

Helen began to cry, and simultaneously a single tear rolled down my face, but my sobs were suppressed. I'd become accustomed to hiding my mental state, I'm never quite sure when he may return and I don't want him to think he has beaten me, I don't want him to think I'm broken.

CHAPTER 39

"DCI Lynch, can I help you?"

"Hello Kell, it's Jenny, at last – something for you."

"Please tell me you've found something completely condemning, and we can go pick this arrogant wanker up and bang him away for life or longer."

"Sorry, I'm afraid this case isn't going to be that cut and dry. However, I can confirm that the information Sally shared from her *'Parisian man friend'* has proved to be more valuable than we might have first anticipated. Now although we recognised in our own minds that these European murders possessed an almost identical MO to our killings, a definite link between French girl Aude Boucher's case and the mystery DNA found at the scene is corroborated. As per routine procedure, I took swabs from the body of Janet Storer, inclusive of her fingernails. Now as well as the dirt, her own skin deposits, fine hair from sofas, clothing, etc that most people collect behind their nails from everyday life, despite the fact we all consider ourselves to be pristinely clean, we also discovered DNA samples and a small amount of blood beneath the fingernail of the index finger on her left hand. And I can confirm that the result matches that established and present at the French scene of crime."

"Finally, some sort of fucking breakthrough!" I exclaimed.

"Don't get too excited, there's nothing listed on the database matching the DNA apart from the French evidence."

"Progress with this investigation is like being a drunk on his walk home, one step forward and a stagger backwards."

"Well it depends on how you perceive the situation – are you a glass half empty or half full kind of girl? Remember, we are now in possession of a DNA sample from under the fingernails of a murder victim with links to an additional crime scene in the south of France. Surely with even the best defence lawyers in town on the cases, this will take a lot of explanation in any court of law."

"Agreed, but first we have to nick the bastard and convince the CPS of our case before we can put the animal in the dock, which at the moment isn't happening."

"Patience isn't a strong point of yours is it DCI Lynch?"

"No. Especially considering the fact that the longer this lunatic is on the streets the more dead women manifest themselves."

"We'll find him, trust me – sooner or later he will make a mistake and his arrogance will be his downfall."

"Any thoughts on the OD and suicides you examined?"

"Yes, after analysing the scene at your request, we consider another person was present along with Mr Aikin and Walker the deceased. On investigation, we discovered three sets of shoe prints, two of which matched the street kids and another with no distinguishing features, ie tread pattern, apart from the size, in this case a UK ten, measuring approximately 28 centimetres long."

"Size ten – the suspect footprint found at the Janet Storer scene."

"I don't know about that, it could be pure coincidence. A size ten shoe is common for men in the UK, but my team of forensics are staying to complete a full and extensive examination of the scene."

"When can I expect some results? Sorry, hold on Jenny, Sally is waving her arms about," I explained, holding the phone to my chest.

"Sorry to interrupt Kelly, but we've received an anonymous call from a man who is saying he may have witnessed the Hamstead Heath killer leaving the scene, he's provided us with a registration plate for a silver Mazda, and we are in possession of a name."

"Apologies Jenny, got to fly, something critical has come up," I said, placing the handset down and taking a huge lung full of oxygen. "Who we got Sal?"

"ANPR has identified a Mr Steve Grayson and the PNC provides interesting reading of a man who has a history of violent crime, GBH and aggravated burglary for which he has served time. Plus two alleged incidents of sexual assault both of which were dismissed by the CPS due to lack of witness evidence. And listen to this, recent cases of violence against women, one being his now ex-wife who he beat to a pulp leaving her with a three-day spell in hospital and a collection of cuts and bruises, again with no witnesses, and another on the present Mrs Grayson who failed to press charges after neighbours called us to a domestic. His description matches our man on CCTV seen in the vicinity of Hannah Craven – six foot two, blond crew-cut hair, stocky build and heavily tattooed. He's a proper fucking charmer this one."

"Let's go pay Mr Grayson a visit shall we?"

CHAPTER 40

A small surveillance team took up strategic positions around Steve Grayson's two-up two-down council property. Our aim was to monitor all means of access and any other movement within the house, or rather lack of as, throughout the entire afternoon and into the evening as the winter sun morphed into darkness, observations of any note had been scarce. A Vauxhall Insignia containing Jordan and Sally was perched high on the main road as radio back up, covering the rear of the two-bed should anyone make a bid for freedom. Additionally, a van packed with quick response uniformed officers waited patiently at the entrance of the close, out of sight, but primed to spring into action at a moment's notice. Our Ford Mondeo was positioned to the left and front of the suspect's abode, close to the suspect silver Mazda. An army of kids ranging in age from nine to seventeen and wearing the obligatory hoodies surrounded the car, riding bikes in various states of disrepair, tapping on the windows, pressing faces to the glass, and presenting the two fingered salute before pedalling off down the footpath to the applause, laughter and cheers of their peers, emphasising their overwhelming disrespect for our authority.

"Right, I've had enough of this shit, come on. All positions acknowledge DCI Lynch and DS Turner will be advancing to the property, over."

"Acknowledged, over," times two sounded across the handset.

With a renewed urgency, Gaz and I strutted across the road,

mindful that every single family in this snippet of London would already be aware of our presence. The entrance to the typically sized council estate front garden was a wrought iron gate held in place by one hinge and a bodge job repair of rusty wire wrapped around an equally rusting post, which fell open with a clatter. A nostalgic memory from my childhood of pristine flowerbeds buzzing with insect life and a bowling green strip of grass flitted through my mind, images to be rapidly dispersed by the sight of this plot which appeared more like a landfill site or dog toilet rather than the pride and joy my father kept for many years.

A release of adrenalin began to pump through my body, growing on the approach to the glass panel door with green flaking paint from years of neglect. The DS knocked three times and stepped backwards, inducing a muscular scar-faced Pitbull dog into defence mode with a torrent of ear-bursting barking growls and snarls at the lounge window as an agitated woman bellowed for silence to no avail.

"Who is it?" came the same stressed female voice and frosted silhouette.

"Hi madam, it's the police," Gaz replied.

"What do you want this time?"

"A chat with Mr Grayson."

"No shit, he's not here. Try the Horse and Jockey, he spends most of his waking life there."

"Can you open the door please, we need to speak with you," I insisted.

The door cracked to ajar and a cocktail of stale cigarettes, weed, chip fat and body odour floated out on the warm air. A young peroxide blonde woman with dark brunette roots popped a suspicious head through the gap sporting a multi-coloured black eye and split lip; her gaze sank to the floor in an instant, I assume to avoid any condemning eye contact. A flash of our warrant card was enough assurance to fully reveal herself. The woman was attired in a grubby white towelling dressing gown tied at the waist and flashing far too much cleavage to be comfortable for us; in contrast, she also wore a pair of rabbit character slippers. She scrutinised us from top to toe, drawing long and hard on a cigarette before blowing a plume into the fresh air towards our faces and upwards into the night sky. In the background, the dog rattled the door handle, attempting to join our conversation, a snarling mass of overprotective aggression.

"Don't worry, he can't get out," she assured us, glancing over her shoulder and hurling a cacophony of abuse towards the chaos beyond the sitting room door. "What's Steve done now?" she said, taking another long drag on her cancer stick.

"We were hoping you could tell us, Mrs…?"

"Grayson, Sarah Grayson."

"Obviously been up to his old tricks again," I said, pointing to her face.

"I fell, pissed up."

"What, into a fist?" I asked; she replied with a contemptuous head shake and roll of her eyes.

"So, what is it this time?"

"Can we come in?" Gary asked.

"No ya can't."

"Well we're easy. We can do this here in front of the neighbours if required," I said observing groups forming on both sides of the house and across the road.

"Fine."

"Can you inform us of Mr Steven Grayson's movements over the days between the seventh and nineth of November, particularly on the night of Saturday the eighth?"

"In the Jockey down the road, there'll be loads of witnesses. I left him there about ten because I felt pissed and wanted my bed."

"What time did he come home?"

"Just after midnight. I got up for a glass of water and heard him stumble through the door, he couldn't of done owt wrong that night, he could hardly walk."

"And these witnesses at the location you've mentioned will confirm his presence for the two hours you were absent of his company?" I said, examining her face for signs of untruth.

"Yeah," came the nonchalant reply.

"Is there anything else you would like to inform us of?" I pressed.

"Nope."

I glanced towards Gary in acknowledgement of her defensive attitude which, in our experience, indicated we should terminate the questioning – the phrase blood from a stone sprang to mind. It was blatantly obvious Sarah wasn't going to be cooperative.

"Right, thank you for your time," I said, turning to leave.

"Wait. What's he supposed to of done?"

"Sorry, but we can't divulge that sort of information, thanks again," Gaz responded with a forced cheesy smile before strolling down the path avoiding piles of dog shit, takeaway cartons, and a kid's knackered mountain bike.

"Relocate to the Jockey," I instructed over the radio link.

"Wait boss. We have some movement, confirm the suspect is exiting the rear of the house," Sally announced.

"Pull him Sal, we're on the way."

CHAPTER 41

"Excuse me. Mr Grayson?" shouted Sally, exiting the undercover Insignia. "Mr Steven Grayson, we need to talk to you regarding your location on the night of Saturday the eighth of November, sir? Stop please."

The man glanced up to witness an approaching DC Willis and DC Glover, turned and ran without a reply.

"All positions, suspect is a runner, I repeat the suspect is a runner, he's heading north in the direction of Cecil Close down the alleyway at the rear of Anastasia Drive. He's wearing white trainers, blue jeans, a grey bomber jacket and red baseball cap."

"Received."

Before the message finished Gary took off like an Olympic sprinter moving with mind-blowing speed for a huge man, only breaking stride to dart down a ten-foot alley leading to the path adjacent to the houses. By the time I reached the alleyway entrance he was almost halfway down the narrow passageway. A figure matching the radio description ran past the end of the alley with Jordan in pursuit.

"Stop! Steven, stop!" DS Turner yelled, turning left onto the muddy pathway behind the housing leading to the busy A road running alongside the council estate, his leather brogues fighting in desperation to find any form of traction.

The suspect sprinted past a block of four rabbit hutch two-up two-downs, taking a glance over his shoulder to gauge the pursuit before leaping up an embankment and slipping and sliding over the damp grass towards a six-foot wooden fence adorned in an explosive array of multicoloured graffiti tags, clambering up and over with well-practised ease. Willis grabbed at a trailing leg, receiving a thick lip from the sole of a Nike Air for his trouble, before leaping the obstacle athletically himself, quickly followed by Gary with his more methodical approach.

Grayson paused for thought – his planned escape route was blocked in the distance by uniform officers so instead he opted to dive into the hedgerow boundary separating the housing estate and the dual carriageway. Thick branches ensnared our man, halting his progress instantly and giving the young, fit DC Willis chance to grasp his quarry by the collar. In a bid for freedom, the charming man turned and grappled Jordan to the floor, dishing out a hefty blow to the ribs, a thud clearly audible through the still evening air from my position some metres away. The uniform officers deployed en masse to cut off our man's escape route across the dual carriageway or into the labyrinth of streets beyond where he would simply melt away into the brickwork.

Gaz reached the ruckus before Grayson could break free, with Jordan's hold remaining firm despite receiving numerous additional punches to the body and a well-aimed knee to the face. Before another punch or kick could be landed, Turner smashed rugby style into Steve Grayson's torso, collapsing into a heap of intermingled limbs, mud and grass. In a flash, Jordan jumped to his feet to assist despite sporting tender ribs. As I arrived, gasping for breath, cuffs were being fitted, and I became thoughtful – I seriously needed to work on my cardio fitness.

"Steven Grayson, you are under arrest on the suspicion of

murder," Willis quoted whilst trying to regain his breath.

"You are fucking kidding, I only punched him twice, the bastard shouldn't try to rip me off."

"Steven Grayson, I am arresting you on suspicion of murder. You do not have to say anything. But it may harm your defence if you do not mention when questioned something which you later rely on in court. Anything you do say may be given in evidence. Do you understand?" Jordan repeated, recovering from his short but energetic burst of activity.

"I've not done owt wrong."

"DO YOU UNDERSTAND YOUR RIGHTS MR GRAYSON?" Jordan bellowed, placing a well-aimed knee into the middle of the prisoners back.

"Yeah, yeah, got it."

CHAPTER 42

The team took some time to prepare for the interview, brainstorming all points of interest and ensuring our strategic questioning was the best suited for this situation. Then Jordan and I stepped into the corridor lined by open-plan offices; swathes of nightshift bodies busied themselves on their telephones and PCs or gulped coffee from personalised mugs. We paused, gathering ourselves prior to entering the small but cosy interview room two.

As we entered, we opted for courteous smiles towards Mr Grayson and his solicitor. On initial impressions, the accused appeared to be in his late twenties early thirties with thick stubble coating a pock scarred face which morphed into crew-cut mousey blond hair. Tribal tattoos streaked in a blaze from the collar of his t-shirt climbing his thick neck before intruding onto the skin of his face. Additional ink formed sleeves of dragons, koi fish and flames down both arms, finished with colourful swallows adorning each hand between thumb and first finger. Our suspect sat casually at the old wooden desk, with the names of previous occupants carved into the Formica top, the very same place the two dead street kids had been seated only days before. The fluorescent lights hummed above us whilst we took our seats and shuffled our papers before proceeding to the interview. The suit sat bolt upright with an anticipatory glare towards me and my colleague as we prepared ourselves.

"Good evening again Mr Grayson. I hope you've calmed down now," I stated with a glance over the top of my glasses.

"Yep," came an unimpressed, reluctant reply.

"I'm DC Jordan Willis with sore ribs and this is DCI Kelly Lynch."

"If I may, before proceedings commence, following a brief but concise consultation period with my client Mr Grayson, he has acknowledged he is more than willing to fully comply with any line of questioning this evening. Of course, we will fervently deny any involvement with the cases for which he was arrested, but as an alternative, my client may be able to provide you with witness information to assist you with your ongoing enquiries," Laurence Billings explained.

Grayson sat at the desk, hands clamped together. I deliberately took time to glare directly into his eyes searching for signs of weakness or deceit, none surfaced. The man appeared reasonably calm and collected considering the seriousness of the charges against him.

"For the sake of the recording, the time is 19:37, present are DCI Lynch, myself DC Willis, the accused Steven Grayson and his representation Laurence Billings. Before we continue further, I must confirm that you are aware of and fully comprehend the allegations against you and the reason for your arrest earlier this evening?" A silent nod of acknowledgement followed. "For the purpose of the recording, the suspect nodded his head in agreement. To begin Mr Grayson, can you please tell us your whereabouts on the evening of Saturday the eighth of November between the hours of twenty-one hundred hours and midnight."

"I was in the pub all day, starting in Wetherspoons at about half ten that morning before moving to the local after dinner for the rest of the day and all night."

"And your local is?"

"The Horse and Jockey on Cecil Street, the wife joined me and there's loads of witnesses. I didn't kill anyone." Neither me nor Jordan reacted, our faces remaining dead pan and professional.

"Were you in the area of Hamstead Heath on the evening of the eighth of November?"

"No comment."

"Mr Grayson, this is your chance to tell us what you know. Your solicitor has stressed you will be fully cooperative." He glanced towards Billings.

"No comment."

"Mr Grayson, are you the owner of a silver Mazda 6 registration MA07EZB?" Jordan continued.

"No comment."

"Are you the owner and sole driver of this vehicle?"

"No comment."

"Mr Grayson, a silver Mazda 6 MA07EZB was reported as leaving the scene of a murder at high speed, we can show the photographic evidence from various ANPR cameras en route, the last of which was taken only half a mile from where the body of a young woman was discovered on the night in question. For the purpose of the DIR, Mr Grayson and his representation are being shown evidence item numbers EJW 01 to 05 of a vehicle and the occupants. This is your car, isn't it Steven?" Jordan said pointing with his pen to the CCTV images.

"Alright, yes, it's my car."

"And you are the driver of said vehicle which contains you and what appears to be a blonde-haired woman?"

"Yes but…"

"Do you know the name Janet Storer?" I interrupted,

concentrating on his eyes.

"Never heard of her."

"Well, we think you have Steven. In our possession is a description from a witness willing to testify that he saw you and a woman matching Janet Storer's description driving towards East Heath carpark and you alone leaving at speed on East Heath Road."

"No, I mean yes, but…"

"Were you with Janet Storer on the night in question visiting Hampstead Heath?"

"No, you're wrong, I visited the Heath on Saturday but not with no Janet."

"Well I'm sure you can appreciate how this appears to us – your vehicle travelling to and later leaving the East Heath carpark area, the exact same place a beautiful young woman was to be discovered murdered by a sweet old lady walking her dog the next morning. It's not looking fantastic. What happened Steve? Did Janet lower her guard to your advances, agree to go to the woods, you thinking your luck was well and truly in and when the woman saw the error of her ways and said no thanks, things got out of hand?" I said, pushing on and observing the anger rising in his eyes.

"No, no, I was in the carpark with a friend, it's not a crime, and yeah, she's blonde, we got a phone call, and we left."

"No – *you* left Mr Grayson, alone. We have witnesses and photographic evidence."

"My friend ducked down."

"If you were just there with a friend, why did you leave the area like you robbed a bank? Are you positive you didn't take our victim for some fun which all went wrong?"

"Right, can I interrupt please? May I remind you my client has kindly offered to cooperate in full to any line of questioning in an attempt to clear his name. We possess a substantial list of witnesses to clarify his opening statement. I understand the seriousness of the allegations but please accept his testimony."

"I am prepared to consider Mr Grayson's account of events earlier in the day but considering his long and illustrious violent past with an undeniable preference towards the female of the species, I expect you can compute our pressing urgency Mr Billings. So, with all due respect, allow us to carry out our job."

Jordan stared toward his notebook awaiting silence before continuing. "What time did you arrive at the wood?"

"About ten past eleven. I can't be a hundred percent sure, I never took much notice."

"Would you like to tell us what you were doing in the area at that time of night?" I probed.

"Not really."

"Listen, shall we be frank? Personally, I do not care at present whether your activities on the evening in question were perhaps not, well, altogether kosher. If you are innocent of the charges against you as per your claim and can assist us in our enquiries, I suggest you do so. Without meaning to be insulting, we have a lot bigger fish to fry here Mr Grayson. A lot bigger than a small-time drug dealer, petty thief or someone who struggles to keep their hands to themselves. To emphasise the fact – young women are being murdered across London. That is our focus. This is the course of action we are pursuing unless you have something you don't want us to discover."

"I've got nothing to hide. I go with a friend to smoke weed that's all."

"A bit of advice, it's considerably safer to indulge in drugs at home," I joked, trying to cut the tension. I sensed Mr Grayson starting to strangle himself as the seriousness of the situation kicked in.

"Mr Grayson, I can assure you we won't be nicking you for smoking dope with a friend, not today. But as DCI Lynch mentioned, if you insist on partaking in recreational drugs, do so in the luxury of your own four walls."

"I can't do them at home."

"Care to enlighten us as to why not?" Jordan asked.

"Because the person I smoke weed with shouldn't be with me and I shouldn't be with her, do you understand me?"

"Sort of Mr Grayson, but for our enquiries and the recording you will be required to be one hundred percent honest with us – more specifically, innuendo and mere speculation will not cut it as witness statements or an alibi. May I remind you of the reason for your arrest – the body of a young woman was found not a five-minute walk from where you have admitted to being parked participating in drug abuse. Do I make myself clear?" I pushed.

"Yes," he paused. "I'm having an affair – is that what you need to hear? I wait until our lass goes home pissed, pick my lady friend up from work and drive over to the carpark, where we do what adults do together and after that we smoke some drugs. Things at home are not brilliant."

"Is that why your wife is sporting a black eye Steven? Domestic violence is frowned upon these days by judges."

"DCI Lynch, may I remind you my client is here to assist you with your enquiries regarding the murder of Janet Storer, not on a domestic violence charge, and the accusations you present are mere speculation," Billings shot me down.

"Our apologies, and I'll remind you Mr Billings, your client was arrested as a suspect in a murder case. We need answers and we need them now. To continue, does your mistress possess a name Steven? We will need to talk to this woman for clarification of your story," Jordan requested.

"Will it be necessary to involve her? It's a bit awkward as you can imagine."

"All affairs are problematic Mr Grayson and yes, as police officers, it will be obligatory to speak to her. Can I remind you yet again you are the prime suspect in a murder case and perverting the course of justice is a serious offence," I said increasing my seriousness.

"Listen, if her hubby finds out about us, I'm a dead man – he's a proper nutcase, and god knows what he will do to her."

"Tell us her name Mr Grayson," I said switching to bad cop and adopting his formal name to emphasise my growing impatience.

"Beverly Newton."

"Oh dear Steven, you do like to live dangerously, don't you? On the bright side, you don't need to worry for ten to fifteen years, because her husband was banged up in July for armed robbery and attempted murder, providing of course his appeal is dismissed, which we cannot guarantee. A lovely bloke wasn't he Jordan? Apparently spat in officers' faces when arrested, always a pleasant experience, receiving another person's phlegm in your face. I presume this is the same Bev Newton who lives with Paul Hull?" I explained.

"Yes."

"Don't be overly concerned, no one will suspect anything out of the ordinary if a pair of coppers are visiting their house, it's normal protocol for them. In any case, your sordid love affair doesn't interest us. What we are interested in is the events of Saturday the eighth of November concerning you or what you may have witnessed whilst at the woods, so please continue."

Mr Grayson took a huge breath of air. "Well after a shag we smoked some weed as per usual, then Bev got the munchies, that's when we decided to leave and call in at the garage for food before I dropped her off home. But she got a text message from a friend explaining some idiot in the pub was gobbing off about our fucking affair. It pissed me off, so I went to sort the bastard out. This bloke has caused trouble for me before. The reason I ran earlier is I thought it was sommat to do with me giving the kid a right kicking."

"Carry on Steven," Jordan said, leaning forward as if watching a soap on TV and the juicy ending was about to be broadcast.

"Well as we were leaving the carpark another car came flying through the entrance. Bev ducked down in case it was anyone we knew. But it was a flash motor, one of those Evoque thingies, a pale colour, possibly white, I'm not sure, the light was pretty shite."

"Anything on the reg plate Steven?"

"No sorry, a new shape which might help a bit."

"Thanks Mr Grayson, please continue," I said deflated but I suppose I was being overly optimistic to think this would be easy. Even if we did have the registration number, would a calculated killer use his own plates when committing his crimes? I doubt it, but worth a stab in the dark.

"Well as I turned towards the exit my lights flashed into their car, the woman in the passenger seat was stunning, I clocked her in an instant because her golden hair almost glowed."

"For the record we are showing the suspect images EJW06 to 10. Are any of these females familiar?" I asked, presenting photos of various missing women including Janet Storer.

"Yeah, that's her, I'm sure." He pointed a grubby finger.

"One hundred percent sure?"

"Ninety-nine. Hey is this her, the dead woman?"

"As you are aware we can't divulge any information regarding our present enquiries Mr Grayson." I shut that door quick.

"And the driver, can you describe him? Any distinguishing features?" Jordan stepped in.

"I didn't get to see the bloke's face, but I can tell you he had short blond hair, and was an enormous man, he filled the seat."

"When you say enormous, do you mean obese?"

"No, not at all, he's a gym monkey – his arms and chest were huge, he was a mountain of a bloke, that's all I can tell you. Me and Bev go regular, people come and go all the time, it's a bit of a hot spot for couples who require some privacy, but neither of us can remember seeing this car before. And he was in a rush that's for sure, we almost crashed at the entrance."

"No tattoos, or anything distinguishing?"

"No nothing."

"Thanks Steven, you have been most helpful. Oh, and we will be talking to Bev to confirm all the evening's events so make yourself comfy in the cell," I confirmed.

"This interview is terminated at 20:08. Don't get too excited, you aren't going anywhere yet – there's an assaulting a police officer charge to deal with first," Jordan beamed.

"Please don't let my wife know anything, this would destroy her if she found out," he said as anger flashed in his eyes.

"Our team will do their best to keep your bit on the side under wraps but no promises. If your marriage means so much to you, consider knocking the affair on the head and stop slapping your wife about," I advised with an element of spite.

We left Mr Grayson in the interview room and instructed the desk sergeant to hold him for the maximum remaining hours to allow the investigating officers time to fully corroborate his story.

"Guys, listen in, we are discounting Grayson as our prime suspect. The man possesses a list of alibis as long as my arm and CCTV footage to back up his movements on the night in question. He has, however, kindly confirmed that Janet Storer is the woman he witnessed in the other car they almost collided with whilst leaving East Heath carpark. The gentleman accompanying her is described as a gym monkey with short blond hair and zero tattoos on his forearms. I think we can all acknowledge what this means without going into much greater detail. The man highlighted in the CCTV we possess doesn't match Mr Grayson's description, meaning we now have two possible suspects – the tattooed gentleman with Hannah Craven on her fatal night out and our new man, the chauffeur of Ms Storer, who incidentally drives a new shape white Range Rover Evoque, no plate details unfortunately. Can someone scan any footage from the road cams, ANPR and private security devices covering the roads to and from the Heath, including B roads, to see if we can pick something up, please? Absolutely anything. Hey guys, let's be perfectly honest here, we are dealing with a thousand and one routes into and out of the area and a single white Evoque, which are, as we know, like wheelie bins throughout the country – every fucker seems to have one. To cut to the chase, we may well be pissing in the wind attempting to trace this car but there's not much else to go on."

"On it boss," Jordan announced standing to go to his desk.

"One last thought from me, I know Grayson's statement indicates the person he witnessed with Janet Storer was tattoo free but take into consideration it was dark and he was under the influence of drugs and alcohol. I suggest we follow up on our original CCTV image of the inked man who still hasn't come forward. Someone please compile a search of ex-cons with full sleeve tattoos on both arms focusing on men with a history of violence particularly towards women, cover all bases here."

CHAPTER 43

For cases like the one we are investigating at present, days can quickly turn into weeks and weeks into months but hopefully not months into years. The LSCIU had put personal lives on hold for two months, enduring arduous days of long hours in a desperate attempt to reveal some sort of incriminating evidence, anything to give us a breakthrough in this case before more women vanish from the face of the planet and materialise face down in a crude makeshift grave somewhere in London. Each of us has trawled through endless hours of CCTV footage, studying nightlife venues, transport routes, places of work. We've delved into the private lives of the victims, unearthing all manner of personal preferences, all in the vain hope of discovering a clear mugshot or a lead to the mystery Casanova. The line of questioning is persistent – family, friends and colleagues not only in and around London but up and down the country from Blyth in the northeast to Dungeness on the Kent coast. A time-consuming task, in this instance giving an almost fruitless return, appearing as if the killer may have rather intelligently also accounted for the family's and friend's angle. Most of the victims and missing persons believed to be associated with this case have recently moved away from their long-term homes for new jobs or to escape sour relationships or family disputes. Hannah Craven, Janet Storer and Becky Holt were all witnessed in conversation with a male in local bars, his description uncannily similar, however during the investigative process, in recordings showing the person deemed the prime suspect, he was always conveniently obscured from the cameras, although his stature and description match that of the information given during the interview with Mr Steven Grayson apart from the ink.

Gaz discovered a report dated last year from a friend of Ellie Clark, one of the dead prostitutes, who had approached the uniform plod on the street. I say friend in the loosest terms possible, a more fitting description would be pimp. As he explained, it was down to him and a colleague who remains anonymous to provide for and protect the girls.

"We find dos bitch clients, n watch their backs. One of dem took uh beaten buy uh customer, he wuz sorted by my boyz. You need to protect da merchandise, do y know what I mean? n when dem ladies needed to trip da light fandango we gived dem what is required. Uh rattling bitch is not attractive one, y get me bro," he explained to uniform in his own street slang.

This charming person went on to describe a young lad, tall, slim build, short dark hair, driving a silver Mercedes, 07 plate. A bit of a loner who wasn't shy with his money, and a regular visitor to Ellie, specifying her company only, described as besotted by the girl to the point of obsessive. Under no circumstances would this person be tempted away from his beloved young prostitute Ellie. Now according to Mr Pimp, this kid mysteriously vanished weeks before the street girl. After following up several leads and eventually locating the young lad and his family the story quickly became clear. This young lad did indeed use Ellie to relieve his sexual desires – but as a last fling before he became too ill after being diagnosed with terminal pancreatic cancer; he died only months later.

So, we continue wading through mountains of information gathered over the last few months, studying each sheet of paper until the print becomes a blur – interviews, witness statements, descriptions of the man believed to be our killer by so many different sources which invariably contradict each other: dark hair, blond hair, ginger, bald, tall, short, fat, thin, muscular, clean shaven, bearded, moustache, you name it and we've had it, all of which require investigating by someone, most of which lead to nothing. As requested, all notes are scribbled across the white board, crammed in a random nondescript manner, scrawled in different colours and various directions, no lines, no rules and they made no sense yet. Organisation becomes boring and mundane, random focuses the mind, you need to focus the mind to follow the words, the theory being that nothing gets missed. The pieces of the jigsaw were building right in front of us, we all knew it, but we had far too many pieces missing to finish the whole picture. The free phone information line promoted at the press conference was considered successful, which of course it was, it's a practice we adopt regularly; we received thousands of calls providing a plethora of information regarding the case – some relevant, some complete red herrings and others I'm sure who only rang for the conversation.

CHAPTER 44

As promised, the present squeeze Mr Harrison provided me and the teenager with a much-needed day out at the rugby, managing to secure complimentary tickets which included free food and drink in a rather impressive hospitality suite to view the game. A couple of the more prestigious players attended our box prior to the warmup for a Q and A session, names which I embarrassingly didn't recognise. I must confess, I don't understand a great deal about rugby, my father's sporting preference being football, football and a bit more football for good measure. I was an avid Hammers fan, drilled into me since birth and probably whilst in the womb by natural process, but I could become accustomed to being spoilt rotten, waited on hand and foot with the bonus being the scenery isn't bad either. Hunky players are easy on the eye for sure. My son beamed towards me, apparently meeting one of his England heroes was the highlight of his life, chatting and taking the opportunity to apprehend said player for the regulatory selfies and snapshots before excitedly dispersing them across social media for his friends to peruse at their leisure.

Personally, I felt like a spare prick at a lesbian wedding with James and Jacob enjoying the match together, enthusiastically pointing out top plays, discussing a more preferential solution to a particular situation, scoffing at the opposition and disagreeing with the referee on a regular basis. Two buckets of Sauvignon Blanc eased my pain alongside the unquestionable fact that my boy appeared happy for once, the icing on the cake to a day of free-flowing alcohol, gorgeous food and rugby players' bodies.

Another factor to add to the glow of pleasure was that my overprotective son not only tolerated the new man in my life but bonded to a point I can only describe as bromance. For the first time in years, an overwhelming feeling of being happy, content and relaxed flooded over me, despite the pressure cooker of work. And my intriguing, unfamiliar sense of happiness was solidified with a smile from my man and a thumbs up, inclusive of a cheeky wink – a rare moment of elation that was rudely interrupted by the dreaded ring tone of my mobile phone. *Office* appeared on the screen. I stood to take the call, making my way to the rear of the suite, away from the noise of the baying crowd.

"Hello, DCI Lynch speaking," I whispered, why I'm not sure – the overwhelming roar of the fans was almost ear bursting as the home team touched down for a try.

"Hi Kelly, only me. I'm so sorry to bother you on your day out, how's it going by the way?"

"Interesting Gary, even if you don't comprehend what you're watching or what's going on. But on the bright side, eye candy is in abundance if you know what I mean?"

"Ha-ha, all muscle, cauliflower ears and battered brains – it sounds delightful. Well, you enjoy. I'm ringing to tell you Jordan and myself are going to visit the King's Arms pub not a million miles from St Mary's where Hannah Craven was found. A Ms Candace Jackson has raised concerns regarding a friend who hasn't turned into work for a few days. As you appreciate, we wouldn't normally be overly interested in such a situation but guess what?"

"She's blonde and beautiful," I answered before he chanced to inform me.

"Correctamundo, and she's only recently moved down here from the Leicester area after breaking up with a nutcase boyfriend. Personally, I think this is too coincidental to ignore. So, we'll nip over, listen to the friend's concerns and keep you informed of proceedings."

"Brilliant, if you need me, someone will have to pick me up. I may have had a couple of glasses of wine, large ones."

"No probs Kell, it might lead to a blank, but my gut is impelling me to check this out."

"Keep me updated."

CHAPTER 45

A young African-Caribbean woman, stunning in every conceivable way, stood behind the bar of the King's Arms pub, attempting to busy herself wiping down the bar and replacing used spill mats for clean ones. A blaze of expertly applied makeup highlighted her deep brown eyes and luscious lips. Long jet-black hair containing streaks of gold flowed down in a torrent of braids from a top knot tied high on her head and intertwined with a colourful array of matching ribbons and beads. Tight ripped jeans clung to her impressive curvaceous assets like an additional layer of skin and a scarlet lace vest revealed more flesh than it covered, accentuating plump breasts. A dazzling peacock butterfly and sunset lily tattoo meandered its way from her right shoulder down her back before disappearing into the skimpy crimson material. The whole appearance came to a crescendo with a clutter of multicoloured bangles loosely applied around both wrists and hands of golden rings. From across the room, she checked us entering the lounge via the door from the side carpark, continuing her bar cleaning before moving onto drying wine glasses with a tea towel, examining the rims for any stubborn lipstick marks the dishwasher may have missed. An old guy with a flat cap and weathered face sat in a dimly lit corner at one end of the bar, precariously balanced on a high bar stool next to the display of salted peanuts and a poppy appeal charity box, his walking stick as reassurance propped close to him against the wall to his side.

"Hi guys, I'll be with you in a second," the young woman said.

"Afternoon, we're looking for a...?" I stopped to check the

notebook in my hand acting as a prompt, "Candice Jackson."

"Yep, that's me," she replied, leaving her glass cleaning to one side and leaning with her elbows on the bar, ignorant to the instant cleavage promotion.

"Hello Ms Jackson. I'm DS Turner and this is my colleague DC Willis, do you mind if we talk to you about the missing persons report you filed this morning?"

"Yeah, no problem, you lot are on the ball, aren't you?"

"Well, we aim to please," Jordan said with a smile.

"Candice, tell us what concerns you have regarding your mate Helen Richardson?" I said, taking a tall bar stool.

"My Helen hasn't turned up for work for two days and it's not like her, usually she's an exceptionally reliable girl, in fact she's Mrs goody two shoes, never missing a shift and always half an hour early."

"I'm aware this might appear an obvious question, but we do need to ask if anyone has tried to contact her?" Jordan enquired.

"Yes me, no reply at home or via text. I'm quite worried now, because for a fact, my girl is broke, she needs money for bills, Mr Bank Manager took to chewing her ass weeks ago. See she'd worked a lot of extra shifts and was due a fair wedge. Which is the reason I'm so concerned about her – ya understand, yesterday was pay day, and she did a no show, her wage packet is still in the office."

"Right, tell us the last time anyone laid eyes on or made contact with Helen."

"The girl worked her afternoon shift, then Sian one of the other girls phoned in sick which isn't a massive shock, she's one lazy cow let me tell you for nothing. My girlfriend, bless her, worked a double shift with me. We get busy on a Wednesday night with cheap beer and the quiz, students flock in their droves – you should try it guys, it's a cracking night."

"We might do aye boss?"

"Why not. Candice, to clarify – you're certain this is the final time you saw her?"

"Yep, but she texted me to tell me her new man picked her up."

"New man?"

"Yeah, Dave, the new fella, a top bloke. According to the gossip he's moved in around here after a messy split with his wife; dis man has taken quite a shine to our Helen."

"Do we have his full name and address?"

"I just know the bloke as Dave. George? Mr Stewart?" She turned to the old man perched precariously on a stool. "Sorry, he's deaf as a post, oh a warning – don't mention the war, you'll be here for hours, GEORGE!"

"What?"

"Can you remember what Helen's fella is called and where he's at?" she yelled.

"Yeah course I can. I'm old not facking stupid."

"These are policemen, they want some details," she bellowed, again exaggerating her lip movement should he need to read them.

"The solicitor? He's a nice fellow, from Ealing way I think he said, but he lives in the big house on the corner of Earls Avenue now. The boy's facking loaded, always got wads of cash on him, generous too but I can't remember seeing him for a couple of weeks, his ex has been giving him some shit."

"What's his name George, can you recall?" Jordan shouted, also sub-consciously exaggerating his lip movements.

"David… bloody hell, what was his second name? Oh I know, Roe, that's it, Mr Dave Roe. This body might be facked boy, but my head's still as strong as a young man."

"And what did he look like? Can you describe him George?" Jordan continued, poised with pen and notepad.

"Yeah boy, tall bloke, aged about 30 I guess, handsome-looking chap, short blond hair and fit boy, he has muscles on top of muscles – his bloody arms are bigger than my bloody legs."

"Brilliant Mr Stewart, anything else we may need to be aware of regarding Mr Roe?" pressed Jordan, noting down an all-too-familiar description.

"Let me think," the old man mused whilst taking a slurp of ale, "oh yeah, his arms are covered in ink boy, from top to bottom, all the colours you can think of." The frail man painted a common picture.

"Is there anything distinguishing about the artwork?" I interrupted.

"Swirls of black and colour, all different and a Koi fish on his forearm."

"Thanks George you've been most helpful."

"Helpful enough to buy me a pint boy?" His toothless smile prompted Jordan to take the change from his pocket and toss the handful of coins on the bar with a nod of consent towards Candice.

"Candice, what can you tell us about Helen? Obviously, we are in possession of a photograph of her, I presume sent in by yourself. What about her personal life?" I continued with the questions, knowing in my head what we might be dealing with here, unfortunately for Helen.

"She's my best friend. The girl has a heart of gold and jeez she would rock the socks off any man if she wanted, but she aint like that. I'll tell you boys now, if I had her body and beauty, I'd be paving my way with notes in one way or another, yep she could have whoever she wanted."

"Apart from Mr Roe, any other male interests?"

"An ex-boyfriend in Leicester, the reason my girl moved down to the big smoke. Dat arsehole beat the fuck out of her. A beautiful girl like her and all he wants to do is cause damage, the wanker," Candice explained with a face of utter disgust.

"We got a name for him, Candice?" Jordan continued as I carried out a quick scan of the bar areas.

"Grant is all I can tell you, he might still be on her Facebook page, she likes to keep an eye on the prick and warn other girls off. Do you think this arse is something to do with Helen's no show?"

"It's a line of enquiry we will pursue, anything is possible. Any cameras in the establishment?" I asked, breaking her train of thought.

"The only one I'm aware of is on the entrance but it's not worked for months. The boss says the wires are damaged. He's having new ones fitted in the building and on the porch, those blue tooth thingies. I don't understand much about it, technology is wasted on me unless I can text, shop or catch up on social media and shit."

"So, Wednesday at work was your last contact with Helen?"

"No, she left early because she was off her feet from a double shift, but she sent me a message later after eleven – here, you can read it."

She handed over her mobile for me and Jordan to peruse the text reading, 'Hi babe, you'll never guess but Dave turned up at my flat, story is his ex-missus is giving him a lot of grief over money, going for food at the fox, giving the poor bloke the cold shoulder but glad to be with him TBH, don't ever tell him the last bit, ha ha ha see y soon xxxxx'

"And this was all?" I said, handing her phone back.

"Yep, Thursday morning, pay packets were ready for collection and she didn't show, no show Thursday evening for her shift, nor Friday, and as I said, my girl is not answering calls, texts or her flat door."

"Cool, brilliant, to recap, please feel free to interject at any time. Your friend Helen Richardson is described as blonde hair, blue eyes, beautiful, five foot eleven," I began my summary of facts.

"Stunning, not just beautiful, fucking stunning," Candice interrupted abruptly correcting my description.

"Stunning agreed, arrived here in London six months ago after a failing violent relationship, and has worked here for?"

"About four months," Candice provided the answer without any further prompting.

"Thank you, are you getting all this Jordan?"

"Yep, carry on."

"Right, Mr David Roe, approximately six foot two, stocky muscular build, short blond hair, tattooed, solicitor from Ealing, recently separated and moved into the area, on Earls Avenue. The two dated but Mr Roe has been AWOL lately dealing with the ex until Wednesday evening when he met Helen eating humble pie and took her out for supper, any idea where?"

"The Fox and Hounds on Carson Way, it serves food late," Candice informed us. "Do you think this is the angel killer who George told me about in the newspapers?" she asked painfully.

"Probably not, don't believe everything you read in the papers. Remember, statistics prove the percentage chance of anyone being involved in violent crimes of this nature these days is extremely rare, and most incidents are exaggerated by the press for sales purposes, hence why they only focus on the extreme cases. Remember, daily mundane police work doesn't sell papers. All we are doing is chasing up mispers, missing person reports, as per the boss's instructions," Jordan lied, he had recognised the MO as I had. Hopefully, Candice was provided with an air of reassurance as we vacated the King's Arms.

"Why didn't you ask them to do an e-fit Gary?"

"Because in Candice's mind, her friend is only missing, we ask for an e-fit she knows we think this is more."

Before reaching the car I rang the office; my concerns were far from the tales of consolation delivered to the young barmaid – now the priority for us was to find this woman ASAP.

"Hi Sally, Gaz here, can you do me a massive favour?"

"That depends on what, and nothing sexual," she replied in her usual jovial manner.

"I need a search on a Mr David Roe, we believe he's a solicitor from Ealing, approximately 30 years old, six foot two, stocky muscular build, short blond hair, tattooed arms, only possible address we can confirm is Earls Avenue."

"No problem, I've got all that, give me half an hour, I'll see what I can dig up."

"You're a star Sally."

"I know."

CHAPTER 46

"Helen, come on darling, wake up," I spoke as loud as I dare to stir my new companion into life from her caged slumber.

"What's up for god's sake?" she said rising to a sitting position and rubbing her eyes clear of sleep. "Shit Becks, how the fuck did you get out?" the woman screamed with a mixture of shock and explosive excitement.

"Keep your voice down, I don't know if he's still upstairs. I'll explain whilst I try to help you."

"How the hell did you escape?"

"He's fucked up mate. I got out because Mr fucking perfect messed up. When the cage door shuts it clunks twice as the locking mechanism engages. Over the weeks down here I've listened to his routine and taken mental notes. Mine only clunked once this morning – he didn't lock me in properly! He is human after all."

"Help me please Becks," she rattled her prison door.

"Shit, yours is locked. I'll find something to force it open," I said wandering off into the cloak of darkness.

"What about the computer? Try the PC – if we can't escape, maybe you can raise the alarm or send a message to someone."

"Fantastic idea," I agreed, stumbling my way through the murk towards the vicinity of the nearby desk with only the solitary beam of light from under the door to help. After several minutes of fumbling around blindly trying to locate the power button, the device booted into life. The Microsoft logo illuminated the room, staying for a minute or two before fading to darkness. I fixated intensely on the screen praying for this to work, listening out for movement upstairs in the house. Seconds ticked by which felt like hours; eventually, a new page flashed across the oversized flat monitor, flickering light into the now pristinely clean cellar.

"Balls, it's asking for a password."

"Think, what might go through his head, a word he would use?" Helen replied, hanging onto the bars of her cage like some sort of convict doing life.

"God knows, I don't think I want to experience what goes on in his skull. What about lunatic?" I joked attempting to lighten the moment and hide my nerves.

"How about girls' names? The women who have been down here?"

"I only know three, and they are me, you and the woman before you."

"Try them Becks, we don't have much of anything else, do we?"

Janet was the first name I typed in, followed by Helen and Becky, the only response on the screen was 'incorrect password'. As suggested, I racked my brains for words he uses on a regular basis, anything, several sprang to mind and then the light bulb moment.

"I've got it! I've only fucking got it – what does he always call us?"

"His ANGELS!"

"That's what we are in his sick world. He wants to make us heavenly – that has to be the password?"

"Good thinking Becks, try it, we've got nothing to lose."

I entered the word with care – incorrect password. Another

attempt, all lowercase – incorrect password. Again, in capitals, my options rapidly fading – incorrect password.

"Shit, come on," I urged as a pulse of panic rippled through my entire body causing my hands to shake to the beat of the butterflies fluttering in my stomach.

I tried again, ANGEL – and this time a bright flash blinded me temporarily, and through the blur the welcome page booted up.

"Fuck me, I've done it, Helen – I'm in!" I exclaimed elated, rushing over to the other woman and embracing her hands through the steel bars.

"We've fucking done it girl, we are getting out of here!" Tears rolled down her face in a flood of emotional relief, her fingers gripping mine tight. Our brief moment of euphoric jubilation was broken by a piercing alarm followed by a series of dazzling strobe flashes emitted from the desktop screen, inducing a jump of the heart before darkness and an eerie silence ensued. Both of us glared in the direction of the screen, frozen to the spot, not daring to breath. Another flash of blinding light caused me to squint the overwhelming eye strain away. As my vision cleared, his face appeared, accompanied by more strobe flashes across the monitor.

"Oh dear, the password is wrong girls, naughty, naughty. I am on my way home, ha ha," bleated out his annoying animation continually for several minutes before his image vanished to be replaced a split-second later by live footage of me and Helen.

In a second of blind panic, we span to face each other, neither of us speaking a word. Both PC speakers continued spouting out the incessant message on a repeat loop. A quick glance deep into Helen's eyes showed the complete fear exploding from her brain as the hope of escape drained from her soul. With utter rage burning within, the first thing which sprang into my mind was to run towards the PC, rip the wires from the monitor and hurl the bundle of technology through the dank air; it bounced along the tiled floor with a satisfying crash before a pleasant silence fell upon the basement, restoring the room into darkness apart from the spit of illuminated hope from under the door.

Panic-filled adrenalin surged a sickness through my whole body, every muscle, bone and sinew; my heart began to pound through my chest and my hands shook in an uncontrollable manner as the stark realisation hit me. The entire time, every minute of our imprisonment down here in this dark cellar, this bastard had been watching us, and now he was heading home to do whatever his sick, perverse mind might formulate to punish my act of revolt.

My mind switched back to Helen, still imprisoned and I began hunting frantically amongst the gloom for something to prise her cage open with, only the beam of light from underneath the door at the top of the stairs to guide me, but I found nothing of any use. The quarry tile floor was now spotless, cleaned to a polish to rid the place of Janet's blood. The walls on one side of the cellar were lined with several filing cabinets and two wooden cupboards, their doors adorned with centrefolds displaying their naked assets, all secured with chunky, substantial padlocks.

"Listen to me Becks, save yourself and fetch help. He won't hurt me, I'm sure."

"No, I'm not fucking leaving you here girl, not a chance," I hollered, gripping the bars of her prison gate and tugging at them with all the might I could muster, but they held solid, the thin metal biting into the skin of my fingers.

"You kick at the same time," I suggested.

"I'll try," she said, panic and fear showing clearly in her eyes.

"Ready, as a team, I'll count you in – one, two, now!" Helen lay on her back, launching her tan leather ankle boots in tandem towards the mechanism as I yanked simultaneously, but again the door remained solid.

"Come on, after three, go!" Helen's foot hit the lock again, this time with an impressive thud, but the steel frame again remained intact.

"Come on again, now!" No movement again, not the slightest bit of damage had been caused, and fatigue began to set into my arm muscles. Our rather poor diet and lack of exercise was not the ideal preparation for the unexpected exertion required.

"Keep going," I panted, catching my breath with my tender hands resting on my knees.

"Go Becks, raise the alarm, do whatever you need to, but get out."

"No come on, we can't give up, kick Helen, fucking kick!" I encouraged, fighting the metal with my full weight, wrenching my arms over and over in a frantic but pathetic rage, the bars again cutting into the soft skin of my fingers.

My new friend kicked the lock with all her might, once, twice and a third time before the cage door gave an unexpected flex, the frame bending for a split-second before springing back and trapping my right hand in between the steel and the rigid box section, ripping a deep gash into my flesh and shooting pain signals to the receptors in my brain.

"Ow bollox!" I bellowed as a natural recoiling reaction to pull my hand free resulted in a deeper laceration across my palm. The claret oozed in an instant, with a steady flow dribbling down my forearm.

"Jesus, fucking hell!" I cursed again.

"Are you alright Becks? Shit, what have you done?"

"Cut my hand, but I'll live."

"Is there a lot of blood?"

"A fair amount to be honest."

"Here, wrap your hand in my scarf to stop the bleeding."

"Honestly I'm fine, a bit of bark as my dad would say," I assured her using her donation as a makeshift bandage to contain the flow. The phrase I had employed, the words I uttered stimulated a vision of my father. The mental image of his kind thoughtful face hit me like a brick and the stark reality of our desperate situation flooded over me, causing a surge of emotional exuberance.

"Right, I'll be back soon, I promise," I said, holding her hand for a moment through the bars as a gesture of reassurance, gazing sincerely into her eyes. "I promise I will find help."

Without further hesitation, I fumbled my way intently forward to the beam of light filtering under the door, stumbling over the first step and falling heavily onto my hands and elbows. I felt a rippling shock in both wrists and a searing red-hot poker agony shot up my forearm and exploded into my brain from the gash on the palm. Pain was now an inconvenience I needed to put to the back of my mind and I scrambled up more stairs on all fours towards the encouraging sign of freedom, more than aware this may be a road to nowhere taking into account the trio of hefty bolts on the other side of the door and the lock which clunks twice when operated. But for Helen's sake I had try my upmost to raise the alarm. The woman was beginning to weaken, her state of mind buckling with the constant absence of sunlight, lack of food and sleep deprivation. I needed to find a way out of here sooner rather than later.

Through the darkness I ascended the final steps before clumsily making my way along the wall of the narrow landing, metres from the oversized wooden door. Anticipation built in the pit of my stomach and nerves caused my whole body to shake. The sickening feeling drew bile to my throat, forcing me to swallow hard, and fatigue started to take the air from my lungs like a debilitating disease. I paused for breath before approaching the door, I guess through fear as much as exhaustion. The shaft of dust-laden light shone bright from the bottom sill, a simple source of hope, of freedom, just inches away.

The brief silence was broken by several loud thuds against the oak door followed by a deep, rumbling thunderous growl and a crescendo of ear-bursting ferocious barking. Panic exploded through my body as I heard the three door bolts slide aside before the two clunks of the lock. A huge black dog burst through the wood-panelled door, slamming it hard into the brickwork. A blaze of bared teeth, drool and aggression accompanied a spray of daylight which coated the dank cellar.

In the background, Helen screamed. I turned on my heels and fled blindly from the salvation of the light and back into the cloak of darkness. The black beast followed, gaining on me by the second with ultimate ease, only for it to be halted abruptly by a steel leash which ended the animal's progress towards me but certainly had no calming effect on its determination. The man, our prison warden, entered the cellar, a broad grin across his face, the dog chain tight in one hand, wrenching his muscular arms. He clicked his fingers twice and the hound sat, full of obedience, although its attitude remained intact as corroborated by the continuous snarl.

What contributed to the next set of events I'm not entirely sure. I remember tripping on the top step and spiralling out of control down the stairs, bouncing on my ribs, arms and hips. An agonising pain shot through my right ankle before I came to an undignified halt close to the remnants of the desktop computer on the cold tiled floor. Blood oozed down my face and an egg swelled over my right eye. The fluorescent light flickered into life above me revealing the deformity of my painful right leg. The man above me simply laughed at my pitiful effort to escape.

"Silence dog, here!" he shouted above the chaotic din with an authoritative tug on the chain. The hound obediently returned and sat at his feet, all the aggression subdued to a wag of the tail, content in the fact his actions had pleased his master.

"Oh dear, Becky that doesn't appear brilliant does it? I bet that's painful." He continued to amuse himself at my predicament. My strenuous attempts to move my battered body became futile. The flood of pain was too intense, causing me to collapse back onto the chilly tiles, inducing an impulsive lung full of stale cellar air. Exhaustion overwhelmed my beaten body; my heart pounded, craving oxygen to gradually appease my weak muscles.

A cold sweat began beading from every conceivable pore, and every limb vibrated violently, fighting back the frustration and anger. The ankle pain increased as my adrenalin levels subsided and all the symptoms of shock engulfed my body. Rivers of tears began to flow down my face betraying a weakness I had tried to keep hidden from him for such an age. The harsh reality hit me – this occasion might have been our only opportunity to get ourselves out of this hell hole before he makes us into angels. A chance now drifting from our grasp, as I lay there battered and bruised and at the mercy off some psychopath. Helen was silent, her knees tucked into her chest in a defensive ball, backing herself further into a corner of her still secured cage, her grubby blanket pulled tight around shaking shoulders as an attempt to disguise her sobs.

"Woman, did you take me for a fool? Did you think for one minute I'm an idiot? I've been watching you since day one. Every movement made, every tear shed. The bravado you portray to conceal your emotional state when I visit is Oscar winning. It's been an entertaining game, but this is the last shake of the dice for you I'm afraid. There will be no glorious ending for you, no flight to the heavens where you'll line the way for others. No, no, no – you're not perfection anymore, you're all broken. You simply do not fit the specifications, another will do your job, complete my mission," he informed me as he descended the stairs, his loyal mate never twitching as he stood sentry at the cellar door.

A bucket-sized hand and muscular arm dragged me by my hair and blouse to the cage, dumping me like an undignified sack of potatoes without an ounce of compassion before slamming shut and locking the gate with two clunks followed by an accompanying burst of uncontrollable laughter. I sat in agony, again examining the peculiar angle of my ankle.

"What am I going to do with you now Becky? Have you seen her Helen? Look at her! I SAID FUCKING LOOK AT HER!" he bellowed. She turned from her safe place in the corner of her cage where she'd buried herself like a chastised dog curling away from harm's way when he's chewed your best shoes. Her body shook vigorously and her petrified tear-filled eyes met my gaze momentarily with an accompanying sorrowful smile.

"This is what happens when you let the evil inside take over your mind. This portrays weakness Helen, please don't become a weakling," he explained. Her eyes plummeted south almost submissively before she turned back to her safe place, pulling the grimy blanket back over her head.

CHAPTER 47

"Hello Gaz."

"Sal, what you got for us?"

"Well if Mr Roe's description is correct as per your detailed report, he's doing exceedingly well for his age. The person I have in front of me is a partner at Roe Solicitors in Ealing, he was investigated five years ago regarding an allegation of sexual abuse in the workplace, for which he was found not guilty, surprisingly."

"Brilliant, this sounds promising."

"Hold off the celebrations for a minute. This man is also sixty-two years old, approximately five foot six, bald and married to Mrs Silvia Roe for forty years with two kids both now adults. Address is on the outskirts of Stevenage, and he owns a villa near Mercia where he and his wife spend most of the year and which is their present location. So, I'm taking a wild stab in the dark that this is not our man."

"Shit, thanks Sal."

"What now?"

"We might be wasting time here, but me and Jordan are going to ask some questions down at the Fox where we believe they were going for food. I'm sure they'll have CCTV to check, but the odds are she never got there. Yet again, I need a favour from you whilst you're lazing about in the office."

"My parameters still stand from last time – nothing sexual."

"You wish. Can you locate any cameras around the vicinity of Ms

Richardson's flat, especially last Wednesday night between the hours of 21:00 and midnight please, which is the time period our missing woman is believed to have met up with said boyfriend."

"On it Gaz."

Sally ended the call and headed towards the mess room and the kettle before settling down to carry out the request. Her desk phone rang as per all day; she cursed before answering.

"Hello DC Glover speaking, special investigations unit, how can I help?"

"Hi Kelly speaking, do we have any updates I should be made aware of?"

"Nothing to assist the enquiry as such Kell. Gary got a lead from the boozer where Helen Richardson works on a David Roe, a solicitor from Ealing, apparently a six two, blond-haired hunk she was dating. But it's only led to a sixty-two-year-old bald bloke. I'm currently scouting the CCTV footage from the vicinity of her flat on the night of her disappearance, Gaz and Jordan are checking the Fox and Hounds on Carson Way, apparently she told the friend they were going to eat there. Oh, one more thing, your ex called, he's been trying to locate you all day, insisting it's important he talks to you."

"A bit weird, it can't be anything Jacob's done because he's been with me and James all day. Strange, unless that's his problem of course. Cheers, keep me updated."

"How was the rugby?"

"A brilliant day out. What can I say – delicious food, wine on tap and hunky men, every lady's dream day?"

"I'm so jealous right now. And when are we going to meet this ideal new man?"

"Soon Sally, soon."

"Are you falling for him Kell?"

"The man's growing on me which is all I will commit to, and Jacob adores him. But," I pause for a second to regather my train of thought, "haven't you got proper investigative work to do, rather than pry into my private life?"

"On it boss, see you tomorrow lovebird."

CHAPTER 48

"Evening Darrell, I'm told you've been phoning me. Now listen, if this is regarding James taking me and Jacob to the rugby, it's not on."

"Get over yourself please, this is nothing to do with elements of your private life. I'm worried about Fiona."

"What happens between you and her does not concern me anymore."

"The person you used to call your bestie is missing, and with all these news stories about this angel killer flying about, his preference for blondes, wining and dining them before abducting and murdering them…."

"Whoa, whoa, whoa, Darrell – slow down. What makes you think this is anything at all to do with these murders?"

"On Thursday evening we had a monstrous argument and, as per usual, she stormed out of the house straight to the nearest pub and drank herself into oblivion. You above all have experience of her when she drinks, she's a fucking nightmare."

"What's so unusual?"

"Fiona didn't come home until Friday afternoon. I waited up all night and pulled a sicky."

"Well at least you showed her you care which is nice."

"I don't appreciate the sarcasm, this is a serious matter."

"Soz."

"Thank you, she apologised for her behaviour, blaming the stress at work along with trying for a baby for her current state of mind as well as hitting the booze."

"Well this is an insightful glimpse into your idealistic life with my ex-best friend, but again, I cannot grasp for the life of me what the fuck this has to do with me. As far as I'm concerned, you've made your bed, now fucking lie in it."

"She slept with someone else Kelly, he charmed his way into her knickers, taking advantage of her heavily intoxicated state, leaving her in the hotel room asleep."

"I take it the wedding's off?"

"Do you mean to be so callous?"

"Sorry, occupational hazard. If you're ringing for the sympathy vote you are barking up the wrong tree."

"I can't get hold of her Kelly, she's not attended work or been in touch with friends, and she's been missing over twenty-four hours now. A mate told me she last saw her getting into a black BMW with a man who matches the descriptions of your suspect in the papers."

"Calm down Darrell, if it's any consolation, there are thousands of men across London who will match his description, but I will give your concerns consideration I promise. Send me details of the area she disappeared."

"Thanks Kelly. How's the new man?"

"I'm not prepared to discuss him with you, bye Darrell."

CHAPTER 49

Three bolts on the cellar door slid with a hefty thump, one, two, three, and the lock clunked twice before the door was flung open in a blaze of artificial, eye-dazzling light. The thud of footsteps above caused a non-negotiable surge of adrenalin, increasing my heartbeat to bass drum status in my chest; this was followed by uncontrollable shaking of the hands, and the sickly feeling now so familiar to me which emerges from the depths of my stomach, assisted by the fluttering of a million wings, leaving a bitter, vile taste in my throat. For the first time, I'm here alone with him; Becky has gone, taken away during the night, probably never to be seen again. She didn't receive her wings or clean clothes, she was unceremoniously hauled up the steps, screaming with the agony of a broken ankle and gone to God knows what fate he had concocted in his sick mind.

I have made an active decision not to provoke this man in any way whatsoever, promoted by an overwhelming urgency of self-preservation. If he speaks to me, I engage with him but keep conversation to a minimum; I'm eating and drinking just enough to keep me alive, conscious in the knowledge that I need to maintain energy levels should the occasion present itself to escape this living hell, but also aware of his adopted method of applying drugs to necessitate his requirements and subdue any protest.

"Hello Helen, my darling, I have a surprise," he bellowed down from the door.

Cowering in the corner of my cage, I pulled the stinking blanket around my neck, not wanting to know what, or more likely who, he had decided to introduce to this world of shit.

"This is Fiona, she's one of the last parts of the jigsaw. The final part of my mission and I can rest in peace. Sorry, I meant to tell you – Becky had to leave, I do hope you two didn't become too close because she's fish food now. The Thames possesses numerous legendary qualities but one which is often overlooked is for hiding bodies or shall we say inconveniences, bodies sounds so callous."

A ripple of emotion shuddered throughout my entire body as I fought back the tears already filling my eyes, determined I would not give him the satisfaction of observing me in this state. Becky continually emphasised "don't give the bastard anything, don't let him witness a weakness". But now she and her mental strength had gone, and another woman was about to begin a nightmare of her very own.

"Now Fiona is lovely, a little feisty, but all the same. So be a good girl and make her welcome. She is an angel like you Helen, and soon girls, this will all be over; my mission will be complete."

CHAPTER 50

An early morning slumber was broken by the abrupt rumble of my iPhone skipping across the bedside table. I grasped thin air twice towards the vicinity of the irritating din before locating the device which I held above my face with a squint to witness a London number streaking across the screen.

"Hello, DCI Kelly Lynch," I said, trying desperately to sound like I hadn't been rudely awakened.

"Good morning Ma'am, Sergeant Peter Jones speaking from the Thames River Police, sorry to call at such an ungodly hour on a Sunday morning."

"Morning sergeant, no problem, what can I do for you?"

"In the early hours of this morning, after reports from late night revellers, we pulled a young woman from the Thames, close to Tower Bridge. She'd been in the water quite some time, but fortunately she is alive, just! The paramedics rushed her to the KCH where the young woman is recovering from the effects of hypothermia and a severely broken ankle which will more than likely require surgery, amongst other minor injuries."

"Great sergeant, but why does this concern my department? Attempted suicide is not exactly our particular forte!"

"The woman is claiming to be Becky Holt, one of your missing women."

"Shit – really?"

"Yes Ma'am."

"Thank you for the information. I'm on my way, can you please send all the details through to this number?"

"No problem."

Within minutes, I had dressed and messaged around the team with Jordan offering a response to meet me at King's College Hospital. Was this our prayers answered? The breakthrough we'd been waiting for? That single miniscule mistake made by our scrupulous killer which might give us a chink of light at the end of the tunnel.

DC Willis stood outside the A&E foyer, leaning against the wrought iron fence to the side of the ambulance bay and drawing on his vape before bellowing a plume high into the drizzly sky. The collar of his long black trench coat was turned up high and a scarlet woollen scarf was wrapped tight around his neck to hamper the icy biting breeze, a chill to which I had paid no attention. My brain was in overdrive, spinning out of control at the prospect of this woman revealing all the facts required to find the man killing these beautiful blondes.

"Morning."

"Morning Jordan, are you ready for this?"

"Born ready boss," he laughed.

"Let's do this."

The teenage receptionist at front of house appeared fresh, gorgeous and worry free considering the early hour, making me feel like a decidedly ancient and weather-beaten forty-something-year-old. Her shoulder-length layered brunette hair lay perfectly in place around her stunning features. A gleaming snow-white smile greeted us until she finished her headset phone conversation. The young lady was most helpful, impressively directing us from memory straight to the private room containing Becky Holt.

The suggested route proved to be an endless maze of identical corridors, magnolia walls, grey laminate floors speckled with brown and black smudges, white swing doors sporting bright green fire exit placards and safety glass windows. Our only solace was the royal blue line painted at waist height on the walls confirming the directions given by the fresh-faced brunette. Nurses and porters buzzed busily up and down the halls, manilla folders full of doctors' notes and X-rays in hand, some taking the opportunity for a bite of a sandwich whilst on the hoof. Two uniform coppers stood sentry outside what we could only conclude was the victim's room.

"Good morning chaps, we are here to talk to Becky Holt," I said, flashing a warrant card.

"Thank you Ma'am, but the doctor expressed strict instructions not to allow any visitors, unfortunately that includes DCIs too. She's had enough strong pain relief to fell a bull elephant and she needs to sleep – doctor's orders. God knows what this woman has been through. When the TVP dragged her from her little dip in the river, the poor woman was all but done in, totally exhausted with half the Thames swilling around her gullet. I'd say she's very lucky, they almost lost her, but paramedics were at the scene in minutes. Doc says she requires rest and recuperation. Sorry." The expression on my face told the story of annoyance and extreme frustration; the minuscule amount of patience I do possess was being tested to the limits.

CHAPTER 51

"Don't worry guys, come in. I can't sleep," came a croaky voice from the other side of the door.

The private room was warm and welcoming, the air stained with the obligatory disinfected taint. A pair of midnight blue NHS blackout curtains were pulled closed, shutting out the horrors of the outside world, with a single bedside lamp providing adequate lighting to negotiate the sparsely furnished room. Directly in front of us, a familiar young lady wearing the standard surgical gown sat up in bed with a pleasant smile of greeting. Becky's face was a hue of purple and green but still her stunning beauty was evident for all to note. On her left hand was a wrap of expertly applied clean bandage and her right foot was slightly elevated in a temporary cast. Only the almighty could appreciate what this woman had been through over the last few weeks, and still she managed another forced smile in our direction as we strode towards her bed.

"Strange, I'm so tired, but my brain and body will not allow me to sleep." I shot a sympathetic expression towards her.

"Hello Becky, fantastic to finally meet you."

"Thank you, I suppose you want all the gory details?"

"In your own time, there's no rush at the minute."

"No, I would like to do this for Helen. She's still with the vile pig and I promised to help her if I got out, so no time like the present."

"Can I be presumptuous and assume this is Helen Richardson?"

"Although we talked, I never found out her surname." She paused to push herself up the bed, pain fleeted across her face.

"Does he have a name, this man?"

"The lunatic uses numerous pseudonyms– David and Nathan are the ones I'm aware of."

"Do you have any idea at all why he is doing this?" I asked.

"For some reason, he keeps spouting on about a mission he must complete, what he means is anybody's guess."

"Did you have prior knowledge of this person before your abduction?" I posed the question to which we already knew the answer, but for investigative purposes, appreciating the process from the victim's point of view helps with the analysis of a killer's mind; it provides a deeper understanding of why he's murdering these women in the style he is and reveals a previously hidden piece of the jigsaw.

"Yes, I'm an estate agent and he booked a house viewing with me. Of course, he appeared utterly charming from the off – eloquent, educated, handsome, fit, forthcoming and easy to talk to. That particular house wasn't quite what he was looking for – it was stunning in every aspect apart from the location and he enquired as to the possibility of locating a property closer to the airport to facilitate his job as an airline pilot. What can I say? I was impressed, what girl wouldn't be?" she shrugged. "After chatting for some time, he took my number and insisted he would be in touch. Later in the evening he rang me, not in a professional capacity, but to ask me out for a drink. I'd split with my fiancé months before and, after a moment of consideration, I thought sod it, why not – jump back on the horse so to speak. In total, we met three times within a week. He was a joy to be with, taking me to expensive restaurants, buying me a gorgeous bouquet. I should have realised something was amiss with him – how many blokes buy a girl flowers nowadays? No offence intended."

"None taken and a fair point well made. Can you remember the places you visited with him?" Jordan continued.

"Maybe later, I'll need to think. My head's still a bit fuzzy, but I can tell you he always paid with cash."

"Don't worry Becky, please carry on in your own time," I suggested.

"Following several what I would consider exceptional dates, I slept with him before he vanished from the face of the earth, so his ruse worked. The only thoughts I could muster were that I had been well and truly played, and I wouldn't lay eyes on him again. It turned out I was wrong – weeks later he reappeared out of the blue, all apologetic." She paused. "Did you find Janet?"

"Yes, was she with you?"

"The twat managed to break her, bless her. She became a total mess in the last few hours. This animal kept us caged in a cellar, although to be fair he always provided fresh food and water and occasionally he would let us shower. But on one occasion when he paid us a visit Janet received her wings directly in front of me."

"We've seen the wings – but why?" said Jordan, turning the palms of his hands towards the ceiling, emphasising his question.

"I really don't know. That day for some reason he wanted me to witness my fate so to speak. As you can imagine, it was fucking horrendous. The poor woman screamed the fucking place down, and I was completely helpless, there was nothing I could do for her apart from beg him to stop. In her heart at that moment, she realised it was the end for her. The horrible bastard showed no sympathy or empathy towards her, nothing. He's obsessed with his mission to release us from our lives of evil and become heavenly."

"Can you tell us anything with respect to the place where he kept you – the area, town, distinguishing features?" Jordan asked.

"No sorry, I can't. I guess he drugged us with something, I'm not sure how I got to the cellar where he kept us. I can't remember anything about the night he took me, apart from jumping in his car for us to talk. My first memory is of waking up feeling like shit, cold, confused and imprisoned. A stark realisation hit me like a lorry as I realised my predicament with the recognition I was in a whole world of crap and had absolutely no influence on the situation. Find Helen, won't you? Save her."

"Let me assure you our priority is to locate the missing woman ASAP which is why we require as much detail as possible from you Becky, anything at all which might give us the single snippet of information we need to finish this and catch this bastard. How did you end up in the Thames?"

"Every day without fail he leaves the house. The man is notably routine based – OCD springs to mind. Alone in the gloom you learn to remember his actions. He feeds and waters us first thing in the morning, checks the cage doors are secure, boots up his PC and casts an eye over his emails; once finished, he climbs the wooden stairs two at a time, slams his cellar door shut and locks it behind him. The lock clunks twice before three bolts slide into place one by one. For the rest of the day we sat in darkness, an endless cloak of fucking darkness with only a small splinter of light penetrating under the door at the top of the stairs. Any social interaction was limited to feeding time or for us to receive our wings. Apparently, an essential element to liberate us to the heavens. From his perspective, conversing with us meant we were human, and he couldn't allow any sort of relationship to bloom – he wants to view us as prey, inanimate objects in place to assist him to complete his mission."

"What is his mission?" I asked.

"As I said earlier, god only knows."

"Sorry, please continue."

"Thanks. One morning, he didn't lock my cage securely and I managed to escape. Initially, I tried to help Helen, I tried so desperately to help her, but I couldn't muster the strength. An idea struck us to log onto his computer, a chance to inform somebody, anybody, about our nightmare situation, albeit slight. This was the point when we discovered he had been watching us the entire time, our every move, all the conversations we thought were private, our plans to escape – he was big brother. The reason he always appeared to be one step ahead of us. I sprinted up the steps in the near dark to the only exit to be met with a sadistic smile beaming across his face, and a huge black snarling dog by his side. As I fled into the darkness, I tripped down the stairs from top to bottom, hence the bruises. Stupid cow – I must have looked completely pathetic crawling about, crying and wailing in pain. He stood over me laughing."

"Did he use the computer for anything else other than emails, that you are aware of – browsing for example?"

"To find girls, he uses social media and dating sites."

"Which means he must have profiles, we'll have the techies investigate," I said to Jordan.

"Was he violent towards you? Did he beat you or anything?" DC Willis pressed on; my concentration was amiss for a second as my mobile buzzed in my coat pocket.

"No, he never laid a finger on us, in his mind, our perfection was his only concern. The man never showed any interest in us until those last few hours. Janet was given her wings, allowed a warm shower, dressed to look stunning, released from her cage to eat at the table, which was unusual, and afterwards he took her away. I didn't see her again. And how did I end up in the Thames? I do not have a clue. Amongst his fits of laughter, he informed me I was broken, imperfect and simply would not do; all I can remember is drinking some water followed by the police pulling me out of the river."

"This depends on what perspective you take on your last few weeks, but you can consider yourself an extremely lucky lady; it probably doesn't appear so now, battered, bruised and in a hospital bed, but at least you are still here," I explained in a vain attempt to humour her.

"I would do the lottery tonight if I were you," Jordan said raising a smile.

"Finding Helen would do," Becky replied, tears welling in her crystal blue eyes.

CHAPTER 52

Annoyingly, my mobile buzzed in my pocket yet again; the joys of modern technology began to test my patience.

"Excuse me," I said heading out of the room momentarily, leaving Jordan to continue with the interview, scribbling childlike scrawl on his notepad which is only decipherable by himself. The information Ms Holt had begun to relay was vital to the case – without a doubt, this woman was providing us with a valuable insight into the workings of our killer's mind.

The screen revealed text messages, three in total, one from Darrell, "*Any news on Fiona yet?*", which I ignored for the time being, and two from Ben. "*Have you remembered you are supposed to be picking me up xx*" Balls, no I hadn't, and a second message an hour later. "*Don't worry Kell, taken the morning off, but if you could pick me up about dinner time that would be great xxx*"

"*Shit so sorry I forgot, got called into work early. I can run out for you now if you want or lunch will be fine.*"

An instantaneous reply vibrated in the palm of my hand. "*Didn't fancy working today ha ha, and walking dog now, day off I think*"

A thumbs up emoji and two kisses were sent in response. Jordan popped his head around the door.

"Ma'am, Becky is offering to give a photo fit. I'll call the team in, she's in no state to attend the station."

"Thanks, sorry about my bloody mobile, the damn thing hasn't stopped all day," I explained as a phone alert sounded once again. "For god's sake, what now?"

"Mum we forgot it's teacher training day at school, not got keys. What y want me to do????"

"Oh bugger, I'm at hospital with a witness ATM, can you go to the office? I should be back just after dinner time when I've dealt with this"

"No problem, I'll go chat to Sally xx c y soon mum"

"Behave yourself she's too old for you"

"ha ha ha xxx"

For the rest of the morning, we progressed the cross-examination of the victim, despite the fact her exhausted, dishevelled appearance indicated we should consider letting her rest, but memories and facts fade with time. The first twenty-four hours of any investigation are the most important. Slowly and surely, we began to unlock doors. This battered broken female revealed valuable knowledge regarding the man behind these kidnappings and killings, providing a profile not dissimilar to the one the LSCIU had concocted from the miniscule amount of evidence presented. That of a man who so desperately required capturing. All our team were aware through bitter experience that every single drop of information we could squeeze out of this woman now would hopefully save lives in the future – and with a bit of luck that of Helen Richardson.

Exiting the ward with an assurance to the victim of "I'll be back soon," I left DC Willis in attendance awaiting e-fit artists for her description. I headed back towards the exit, glad to be out of the stifling heat hospitals endeavour to promote. The science behind the facial recognition techniques is amazingly accurate nowadays compared to a few years ago when they all resembled creatures from an alien planet. Team optimism was on the up as we knew that once the e-fit was complete we could reveal this to the public, certain in the knowledge that we would be overwhelmed with a plethora of additional information. My phone vibrated once more, the annoyance inside me started to boil over. It was an unknown number, not an uncommon occurrence when the unsympathetic press are probing for an inkling of story.

"*A house of birds on a mound of trees, this is where you need to be, with this in mind you'll see, today's the day I set my angels free*"

"Shit, the bastard!"

"I beg your pardon Madam," an ageing innocent balding man with spindly features slopping a mop around the floor behind a slippery surface sign questioned my behaviour.

"So sorry, I apologise," I said, acknowledging my foul language whilst darting out of the automatic door into the cool refreshing air with phone stuck to my ear.

"Hello Kell, what do you want now?" answered Gaz, joviality in his voice.

"The arsehole messaged me."

"Who?"

"The killer! *A house of birds on a mound of trees, this is where you need to be, with this in mind you'll see, today's the day I set my angels free* is what the message reads."

"How the fuck did he get your mobile number?"

"God knows, we can worry about that later. Find me a fucking bird house and a mound of trees before another woman dies."

CHAPTER 53

Milling around the hospital front, unable to settle in one spot for more than a few seconds, these are the times when I miss smoking. A young man with a mullet of ginger hair and an impressive Viking-esque beard drew a deep breath on his freshly lit cigarette, the familiar aroma drifting towards me on the breeze. For a brief second, as I marched back and forth across the external hospital foyer, I savoured the soothing bouquet of tobacco and nicotine which was once a necessity in my life. This was an exercise unknown to myself, adopted by my subconscious mind to ease my nervous tension and anxiety whilst awaiting the vital information required from the office. The automatic doors became an annoyance, obediently kicking into action and opening and closing with each of my passes, so I stood with my back towards the wall, within touching distance of the red head who glanced up with a sweet smile.

My focus returned to the works mobile and the killer's cryptic message for the hundredth time, reading the words over and over in silence, praying for something to jump out at me from the jumbled verse, while simultaneously hoping for another dose of passive smoke with the calming effects the addictive drugs provide. Taxi cabs adorned with advertising slogans, company logos and contact numbers in all the colours of the rainbow and various script styles pounded the rank with a constant flow of patients, hospital bound for a multitude of ailments. The blur of flashing blue lights pulling into an ambulance bay grasped my attention from my intense world of thought, its cargo, a fragile old lady with cuts and bruises to her face and a sling supporting a painful left arm.

A suited gentleman walked with purpose from the extortionate hospital carpark towards the entrance. Taking a second glance, I recognised his face in an instant, with its broad chin, bent nose and grey grizzled cropped hair. Robert Dent is the officer trained and appointed to produce e-fit images within our area, a person I have only met on one other occasion. For a moment, he passed me by, continuing into the foyer before turning his head with a quizzical glance.

"DCI Lynch?"

"Correct, Robert, I presume?"

"Yes, are we in here Ma'am?" he said pointing a hand through the hospital doors.

"We are, how long do you think you'll be?"

"The process can take hours depending on the descriptive powers and the recollection abilities of the victim or witness. I am hoping this won't take too long. I'm guessing Ms Holt will find zero problems with her ability to recall facial features considering the time she has spent in the presence of the person in question."

"Let's hope not, I need to circulate this image into the public domain ASAP."

I headed back through the automatic doors into the disinfected subtropical climate before the temptation to scrounge a smoke from the ginger dude overwhelmed me, breaking months of unblemished will power. An uncomfortable plastic chair in the waiting room down the corridor from Becky Holt took the weight off my aching feet whilst I awaited the results of our victim's powers of description. As usual, impatience and boredom engulfed my mental state as the minutes morphed into hours, causing an impromptu flick through the gossip-filled glossy magazines containing irritating, untalented nobodies promoted to fame, fortune and ultimate stardom for achieving fuck all other than being annoying gob shites on some over publicised reality show. Any interest I possessed in the magazines rapidly dwindled at the fear of the brain cell destruction they might cause; I opted instead to concentrate on the considerably more interesting sparrows going about their business in the shrubs and trees through the waiting room window, alongside checking the endless stream of emails and barrage of messages occupying my time. The door to Becky's room opened and DC Dent appeared with a smile.

"The young lady has provided us with something substantial." He paused. "I'm optimistic the image will be an accurate representation of the suspect, she became extremely insistent with certain features."

"Thank you, has the witness statement been signed?"

"Yes, all done and dusted."

"The last thing we need are any slip ups. When can I expect the results?"

"As soon as I'm back in the office I will process the data onto the police files and email your team, within the hour."

"Brilliant, thanks."

The narrow, reinforced glass panel of the fire door revealed Jordan still scrutinising Becky Holt and sitting in a chair far more comfortable than the arse numbing plastic I had been parked on. I paused for a moment to admire the bravery of this young female and the pleasing effect she has on the eye. Considering the bruising and toll of her ordeal, an undeniable beauty was evident with a confidence and sparkle returning to her by the minute. Ms Holt glanced up and spotted my mug through the glass, alerting my colleague to my presence. I waved for him to join me and smiled for effect.

"Yes, boss what can I do for you?"

"The bastard's messaged me, look here," I said, showing him the text from our killer, headed unknown number.

"What the fuck does he mean? Let's take a seat and write the words down. I see things better on paper," Jordan suggested, taking a section of plastic bench in a small waiting area outside the ward. "Read it out Kell," he insisted, scrawling in his pocket notebook in his infantile scribble as I recited the text with emphasised care.

"He wants us to find him, that's blatantly obvious, I'm positive this is what the message is about, but he doesn't want to provide an easy route and spoil his day. So, mound of trees, let's break the verse down, trees? Copse, woods, thicket, forest, jungle. And pile, hump, hill, ridge, bank, forest bank?" the DC suggested with a quizzical glance.

"Forest Hill, shit, Forest Hill!" The penny dropped. "But where?"

"Well boss, a bird house is a dovecote, aviary, cage, roost or nest maybe?"

"Correct," I replied as Jordan busily typed into his mobile office, his face focused on the technological miracle held within the palm of one hand.

"I've got it Kell – Aviary House, Forest Hill, it's got to be worth a visit surely?"

CHAPTER 54

An old-fashioned ring tone echoed across the office breaking the silence induced by the concentration required for our task and the shock from the call received from the boss an hour previous.

"DC Glover, can I help?"

"Hi Sally, Sergeant Banks, front of house speaking. I have a Mr Jacob Lynch here to visit you?"

"Send him through please," I instructed, glad of a small but well-deserved break from cracking the coded verse sent by the killer.

Within minutes the office door flew open and the young man strolled through it, sporting his usual infectious broad dimpled grin which in the future, when older than his tender fifteen years, will surely render most women an instant gibbering wreck.

"Hello gorgeous, how are you today and what are you doing later?" he said perching himself on my desk and dropping his school bag by my office chair.

"To be honest you are a little cutey, that's a fact, however the other undeniable specifics I am obliged to highlight before your affections for me spiral out of control are that I am way too old for you and also married."

"Little cutey, ew gross," he replied, his beaming smile turning to an expression of utter repulsion.

"Thank your lucky stars boy, she'd suck you in and spit you out in bubbles."

"Cheers Gary, I don't think Jacob needs to hear such graphic information."

"I'm not bothered Sal, and you know where I am when you're stuck for a little male company," he offered with a cheeky wink alongside his model smile which will break hearts at some point in the not-so-distant future.

"I appreciate the offer, but in all honesty, I can't imagine your mother greeting that sentiment with such overwhelming enthusiasm."

"Your loss babe," he said heading in the direction of the window. "Where is Mum?"

"With a witness," Gaz interjected.

"Will she be long?"

"Anyone's guess mate. Sally, the email from Robert Dent has arrived."

"Well let's take a peek then." I clicked the icon resembling an envelope to open my mailbox with Jacob still glaring onto the street below at the ant-sized people running the rat race.

The phone rang out on Gaz's desk; "the boss" he mouthed and answered immediately.

"Hello Ma'am, yes Kell, I have been studying the message, unfortunately not come up with owt yet though. OK, we'll be about forty minutes, don't go in without us. I'll arrange some back up en route."

"We on the move Gaz?"

"Yeah, we think Jordan is onto something, Forest Hill, we need to go now."

"I'll wait here, shall I?" Jacob suggested with an element of a sarcastic tone.

"We'll sort something out for you mate," Gary promised whilst retrieving his coat from the wooden stand in the corner of the office.

"Bye Sal, remember, anytime," Jacob said, blowing a kiss my way.

"Thank you, but no thanks – your mum would string me up."

"One more thing."

"I'm serious sunshine, we have to move – this is important police business."

"Why do you have a picture of James on your PC monitor?"

"What?

"James Harrison, him on your desktop."

"Come again boy," Gaz quizzed, concern etched across his face.

"Yeah, this bloke on the screen – he's Mum's new squeeze."

"Are you *sure* Jacob?" I emphasised the word sure.

"Of course man, a spit."

"Thanks pal," I said, locking my computer with a glance towards Gary; shock and panic pulsed through my body in equal proportions.

"Stay put, we'll get some house keys to you," I promised, cool and calm as I dashed out of the office on the coat tails of DS Turner.

"We need to warn the boss, Gary."

"Trying now," he replied. "Shit, the answer phone."

"Let me go back and run the boss's man friend through the database, see if I can dig up some dirt. We need an insight into what we may be dealing with here."

Gaz stood pondering the situation for a second. "Go find out what you can and keep us informed," he agreed.

CHAPTER 55

Before I started diving into the former world of the gaffer's boyfriend, Jacob and his adorable persona were despatched to the waiting area front of house under the strict supervision of the desk sergeant. The last thing I needed was for our young mate to notice any of our intensity and uncertain concerns for the safety of his mum. With Jacob safely stowed away out of sight, I began my search and half an hour later I had enough information to raise serious concerns regarding the safety of the boss.

"Hello Gary, how are you getting on?"

"Shit! There's been an RTA en route, a three-car pile-up and an overturned lorry, it's fucking grid locked. We aren't moving anywhere for a while, even on blues. How about you?"

"All I can say is holy fuck. Seriously, we need to find Kelly and any others ASAP, this is worse than we had anticipated if that's possible with a murder case."

"Bollox, they're starting to clear the wreckage now. I'm hoping to be underway in the next twenty minutes or half hour according to the officers on scene, but even on blues it'll take us a while to reach Forest Hill."

"I'm on the way Gary. I've managed to round up a van full of muscle and alert the firearms unit to attend," I said, jumping into the passenger side of a marked car with a squad of uniform officers togged up to the eyeballs ready for action in a riot van at our rear.

CHAPTER 56

D C Willis and I viewed the location in question from behind a once cared for hawthorn hedge, its dense branches now providing ample cover. Aviary House was situated on the outskirts of Forest Hill, a leafy residential area popular for its trendy cafes and bars and a brace of small but essential nature reserves within spitting distance of Dulwich Woods. The impressive, detached residence, an old farmhouse barn conversion, was strategically placed towards the end of a fifty-metre meandering gravel driveway riddled with intrusive weeds and topped with a sea of mosses and discarded leaves forming rotting banks to the outside edges of the drive. All of which was enclosed by a canopy of intertwined willows and untended shrubs giving a natural tunnel effect which I can only assume would be greatly exaggerated through the summer months when all the branches are laden with fauna.

From our secure roadside hide, we observed the plot. The perimeter of the property bit into an invading treeline containing a plethora of ancient oak, beech and horse chestnut trees and pockets of bramble. To the opposite side of the vast grounds, a ten-foot wooden fence provided privacy from the local golf course; both borders were separated by sprawling gardens, once the pride and joy of their owners now an overgrown jungle where mother nature had reinstated her claim to the land.

Attached to the right of the main body of the house was what could be classed as redundant maids' quarters. A set of French doors opened onto a flat-topped roof leading to a balcony surrounded by a two-foot brick wall with charcoal coping stones to match the rest of the premisses. To the rear of the roof was a barbeque area with a pagoda covered in climbing plants, possibly clematis, making it impossible to see into the wooden structure. The whole set up was partially obscuring the front of the house which was adorned with a huge ornate cross, indicating a place of worship. To the left of the building was an enormous single-storey double garage with one door open, revealing a black BMW displaying private plates, which were legible with a squint of the eyes.

"Well, well, well – a black BMW. I'll run those through ANPR," suggested Jordan, also observing the vehicle and reading my mind, putting two and two together and returning to our car in a stooped walk.

"Good idea," I replied, acknowledging the process would take several minutes, giving time for the support team to materialise. My eyes never left the house as I waited for a sign, some movement, a light, anything to reveal occupants within Aviary House.

Moments later, Jordan appeared at my side again.

"Nothing Kell, the plate doesn't exist," he said, disappointment written on his face.

"Surprise, surprise."

"The support team is on the way but stuck in traffic. What do you suggest boss – wait for the big boys to arrive?"

"No, let's make a move, we don't want to arrive too late for Helen, presuming we're not too late already. As you say, the backup team shouldn't be too much longer."

The skies above darkened with ominous rain clouds as I turned my attention to the entrance of the plot. A pair of neglected wooden gates with peeling white paint, green algae and lichens stood fully open, secured by a metal hook attached to a small wooden post obscured from sight by a wall of thicket. A check for cameras was carried out before we approached, not wanting to highlight our presence and give the advantage to the enemy so to speak. DC Willis spotted a mailbox attached to the gatepost, hidden by the intrusive hawthorn hedgerow; several letters and a heap of spam mail were jammed through the unimpressive letter slot which no doubt was intended to be emptied daily.

"Samuel Cline, never heard of him."

"He might be the previous owner, or our man isn't a Nathan after all," I suggested.

Hugging the left-hand side of the driveway, we kept close to an enormous wild buddleia for cover as the gravel crunched beneath our feet. Through a tangle of branches and twigs, the house was partially visible, revealing an illuminated downstairs room, one which I had not noted from the roadside recce. A silent right-hand signalled for Jordan to stop and crouch behind the bushes which were braced for spring to bring life into their bare stems.

A figure stood in the ground floor window but the distance between us was too far to identify any distinguishing features with the naked eye. A cloak of silence descended over the garden, the bird tweets and song seemingly vanished; even the breeze died, inducing an eerie stillness, apart from the distant hum of the motorway traffic and the adrenalin-induced elevated heartbeat thudding throughout my body. Who was the silhouetted figure in the window I wondered? Was this our man, the illusive killer of beautiful women, the person who had consumed my entire life for months?

"Ma'am, not wanting to appear impetuous but should we move

on?" DC Willis whispered from his camouflaged spot. I turned my head away from the dark figure for an instant.

"You might want to lose the bright red scarf if we want to remain inconspicuous."

"Sorry boss. And is your phone on silent?"

"Yeah, no signal anyway."

"No, me neither, we're on our own here Kell."

"You alright with this Jordan?"

"Yes, come on, let's find Helen," he replied, stuffing the scarlet woollen muffler into his coat pocket and zipping it securely.

"Do you think we should wait for back up to arrive?"

"It might be too late by then Ma'am."

CHAPTER 57

Without any idea as to when our support team might show up, I made a snap decision. We doubled back to the wooden gates and diverted inside the hawthorn hedgerow, keeping to the boundary of the plot and utilising the abundance of overgrown natural camouflage to remain concealed from the house. I was elated I had opted for sensible flat shoes this morning rather than anything with a heel as we trudged our way through the undergrowth around the perimeter of the grounds.

A former lawn appeared in our path and we sprinted the short distance through the long damp open swathe in the direction of the ancient woodland, ducking for sanctuary behind the vast girth of an aged oak tree and taking a moment to gather our thoughts and plan our next move. From this position, the back of the house was clearly visible. In parallel to the building lay a spit of land, once a veg patch I guessed, now a jungle of dying nettles, sticky beak, ivy and thistles invading the rotting wooden trestles left in place adjacent to two plastic compost bins and a dilapidated shed, all consumed by the sea of green. Towards the far end of the house a set of French doors opened onto a small patio area with a rusting glass-topped table containing evidence of life in the form of beer cans and an ashtray. A wind-beaten parasol with a sun-faded flower pattern fluttered in the breeze and four equally weather-damaged chairs sat randomly spaced around the set up.

Jordan took the lead, darting across a gravelled expanse towards the open garage with me in hot pursuit as an icy rain began to fall from the sky. Our eyes adjusted to the dim interior revealing a relatively empty space with only the usual garden implements and lawnmower present. All the items sat thick with dust and cobwebs, an indication as to the last time they were used. The work bench and a tool rack on the adjacent wall were clear of mess or all the other crap we tend to accumulate in garages – unwanted clutter from a family home kept on the off chance it might come in useful someday, only to end up in the bin next time we spring-clean. Jordan pointed out a shotgun central to the bench with polished walnut stocks, fore ends, a decorative chrome action and matte black barrels.

The black BMW sparkled in the fading daylight. I leaned forward, hands cupped around my eyes, glancing through the windows but taking care not to touch the car which could sound an alarm. As with the outer, the internal of the car was immaculate, no visible evidence to suggest who may be the owner or what sort of life they led, and more significantly whether this car was the one we observed Declan Aikin socialising with on CCTV before his ultimate demise.

Past the car was a single teal door connecting directly to the house. From beyond came a clatter, sending our hearts jumping into our throats; both DC Willis and I crouched in an instant behind the shining sports car in a tense game of hide-and-seek, my pulse at bursting point. Jordan signalled for me to stay put and crawled on hands and knees to the rear wheels, casting a cautious eye in the direction of the house; more commotion caused him to recoil back to cover.

"Any ideas?" I asked in a whisper; a silent shrug of the shoulders from my colleague was my only reply.

He leaned back on the rear wheel, holding his phone to the heavens and desperately searching for a signal with a despondent shake of his head. Silence ensued for several minutes and my mind raced for a strategy that would get us out of our predicament. An overwhelming impulse hit me like a wall to find Helen before, well, she became another statistic.

"Fuck this!" I shouted, jumping to my feet, my police cosh in hand, and heading for the partition door with purpose.

The DC followed despite the surprise and concern etched across his face in equal proportions. The pair of us were stopped in our tracks by a deep thunderous growl echoing throughout the garage. Before the aspect of self-preservation registered within my brain, an enormous thick-set charcoal dog with a patch of tan across its chest burst through the connecting door, a picture of slobbering savagery straining tendons, and an ear-bursting cacophony of noise with snapping bright white teeth cut short of taking lumps out of my face by a solid chain secured by a muscular tattooed arm and the face of a man extremely familiar to me, a face I had fallen for, the face of James Harrison. My cosh dropped to the floor.

CHAPTER 58

"Sit boy, quiet," he instructed, an authoritative tug of the chain enforcing the command. The aggressive persona the dog portrayed so convincingly was dispelled in an instant by his master's voice.

"My dear Kelly, welcome to my parents' humble abode," he said, his spare arm guiding our eyes throughout the garage and to the house beyond him. "I did wonder how long you would take to solve my little riddle."

For a moment, I stood aghast, unable to muster any words. A foggy confusion descended, hindering my brain function before years of detective instinct brought clarity to the fuzz.

"What the hell is going on here? This thing isn't Moody – where is he?"

"No, you're quite correct, this isn't Moody. That dog served his purpose and now he's gone, a shame because we'd bonded tremendously. And come on, isn't it blatantly obvious DCI Lynch why you are here? I wanted you to find me, you are part of my mission."

"Your mission?" Jordan spouted up with a sarcastic titter. "And what is that exactly?"

"Silence please young man. You have no business being here. You are but an unfortunate consequence of this situation. An unanticipated blip, and I will deal with you as the inconvenience you are later." He glared in our direction, removing the shackles from his beast which sat obediently, panting, his deep chocolate penetrating eyes focused in our direction.

DC Willis spun on a heel and took off with a burst of athleticism I have never witnessed before, his tan leather brogues toiling for traction amongst the moss-covered gravel. His intent was to reach the security of the car and the fixed police radio within. Both James and the dog remained unmoved by this bid for freedom, watching as my colleague hurtled down the driveway, a blur of arms and legs moving towards the wooden gates with surprising speed. The mutt glanced to his owner and with only a nod of the head, the mountainous hound gave chase, eating up the ground between himself and Jordan with consummate ease, silent as a predator on its approach before the inevitable panicked screams from my friend and the sounds of a savage attack were heard, obscured from view by the base of the buddleia used earlier to hide our presence. A cacophony of snarling bites supported by yells of pain echoed high within the treetops. I watched as James's face transformed from a stern and concentrated glare to a broad smile spreading sadistically across his chiselled face, now glowing with pride and joy at the work of his beast; it was like a parent's elated celebrations at the performance of a child crossing the winning line arms aloft on sports day or scoring the winning goal in the cup final.

"Stop him, please." His piercing ocean blue eyes met mine with utter disdain and a hatred spread across his face. It was an expression never witnessed in any of our previous encounters, a million miles away from the man who had become familiar to me – and dare I say it, the man I had grown to love.

Three toots on a whistle halted the vicious assault with immediate effect.

"Loki, here," he commanded. The only sound evident through the entire garden was the whimpering of my DC and the paws of the monstrous loyal dog crunching on the gravel as he returned to his owner's side. "Good boy, sit and stay. I'll fetch the boy. I wouldn't move if I were you."

CHAPTER 59

"Jesus, why are so many fucking idiots on the roads? Can't they see these blues flashing in their mirrors? People must drive with their fucking eyes shut. Move knob head. Fuck this. Take the next right please."

"This is the quickest route DC Glover," the PC replied from the driver's seat.

"Not today, not in this carnage officer. Head for the A2 and pick up the B207, and let's not fuck about, get your foot down – people are in trouble."

The engine of the marked car roared into life with the riot van full of muscle following close behind, a blare of blues and twos still in full force after sitting in congestion for far too long to be comfortable. The vast majority of the public react to a speeding convoy of police vehicles favourably, but as with any incident, one or two dick heads panic or think their business is more important than everyone else's, and all those prats appeared to be out and about in abundance today.

"Out the way moron. I wish we had time to nick the bastard, who the fuck does he think he is? You are an idiot!" I bellowed out of the window to an apologetic wave from a suit in his Mercedes who had decided to park on double yellows, blocking the narrow side road despite the cacophony of noise and blazing lights behind him implying he should move. The familiar ring tone of my mobile sounded out several times before I located the device in my jacket pocket, buried beneath the obligatory stab vest.

"DS Turner – any news?"

"No, we still haven't managed to establish any communication with the gaffer or Willis."

"Can we triangulate their signals?"

"We've tried with no success. Kelly mentioned an Aviary House; according to our info, there's only one place with that name in the Forest Hill area. I suggest we head in that direction and hope for the best."

"Agreed." I typed in the new postcode and refreshed the destination. "If we make a clear run, our sat nav is predicting an eta of twenty-seven minutes."

"I'm estimating approximately the same, but traffic is shit. And Sally, listen to me – don't enter the premises gung-ho prior to our arrival even with an army of beefy bobbies behind you. A full assessment of the situation will be required before we commence so as not to endanger any members of the public or our own. I recommend once you locate the suspect's house, you surround it but keep out of sight. If we alert them to our presence, we may induce panicked and erratic behaviour."

"Understood Gary. However, I'll tell you now for fuck all, if they make a break for it or the boss manages to contact us, I'm going in, end of story."

"Sally, I'm tell you to hold your position whatever the situation, do you hear me?"

"Soz Sarg, you're breaking up."

"Sally for fuck's sake, wait for more back up – that's a direct order."

"Bad signal Sarg, sorry I missed that." I hung up with a smile across my face knowing full well I would, if necessary, ignore everything the DS had instructed.

CHAPTER 60

The stranger I thought was my lover, a man I had trusted to introduce into my family, escorted me from the garage like a bouncer removing a drunk from his precious venue and led me into a pristine, spacious oak-look kitchen. He locked the partition door securely behind us. A strong grip on my elbow steered me in the right direction while Jordan was encouraged by a single low rumble from his canine guard. The young DC had recovered sufficiently from his ordeal at the jaws of the beast not to require assistance despite a large gaping wound bleeding profusely down the right cheek of his face and copious puncture injuries on both hands dripping onto the tiled floor; numerous protection wounds on his forearms stained his slate jacket, showing claret through ragged rips and tears, not to mention additional injuries to his legs and torso.

Soft classical music played in the background from a radio placed in the corner of a worktop next to a brushed steel American style fridge. Several items of post lay in a neat pile close by, the uppermost addressed to *Samuel Cline, Aviary House, Forest Hill, London.* A breakfast bar with three high stools ran along the partition wall to the garage and a single wicker hug chair with views of the garden stood next to an enormous glossy cheese plant positioned strategically to ensure the optimum hours of indirect sunlight it craves.

"Who is Samuel Cline?" I asked, only to be met with a scornful glance and silence. "Did you kill the two street kids you bastard?"

"It was, unfortunately, a consequence of their own actions. I couldn't risk our mission being compromised. Now shut up."

Loki took to his bed directly in front of the French doors rendering one escape route option obsolete, sitting without any command being given, an air of aggressive intent present in his eyes.

James Harrison opened a cupboard drawer and removed a small bag of zip ties, first securing the wrists of Jordan who showed little in the way of resistance. The hands of my colleague shook vigorously, shock from his prolonged attack at the jaws of the black beast manifesting itself. A glance towards the French doors was met by a Loki glare; a deep meaningful rumble manifested within him as if reading my mind and offering sufficient warning not to approach. My hands were secured behind me, the ties painfully cutting into my flesh.

"Don't even contemplate escape. I would hate for my friend to destroy your beautiful face – and he will, with a click of the fingers." A tender hand lifted my chin and he gazed into my eyes. Only the eyes of James were no longer the warm, inviting, loving baby blues of the man I am so familiar with, but hollow, grey, lifeless pictures of evil, devoid of any of the affection, emotion or compassion he had once shown me.

CHAPTER 61

An unusual amount of activity from the house above stirred my senses into life as I sat in my cage; curiosity flooded over me – why all the noise? Dogs barking, screams, movement and I'm positive I heard a woman's voice – one would presume another woman will be joining us imminently, although judging by the amount of commotion, she's no pushover.

"Fiona, shush." She's wept since minute one – surely the woman has no tears left. I suppose some people manage this unpredictable godforsaken situation better than others and some don't handle it at all. It's not as if your teachers, parents or friends can prepare you for being kidnapped by a nut job and locked in a cage awaiting certain death.

Above us, an all-too-familiar sound startled me from my world of thought as the three bolts slid open and the lock clunked twice before the door swung open spraying a column of natural light across the cellar. Fiona's whimpering ceased and she held her breath and began to shake uncontrollably, cowering into the furthest corner of her cage.

"Wakey, wakey ladies, time to go," came a booming voice from a silhouetted figure as the fluorescent light flashed and buzzed reluctantly before bursting into life revealing a recognisable man. This person possessed the same gym-toned body as Dave but in combination with a stranger's voice and mannerisms, and a distinct lack of oriental artwork adorning his muscular arms.

"You're not Dave."

"Correct, and neither is my brother usually. Take me as the bad cop if you like. Get up and fucking move, it's time to go," he demanded, releasing the cage doors. His words were ones I had hoped never to hear and now I felt numb.

All the features of this man's face appeared identical to our captor – short mousey hair, the crystal sea blue eyes, chiselled chin, all of which would induce an undeniable instant attraction if the situation was drastically different. All the similarities were astounding apart from one deep thick red scar meandering a path around the right eye socket, and the aggressive attitude he portrayed. As commanded, I left my cell; a sickness pulsed from the pit of my stomach through my entire being from head to toe, each inch of skin and strand of hair.

"Stand there and don't fuck me about or you will get hurt," the person said, clamping my throat with a muscular hand to emphasise his words and power over me. The lack of oxygen to my brain brought about a panicked grasp of his chunky forearm and bright lights began to sparkle before my eyes. With a smirk on his face and an annoying air of arrogance, he released me to fall to the ground, holding my neck and gasping like a stricken fish.

"Get out," he shouted, rattling the bars of Fiona's humble abode, his patience lacking. The new woman cowered further into the corner of her cage. "I said fucking move bitch." The monster leaned in, taking a handful of her stunning golden blonde locks and dragging her kicking and screaming from the sanctity of her safe place. A backhand slap calmed her noise and he cast a scornful warning glance towards me to behave. Her sweater sleeve was used sparingly to absorb a single trickle of scarlet rolling down her beautiful face from her nose.

"Hands out now." I looked into the eyes of the woman standing by my side, searching for any fight within, but none manifested itself, and reluctantly we succumbed to his instructions. He took one hand, spinning me around and forcing me face first against my cage before securing my arms behind me. The palm of his hand caressed the cheeks of my backside and between my legs. I could feel his face close to mine and smell his stale coffee breath.

"Stay bitch," he whispered in my ear.

Footsteps skipped down the cellar stairs two by two indicating another presence was joining our merry little band.

"Joseph, what the fuck are you doing? You know these girls need to be perfect, and you're touching this one up for god's sake, and what are the marks around her neck?"

"Sorry."

"Why is the other one bleeding from her nose? Father will not be pleased with you. Learn to temper yourself until the time is right."

"Sorry James, they fucked me about," he lied before hauling us by the shoulder to face both men, standing side by side. Twins – Jesus, why didn't I sus that one before now? The brother James is my solicitor Dave Roe in his full glorious form, ink-covered muscles bursting from a clinging white t-shirt, the person who lured all the women into a false sense of security, into bed and here to this hell hole. A brief look in his direction was met with zero reaction. I'm not sure what I expected, but something – a smile, a glimpse of arrogance, a jolt of sympathy? But nothing, just deadpan and serious.

"I know brother. This will all be over soon, and we will be reunited with our family. Take the angels to the place, everything is ready," he assured his twin, placing an oversized hand on his shoulder.

CHAPTER 62

I lay on the floor of the rooftop balcony above the crucifix I had observed earlier from the roadside recce. In front of me, a two-foot surrounding wall loomed over the driveway and to my rear was the barbeque set-up where a chilling gust whipped a spiral of dust into the air. Lying face down, I struggled against the bindings on my hands and feet, only succeeding in slicing the plastic ties deeper into my wrists and ankles and producing a series of sore grazes in the soft skin of my cheekbone from the sharp gravel of the roofing felt. A tight gag restricted my breathing, which was edging on panic, and prevented any means of raising help or alerting the incoming team of not only our position but also the predicament.

A brief image of DC Willis covered in dog bites and in pain popped into my head with a wave of emotion. I wondered what had happened to him. Was he safe or had he been left in an undignified pathetic heap, still bleeding from the savage attack, exposed to the mercy of the elements? In an instant, my own fragility became overwhelming, raising my pulse an octave and inducing another futile attempt to escape the bindings which only cut further into the soft skin of my wrists and ankles as well as removing more layers of cheekbone epidermis. The near silence was unnerving; the only noise was the distant hum of the motorway and the scratching of an elderberry sapling swaying to and fro against the brickwork, clinging to life by spreading desperate roots amongst the scant moss and debris in a search for sufficient nutrients to sustain itself. A navy-blue curtain with cream swirls danced with the wind in my peripheral vision, within the door frame I had recently been bundled through to my dire situation.

To my rear I heard distant voices closing in step by step to my position. A female was dumped to my blindside, her whimpering and muffled sobs not easing my elevated levels of apprehension. Another body landed in front of me, long golden locks tumbling to the gravelled roof top. Unlike the other woman to my rear, her breathing was uniform and steady, implying a calm, level individual.

"What the fuck we gonna do with the bloke downstairs?" came a gruff voice.

"We'll dispose of him later, he's not a problem, just a hindrance to our plans. Continue with the preparations brother. Samuel will be along soon and this whole nightmare will be over," James spoke reassuringly.

CHAPTER 63

The scatter of deep wounds to my arms throbbed with pain and blood oozed continually, soaking the sleeves of my jacket with a claret hue. A drying sticky scarlet rivulet formed down my neck from a substantial gash ripped into my face by enormous canine teeth. Around each injury, bruising began to emerge in various shades of dark blues, blacks and purple. There were numerous additional bites covering my legs and torso, no doubt leaving similar artistic marks themselves. The enormous culprit glared towards me from his strategic position sprawled in front of the French doors, the only opportunistic escape route I was aware of; his eyes never left their focus upon my person.

"Here boy, you're a good lad." He didn't flinch, my feeble attempt to break his concentration was met by a nonchalant sigh and a lick of his jowls, before lowering his head onto his giant paws.

"Hey boy, where's those cats?" Again, nothing, not even a twitch.

"You want some dinner?" An ear flicked, and he raised his head, showing interest in the word 'dinner'. A shrill whistle sounded from deep within the house which instantly diverted his attention. The beast stood, glared towards me, shook himself down and left the kitchen with one last warning glance from his huge chocolate button eyes before leaving his post unattended.

A quick scan of the kitchen revealed three drawers close by, one of which I would guess must contain something sharp to cut through my bindings. With both ankles secured to the legs of the stool and my arms behind my back, I rocked the bar stool back and forth, slowly shuffling across the tiles, more than aware that if I became over-enthusiastic, I'd end up face planting into the charcoal toned ceramics. Each inch towards the cutlery drawers created a rattle and a screeching echo within the kitchen.

Fatigue soon kicked in and my injuries continually reminded me they were still there, but I was in no man's land – stopping was not an option I could contemplate. A short breather was taken before I continued the rocking motion towards my target, eyes fixed on the doorway, awaiting the return of my furry friend or Kell's fella to interrupt my bid for freedom. The first drawer opened smoothly on the metal runners and with an owl-like crane of the neck I saw only drying towels. Rekindling the shuffling motion that had been so effective to this point, I reached the second drawer at record-breaking speed, before grasping the ornate brass handle, but again, disappointment – baking equipment. On to the last chance saloon; with arms and legs burning with lactic acid and dribbles of sweat and blood tumbling down my forehead, the final drawer proved more problematic than the first two due to the angle I had adopted to pass the edge of the American style fridge. Once opened I shuffled back to see the contents. My heart skipped, the treasure I'd been hunting – knives, and sharp ones at that.

CHAPTER 64

"Sally, where you at love?"

"Blue lighting down the motorway, eta to Aviary House approximately four minutes."

"We're several minutes behind you. Any joy contacting the boss or Jordan?"

"Fuck all Sarg, you?"

"Nothing on phones, straight to answer machine and complete radio silence."

"This isn't good Gaz. We will need to act quickly when we arrive."

"I said don't rush in Sally and that's a direct order. We have to assess the situation first."

"Sorry Gary, you're breaking up again, what did you say?"

"Sally, can you hear me? DC Glover, please acknowledge me, do not storm the scene unless you think persons are in immediate danger, do you hear me? Sally? For fuck's sake, that girl will be the death of me yet. Get your foot down officer."

"Yes sir."

CHAPTER 65

With two giant hands under her armpits, the woman facing away from me was hauled up by the brothers and placed with her back against the wall, her knees tucked into her chest. She sat bare foot, dressed in a work uniform of black pencil skirt and grimy cream blouse with the emblem of the King's Arms public house emblazoned across her right breast, embroidered in an emerald script. She shook uncontrollably, either from the chilly breeze blowing across the rooftop balcony or with fear, I couldn't be sure which. The poor soul looked exhausted and drawn with mascara stains in huge blotches morphing into teary streaks down her high cheekbones under her crystal blue eyes, incriminating evidence indicating this woman has not always been strong. But even in this dishevelled state, her beauty shone through. This was a person I recognised instantly from the images provided by our colleagues in the missing persons department as Helen Richardson. Our eyes met briefly before I too was lifted with consummate ease like a ragdoll and placed beside her by our captors who for the first time I witnessed together with their loyal mutt standing beside them.

"Fuck me, twins – that explains everything," I thought to myself. The possible description and limited CCTV relating to a tattooed man in the vicinity of the victims before their disappearance and the witness statement provided by Steve Grayson profiling a man of similar build and appearance but free from body art in the company of Janet Storer the night before her body was discovered on Hamstead Heath by a lovely old lady walking her dog. Twins – what an oversight on our behalf, all this time our investigation had focused on an individual. Nathan, James or whatever his bloody name was stared deadpan in our direction, his head cocked to one side before heading towards the remaining woman.

The third young woman lay prostrate on the gravelled rooftop. Her appearance screamed night out – knee-high camel suede boots, inky blue skinny jeans which clung seductively to her impressively curvaceous backside and a roman red split-sleeved t-shirt, again cut to emphasise the quality of her figure. As she was lifted by the twins, she kicked her legs and contorted her body, releasing a muffled scream with each thrashing motion before being dropped like a hot stone with a heavy thud.

"Don't be a twat!" grimaced Joseph, kneeling beside her, his giant hand clamped around her throat, squeezing until the fight in her ceased.

"Joseph, stop. I said stop, brother," bellowed James, dragging his brother away by the collar and dumping him unceremoniously on the seat of his jeans before the woman's life could ebb away.

"Sorry, it's difficult for me."

"I know, but you must control yourself. Their time will come and then all will be yours to do with as you please, to elevate them to the heavens in any way you see fit. But for now, we need them as they are, perfection."

The third angel was dumped by my side, her long golden locks tumbling over her ashen face; deep sobs echoed into the gun barrel grey skies. With a deep hollow breath, her head fell back against the brick wall and she turned our way, revealing her identity as my old mate Fiona. In a blink, her eyes filled with tears and overflowed in cascades down her cheeks before she turned away to face the brothers with more gagged screams and a fit of flailing bound legs. The sound of a car engine and the crunch of the gravel drive halted both Joseph and James in their tracks, distracting them from their mission to quash any resistance from this reluctant angel.

"Samuel is here," Joseph declared, taking to his knees, placing his hands together and bowing his head as if praying to a higher being. He was joined by his brother before both stood and entered the enormous house, shadowed by Loki.

CHAPTER 66

With a bread knife clamped firmly in the shut drawer, I went to work on the thick plastic ties binding my wrists, pausing briefly as a rumble of voices descending the stairs was noted. The thick woollen materiel of my jacket sleeve was now slick and sticky with blood and the injuries on my forearms continually reminded me of their presence whilst I vigorously pumped my arms over the serrated blade. In a few short seconds the first binding broke, quickly followed by the second as the footsteps and voices became louder. The two bindings securing my feet to the stool were next on the agenda, but my progress was halted for an instant when I heard the front door open and close. Finally, I was free. Sliding the knife into my inside pocket for future reference should it be required, I headed for the partition door into the garage.

"Shit, locked – and no key."

I scanned the worktops and frantically searched the three drawers, scattering tea towels in all directions, trying not to bring any unwanted attention to myself, but nothing. In the corner, close to the garage door, stood a tall light oak coat and hat stand, matching the rest of the kitchen décor. Several jackets hung ready for use and, in a wooden ring two feet from the floor, was a single black golf umbrella. The first item of outdoor clothing was a wax jacket sized XL; all the pockets were empty apart from the final one which was full of dogshit bags and a few training treats no doubt for the beast who had inflicted my wounds on demand. The next two coats proved fruitless. As I turned to seek an alternative escape route, the stand toppled; I fired my right arm out quickly enough to prevent it falling to the tiled floor and rattling an alarm to everyone in the house. Pausing for a split second, my heart pounded and I listened intently before replacing the coats to an upright position. Pain from the bites pulsed up my arm to remind my brain all was not well. Behind the coat stand was a hook drilled into the wall with a set of keys.

"Fucking bingo!"

The door swung open with a creak and I sprinted into the garage, stopped and span around, grabbing the key from inside the kitchen before locking the door, leaving the lifesaving lump of metal twisted in the lock to prevent the brothers making any kind of speedy exit. Before leaving the sanctuary of the garage, I glanced behind me and across the gravel driveway to where a white Evoque was parked. "Janet Storer's car," I thought to myself.

The coast seemed clear. My heart thumped but any fear was put aside as I made my bid for freedom, sprinting with a limp and crunching up the driveway to the safety of the car. The engine roared into life and the tyres struggled for traction, slipping and sliding on the high grass verge as I sped away down the road, leaving the women at the hands of those monsters.

"Come in all units, come in all units, over!" I shouted down the police radio.

"Received Jordan, go ahead, over," Sally replied.

"We have a situation at Aviary House, urgent back up required, and specialist firearms officers. He has shotgun, over."

"Eta two minutes Jordan, what's the sit rep? Over."

"They have Kelly."

CHAPTER 67

The three brothers made their way up the winding staircase with thick Thornton Manor Axminster carpets and walls adorned with paintings by various artists. One depicted a beach scene and distant lighthouse with waves crashing over a rocky peninsula, another was a historical piece portraying a pair of bay shire horses attached to a wooden plough, the farmer striding behind them, a pipe in his mouth, wiping his brow with a flat cap in his hand in a field surrounded by trees and hedgerow. Samuel gauged the dust left on his hand by the solid oak banister.

"The place needs cleaning."

"Sorry Samuel, we didn't mean to let you down," James said with a disappointed tone.

"Where are the angels?"

"Ready for us to give them their wings."

"Good work brothers, let's finish the mission so we can be reunited with our family."

"Follow me," Joseph beamed.

CHAPTER 68

Jordan was waiting at a T-junction to the right of the main road facing away from us down a country lane with his blues blazing away. He set off at speed with our convoy following close behind down a narrow winding single-track road for about three miles before pulling up on a grass verge a hundred metres away from an enormous stand-alone converted farm property.

"That's Aviary House, Kelly is inside. It's her boyfriend James Harrison, he's the killer, although his actual name is James Cline, I think. I couldn't do anything to help her Sally."

"Calm down Jordan, we know everything – and what the fuck happened to you?"

"A dog, a big bastard too."

"Fucking hell, you're a mess mate, you need to get those injuries seen to, an ambulance is en route."

"I'm not going anywhere until the boss is out of that place," Jordan announced as the armed response unit arrived. Sergeant Hill, a small stocky bloke with Popeye-like forearms complete with military tattoos indicating his service in the Royal Marines, approached with a purposeful stride.

"Afternoon folks, Sergeant Hill, ARU. What's the situation guys?" he asked in a gruff southern accent.

"Hi, I'm DC Glover and this is DC Willis, our boss DCI Kelly Lynch is inside. We believe the man who took her is the angel killer as the press have nicknamed him. We also believe there may be at least one other woman being held alongside her, but apart from that we can't tell you anymore."

"There is one other person – a white Evoque parked in the drive arrived during my time as a hostage, but who, what or where would be pure speculation," Jordan explained.

"What about weapons, layout of the premisses and points of entry?"

"Jordan, this is your baby."

"Right Sergeant, regarding weapons, I observed a shotgun in the garage but apart from that I'm clueless. I was held captive in the kitchen and didn't see any more of the internal layout. What I can tell you is the woods to our left run all the way to the perimeter of the gardens, with the house in full view. On the opposite side of the premisses is a golf course and ten-foot fence, and of course from the road there's a gravel driveway which meanders through relatively thick fauna. Entrance to the house can be gained in three places to my knowledge. To the rear is a patio and accompanying French doors, double glazed, leading into the dining room. To the left-hand side of the main building sits a twin garage which was open when I fled to raise the alarm. An internal door takes you directly into the kitchen diner, and then at the front of the house and central to the building is a porch and main entrance. That's pretty much all I can tell you. Oh, I nearly forgot, the dog, a bloody enormous thing, I'm not sure on the breed but it is well trained."

"Thanks for that. I'm taking a wild stab in the dark our K9 friend did this to you," said Hill, almost admiring Jordan's multitude of injuries.

"Yes, it did."

"I'll talk to my team, but I would suggest the bulk of the vehicles should approached from the road as a distraction tactic, whilst my guys use the woods and the golf course to infiltrate the grounds before you move on the house."

"Sounds good to me, what do you think Jordan?"

"Let's get those women out of there, before we're too late."

CHAPTER 69

A wintery breeze rolled across the rooftop balcony, momentarily floating strands of Helen's golden locks away from her statuesque examination of the surrounding gardens. A wren landed gracefully on the wall besides us, cocking his head and twitching his wings with an accompanying disapproving tut, tut before fluttering away towards the ancient oaks of the woodland. The skies above had turned an ominous oily grey; one large drop of rain fell with a thud, then another and one more.

I turned to Fiona; her face was one of utter despair as tears overflowed from her eyes, and once again she kicked her long shapely legs, scattering gravel with the heels of her boots before slamming her body hard against the wall and rattling her head several times into the brickwork in frustration. More rain tumbled down upon us with an icy sting, but Helen Richardson remained still; the flimsy material of her cream blouse slowly became transparent, revealing an ample pair of breasts and a stylish lacy bra.

The hound suddenly appeared through the open doors and sniffed the air before turning his attention to us, skipping in our direction and examining each of us in turn, glaring with penetrating chocolate eyes. Shortly after, the two brothers emerged with one other person. Joseph took hold of Helen and dragged her towards the edge of the rooftop balcony. Now the fight in her emerged in truck loads as she span herself around and around, lunging to escape like a hooked fish. Joseph held on to her by the collar, his patience growing thin; finally, her struggles were subdued by a slap to her face which reddened in an instant, displaying a perfect palm silhouette across her cheek. He lifted her head with a single finger.

"This will be a lot easier if you comply bitch."

"Joseph, do not damage our angels – which part of that sentence do you not understand? Next time, Loki will discipline you."

"Sorry James."

"Do they have their wings yet?" asked the person behind the pagoda.

"No, they don't," the twins replied.

"You know what to do."

With a nod of acknowledgement, Joseph produced a small blade from the back pocket of his jeans. The rain now classed as torrential. First, he removed the soaked grimy cream blouse with the King's Arms emblem adorning the chest pocket, exposing the white lace bra which he removed next, baring a perfect pair of breasts with bullet nipples. Goose pimples formed across her skin and her body began to shiver. Joseph stood back, admiring her naked body, then stooped with a sadistic smile forming across his broad face and began to caress her left boob while simultaneously running his huge right hand gently over the skin of her back.

"Joseph, that boat has sailed, sins of the flesh are frowned upon, please concentrate on the task in hand," James scowled.

His twin offered a glance of disappointment before he took the blade and sliced it through Helen's skin with relative ease. Streams of blood flowed down her sides, but not once did she flinch, scream or struggle; her eyes remained focused and only on occasion did she show any inkling of pain. In minutes, her wings were finished, ones similar to those I'd witnessed adorning the bodies of the other victims. Claret poured down her ribs and dripped onto the gravel roof.

James passed his brother a claw hammer and he hauled Helen to her feet, cutting the ties around her ankles and walking her to the edge of the building where he stood precariously on the coping stones of the perimeter wall, coaxing Helen alongside. He examined the hammer in his hand and paused.

From the barbeque area behind the pagoda, obscured by the remnants of the clematis, we heard the voice of the third person once again.

CHAPTER 70

The mystery figure loomed from behind us, his arms held aloft as if praying to a higher being as the rain bucketed down upon him, soaking his dress shirt. In his left hand, a trio of all-too-familiar halos were gleaming silver against the dull skies, all sporting the ornate decoration and My Angel script painstakingly scribed with an element of expertise into the precious metal. A blanket of eerie silence fell over the balcony and James dropped to his knees, apparently consumed by the enormity of this person whilst Joseph merely bowed his head to ensure his grip upon Helen Richardson remained firm.

"Father, we have gathered our final angels to aid you on your journey to the Kingdom of Heaven where you will be reunited with our mother, Mary, and baby Delilah. Once you have achieved your passage to Lord God our Father, your sons will join you."

"Angels, this is Samuel, our brother," Joseph introduced.

As the person turned to address us, my heart jumped into my mouth before instantly sinking to the depths of my chest, a place it had never felt before. A sickly feeling rose from the pit of my stomach, surging in pulses through my torso and to my throat and causing me to swallow back vile-tasting stomach linings. My entire body began to shake uncontrollably, from my toes to my fingertips before emanating further, resulting in a gathered weakness throughout my legs; I felt an air of gratefulness that I was seated on the cold, sharp gravel, otherwise I might well be on the floor with little say in the matter.

I blinked once, twice, hoping that my eyes had deceived me, but no, the vision presented was still clear. This was a man I had trusted in entirety, a person I had shared my soul with, a man who had played a substantial part in my life, supported me, been a shoulder to cry on – the man who was father to my son. The person standing in front of me with a broad grin across his handsome face was Darrell, my ex-fiancé. Whoever else this man claimed to be, he was my frigging ex. I had now been duped not just once, by James, but twice as Darrell was in fact Samuel Cline. My head span with confusion. How could I have allowed this to happen and why me? Fiona screamed from the bottom of her lungs; although she was gagged, the noise from her was piercing in between sobs and fits of anger. Samuel crouched beside her and touched a single finger across her lips.

"Shush my dear, Joseph will take good care of you." Samuel stared into her eyes with an almost loving intent, which quickly dispersed to be replaced by the hollow lifeless glare his brother had shown me earlier.

"Soon, my brothers and I will be reunited with our family to live for all eternity in the heavens above, nothing can stop that now. James, Joseph, brothers, we shall complete the mission. Our father spoke of sixteen steps to heaven to be lined with beautiful angels for our rite of passage. Today, we will reach salvation with his God and our kin," Samuel declared, his arms once again raised, his head back as he addressed the grey clouds, heavy rain bouncing off his face. "And you my dear Kelly will be last. I want you to suffer as we have. Joseph, it is time."

The brother gazed upon Helen, delicately stroked her face, cocked his head to one side and drew the hammer back at arm's length. There was a hiss, followed by a crimson cloud which filled the air from the back of Joseph's skull. He fell like a stone before his deadly blow reached its target, toppling from the coping stones and over the edge of the balcony, down to the gravel drive, dragging Helen with him.

"NOOO!" James wailed. "What the fuck?"

"Finish the mission James! Finish the fucking mission! I will meet you on the other side. Loki, with me." Samuel fled into the house, dog in tow.

James acknowledged his brother's command and made a beeline for Fiona.

"Take me you bastard, take me, she's done nothing to deserve this. It's me he wants," I muffled. James removed my gag.

"Fucking speak woman."

"I said take me, let her go, she's done nothing, it's me Darrell wants to suffer."

"His name is Samuel not Darrell."

"Does anyone care a fuck what he's called? You don't have to listen to him James, let her go. We'll work something out, you don't have to do as he says."

"HE'S MY BLOOD."

His brick-sized fist struck me hard on the cheek; the pain shot across my face and exploded into my brain. A second blow came quickly with more force and aggression than the first, and then darkness.

CHAPTER 71

Sergeant Hill and three of his team burst into the bedroom that led to the balcony, guns primed for action, searching each nook and cranny before moving outdoors. Two other armed officers remained outside to guard the landing, having already secured all the other rooms in the house. DS Gary Turner and I sprinted up the stairs, almost floating on the thick Axminster carpet, to be stopped halfway down the long landing by the remaining armed officers.

"I'm DC Sally Glover and this is DS Gary Turner from the LSCIU, our gaffer is inside."

"Sorry but you'll have to wait until we get an all clear from our boss."

From the entrance of the room, we heard an armed officer shout, "Sir, stop, let the woman go or we will be forced to open fire." No response. "Sir, please be advised, if you do not comply, you will be fired upon."

After five minutes of uneasy silence, Sergeant Hill returned, his firearm hung casually over his shoulder.

"It's all yours; the scene is secure."

"Is the suspect down?" I asked.

"You could say that. He jumped. Strange though – he shouted something about joining his dad."

"And the remaining women?"

"Safe, but one will need a paramedic – it looks like she's done ten rounds with Mike Tyson."

The heavy rain had almost eased to a stop as Gary and I headed into the bedroom and towards the scene outside. A photograph of a family stood in pride of place on a chest of drawers, its subjects all smiles: a little girl in an ankle-length summer dress with a lace collar and cuffs, a baby in its mother's arms and three boys, two of whom were twins, all congregated around what I can only presume was the man of the house, attired in a black shirt, trousers and clerical collar. Each person sported a crude crucifix around their necks made up of two single pieces of wood on a shoestring.

Outside, one of the armed officers assisted a stunning blonde lady who looked decidedly dishevelled and weary for her experience, although her obvious beauty and classy, curvaceous figure shone through the shit. Gary took her inside with her armed chaperone. The remaining officer tended to Kelly, cutting bindings around her ankles and wrists before placing her in the recovery position. He wrapped a thick red tartan blanket around her body and rested her head gently on a floral cushion, both acquired from the bedroom I guessed. As if reading my mind, the officer said with a chuckle, "Didn't think they'd be needing them anymore." I smiled back to be polite.

"All units be aware the scene is now secure. Paramedics required on the rooftop balcony, the patient is breathing but unresponsive, please attend ASAP, over."

"Roger that, medics en route, over."

"Received, over."

"Is she alright?" I asked.

"She's had a good whack or two that's for sure, but I'm sure she'll be right, best to get her checked over by the professionals though."

I knelt beside Kelly and brushed hair from her face to reveal a large egg with a weeping cut buried within swelling above her right eyebrow; both lips were split and leaking claret which was now drying to a crust and finally a single string of clotted blood hung in a drip from one nostril, swinging gently in the cooling breeze which had blown the rainclouds on their way, exposing a sunset boasting a plethora of violets, blues, yellows, reds and ambers.

"Kelly hun, it's me, Sally, can you hear me boss?" Her eyes flickered open briefly before settling back into emergency shutdown mode.

"You'll be fine boss, we're here. No one is going to hurt you now Ma'am, they'll have to go through me first."

CHAPTER 72

The gaffer's hospital room bubbled with a whispered conversation between Gary, Jenny McCabe and Sally, a deep and meaningful professional discussion regarding the events of the day. I sat bedside waiting for the boss to awaken. The consultant's assessment revealed a compression to the cheekbone and a hairline crack to the mandible, or for us mere mortals the jawbone. Apart from that, most of her injuries were minor with no lasting damage done, except for maybe the mental aspect but only time would tell on that subject. She stirred a few times and slowly opened her eye as best she could.

"Morning Ma'am, how are you feeling?" I said with a smile.

"Like shit Jordan if I'm honest. How are you?"

"Not bad thanks. I've got more stitches than a Louis Vuitton handbag but luckily no nerve damage. I might need to put a claim form in for new clothes, mine are pretty much fucked."

"Be my guest," she replied, rubbing her jaw which had coloured up beautifully.

"Sally has kindly been to your house to collect essential lady's bits, you know, knickers, bras and some clean clothes," I stuttered, feeling a slight glow of embarrassment discussing the DCI's personals.

"I know what lady's bits are, thanks Jordan."

"Anyway, there's your bag in the cupboard with clean clothes, shoes and your phone. If you need anything else, give us a nod."

"Cheers team. What about the women are they...?"

"Yes, they're alive. Helen Richardson sustained some substantial injuries from her fall, a broken pelvis, both ankles and left femur, she's gonna need surgery and a hospital bed for the foreseeable future but at least she's alive."

"And Fiona?"

"A few scrapes and bruises but fine."

"What about the Clines? Did we get them?"

"The twins are no more, a firearms officer took Joseph out, and James took a leap of faith and came off second best to the driveway." Kelly's head dropped and she examined her hands which had involuntarily begun to nervously twizzle the navy-blue NHS blankets through her fingers. A single tear rolled down her cheek but with the back of her hand it was quickly dispersed.

"I could murder a ciggy, excuse the pun," she said with a forced smile.

"Sorry Kell, strictly no smoking in here. Listen boss, we need to discuss a number of pressing issues with you, but only if you feel up to it," said Gary with a sympathetic tone, as he and Sally approached the DCI's bedside. Jenny took a seat near the door.

"Fire away."

"Sally, do you want to take this? It was you who unearthed the truth."

"Yep, no problem. Did you find out anything during your captivity?"

"Only that my whole life for the last seventeen years has been one huge tale of deceit."

"So, preliminary searches on the name James Harrison didn't reveal much at all on the database, only the odd speeding fine, nothing to speak of."

"Why would they? It wasn't his bloody name. Sorry, carry on Sal, it's not like we're going anywhere soon," the boss said with a sigh.

"No problem. So, I conducted a Google search on the name James Harrison with some interesting results. I found numerous newspaper reports on a young man called James Cline who was adopted by Charlie and Heather Harrison, a couple of entrepreneurs who were minted."

"So where does Darrell come into the whole scenario?"

"Hear me out. James Cline's adopted parents changed his name to James Harrison in an attempt to protect him from his rather violent past, but I'll get to that shortly. It transpires that James and his new parents often took holidays in France and during one of these trips, both Charlie and Heather were killed in a horrific freak accident whilst driving their 1972 MG convertible through the Pyrenees Mountains. Luckily James was ill and had remained at the villa with his nanny, he hadn't travelled with them."

"But there's still nothing pointing us in the direction of why."

"Correct but delving further I found more. Prior to becoming a Harrison, James spent numerous years in different children's homes and with umpteen foster families along with his older brother Samuel, who we now know was your ex, and his identical twin Joseph Cline."

"If it's any consolation, your ex being involved accounts for the lack of evidence at the murder scenes, his forensics training really paid off," Jenny interjected.

"Fuck me, we've really been had."

"Well Kelly, he was considered an expert in his field, don't feel too bad, we all missed the link," Jenny assured her. "Sorry, carry on Sally."

"Cool, I've unearthed numerous cases concerning the brothers regarding accusations of sexual and physical abuse at the hands of foster parents and various care homes. Each case was dismissed without prosecution or so much as a court appearance and the boys were moved on to another promising loving environment. Consequently the boys were separated across the country.

"At the age of twelve, your ex and his newly acquired family were on a holiday in Devon as per usual, staying in the same cottage they had used for years, a place close to the beach with a mooring for a yacht. Sometime during the fourteen-day vacation the entire family vanished in what was believed to have been a tragic yachting incident. A comprehensive search was conducted in the surrounding area from which it was concluded the family had got themselves into difficulty whilst sailing. The bodies of both parents and their daughter were found along with the family's golden retriever. Samuel's body was never discovered, and he was therefore also presumed dead.

"And that got me thinking – two brothers, both adopted, whose families died in freak accidents – coincidental don't you think? The other twin, Joseph, well there wasn't much on him at all, just a minor offence for a breach of the peace around the Leeds area, where he worked as a jeweller, specifically as an engraver. Hence the artwork on the halos."

"That's all very informative Sally but how does this link me to the case and why he wanted me to suffer?"

"I thought you'd ask that, so I researched why the boys were placed into the hands of the social services in the first place. Apparently, police were forced to intervene after Gabrielle Cline, a vicar from Churwell in Leeds, took it upon himself to self-cleanse his family of sin. This was orchestrated in the form of carving angel's wings into the backs of his wife and children."

"Explaining the back tattoos adorning James's back, to cover scars."

"More than likely. Next the vicar presented them with an impressively decorated silver halo before plunging a hammer into the skull of said spouse, their new-born baby girl Delilah and Mary, her three-year-old sister. Sound familiar yeah? The remaining three boys were saved from their fate minutes prior by the police – and get this, the arresting officer was a DC Ged Lynch. Kelly, it was your fucking uncle!"

"Oh fuck! Uncle Ged was the reason I became a copper."

"Yeah, but it doesn't end there. There was a definitive court case in terms of condemning evidence, and Gabrielle Cline was found guilty of three counts of murder and a list of other charges including acts of sexual abuse to children of a non-consensual age i.e., his own kids. But the bastard took the coward's way out and hung himself in his cell by his bedsheets whilst awaiting sentencing. I guess he'd heard child killers and paedophiles aren't exactly welcomed with open arms in the prison community, and I doubt divine intervention was an option."

"Holy shit, the apple certainly didn't fall far from the tree in this case, did it?"

"No boss, it didn't, and we have more bad news."

"Can it get any worse?"

"We searched the house from top to bottom – Samuel had gone."

"But the place was swarming with half the London force. How the hell did he get out?"

"The women had been caged in the house cellar. Whilst forensics were doing their stuff down there, they discovered a door and tunnel leading to a clearing in the woods, a substantial distance away from the house. We found tyre tracks and dog prints but not knowing what he was driving we couldn't trace him."

"So, the bastard's still out there? WHAT ABOUT JACOB? WHERE'S MY JACOB?" she screamed trying to climb from her bed.

"He's safe Kelly, we have plods at your house inside and out, no one's getting to him I promise. Now lay down and relax, doctor's orders. We'll deal with this," Gary reassured her.

"Boss, we have distributed his mugshot all over the country, every port, airport and police station, and launched a man hunt across all London boroughs. We will get him, it's just a matter of time. He can't hide forever," I said with a confident, painful grin which stretched at the stitches in his face. Although underneath my shroud of confidence were elements of doubt. These men had gone to such lengths to avoid capture and to ensure their mission was completed, surely they would have a contingency plan in place for a situation like this.

"Anyone hear a phone ringing?" said Gary with a quizzical look.

"Yeah, I can," I agreed, heading in the direction of the cupboard. "It's your phone Boss, do you want it?"

"I'll take it, it might be Jacob," she beamed.

I dropped my notepad on the bedside cabinet, took the tan leather handbag from the cupboard and passed it to Kelly who rummaged around until she found her mobile amongst all the other items within. She placed the phone to her ear.

"Hello, DCI Kelly Lynch, how can I help?"

"Good afternoon, Kelly. How are you feeling my angel? Do look after my son won't you? I'll be in touch soon. I look forward to seeing you again Kelly. Goodbye for now."

ABOUT THE AUTHOR

Robert Slakki is an author born and raised in a dying industrial town situated in Northern Lincolnshire, bordering Yorkshire and Nottinghamshire, England.

His debut novel, *Northern Monkeys*, is the opening book in a series of three. Released 19th April 2022, it follows Dave Ross through his rather boring mundane life before it escalates into an explosive mixture of sex, violence, love, friendship and survival.

Sixteen Steps to Heaven is the opening title in the DCI Kelly Lynch series where she leads the London Serious Crimes Investigation Unit, a dedicated team of detectives who are tasked with solving some of the more complicated, brutal and testing crimes across London.

Printed in Great Britain
by Amazon